SO SENSITIVE

Books by Anne Rainey

So Sensitive

Body Rush

"Cherry on Top" in *Some Like It Rough*

So Sensitive

ANNE RAINEY

APHRODISIA

KENSINGTON PUBLISHING CORP.

www.kensingtonbooks.com

*To Linda, for your valuable feedback
and warm friendship.
I would be lost without you!
And a very special thanks to Martin,
for your patience and kindness.*

Prologue

Two months earlier...

Gracie couldn't take her eyes off the man leaning against her desk. His dark, wavy brown hair and easy smile sent a shiver of awareness down her spine. He was large, with well-sculpted, drool-worthy arms. Arms that would hold a woman tight. And he was looking at her as if he'd struck gold.

"I don't believe we've been properly introduced. I'm Wade Harrison, Cherry's friend, and you are?"

God, his voice was just as yummy as the rest of him. Deep, a little gravelly, as if he'd just gotten out of bed. It took her a few seconds before she could answer without stuttering. "It's nice to meet you. I'm Gracie Baron, Cherry's new receptionist."

He held out his hand. Gracie promptly dropped the pen she'd been using and let him take hold of her. The calloused, firm feel of him against her skin nearly had her creaming in her panties. He dipped his head and kissed her knuckles. A light brush of his lips and she was ready to surrender.

He winked as he let go of her. She missed his warmth, but forced herself to pick up the pen again.

"It's a pleasure to meet you, Gracie." He looked down her

body, his progress hindered by the desk, then snared her in his dark chocolate gaze as he asked, "So, what do you do when you aren't answering the phone and setting up appointments here at Serene Comfort?"

"I have another job. I'm an administrative assistant."

His brows shot up. "You work two jobs?"

She thought of her dad's utility bills, which were overdue to be paid, again. "Yeah, I need the money to help support my dad."

He straightened and crossed his arms over his chest. "A devoted daughter, huh?"

She stiffened at the term. "Yeah, you could say that, I guess."

More like doormat, she thought bitterly. What was the use in complaining? Nothing was ever going to change. Her father would always drink away his Social Security check and call her in a panic because they were about to evict him for not paying the rent. She was tired of being the fall guy, but she couldn't bring herself to leave him to his own devices. He was her father, after all.

"Do you have a significant other to keep you company when you aren't working, Gracie?"

The way he said her name made her think of silk sheets and candlelight. It was a nice image. Then reality intruded when she thought of his question. "I'm not seeing anyone right now. To tell the truth, I'm not sure when I'd even have the time."

His grin widened. "How about I take you to dinner Friday night? I'd like to get to know you better."

It was like dangling an ice cream cone in front of a five-year-old; Gracie's mouth practically watered at the thought of spending time alone with the delicious man. "I'd really—" A strange tinkling sound interrupted her. She glanced over at the computer and cringed. An e-mail, and she recognized the name in the "from" column. Her creepy secret admirer, reminding her that while she might not have a husband, she did have a man in her life. The fact that she didn't want said man didn't seem to matter to the jerk. Who the hell was she kidding? How could she possibly spend time with Wade when she had an alcoholic father to take care of and a weirdo stalking her via the Internet? Add in two jobs, and you have a woman with zero energy left over for leisure time.

"Earth to Gracie."

"Oh, sorry. I'm ... I'm sorry, but I'm not in a good place right now. Can I have a rain check?"

He placed his hands on the edge of her desk and leaned forward until only a few inches of air separated them. "I can be very patient, Ms. Baron."

The determination in his gaze sent a rush of adrenaline through her body. Why did she suddenly feel as if her days were numbered?

1
_____

Present day

"If you'd give me a valid reason why you won't go out with me, I'd leave you alone. Instead, all I get are snarls. Snarls aren't valid, Gracie."

"I said no, which should be enough. Actually, it is for most guys. You're just mad because every other woman you proposition fawns all over you like you're a bar of chocolate or something. It makes me want to puke."

Wade tried to contain his grin. It wasn't easy with Gracie's description of him. "A bar of chocolate, huh? I don't suppose you have a sweet tooth, do you?"

Her frown turned into a vicious smile. "I'm allergic to chocolate. In fact, just the sight of it makes me irrational, and I get this insane urge to take a hammer and crush it into oblivion."

Wade grabbed his chest, feigning hurt. "Ouch. You're one scary lady."

She sat up a little straighter in her chair and turned her attention back to her monitor. "Exactly. So, go find a cute little bunny to warm your bed; I'm really not interested, Wade."

Wade braced his palms on Gracie's desk and leaned forward. "A piece of fluff can't even begin to satisfy me. Not when I have my sights set on a curvy redhead with a wicked temper."

"Wade, stop bothering my employee."

He turned his head at the feminine voice. Cherry DuBois, soon to be Cherry Ricci when she married the big Italian from the financial consulting business next door. Wade watched Cherry walk toward him, a to-go cup in one hand and a cell phone in the other. Her purposeful strides exuded confidence. He smiled, proud of the woman he'd been friends with for years. After her first husband had asked for a divorce, Cherry had crumpled a little. But making her massage therapy business, Serene Comfort, a success had helped her to see she didn't need a man like Brody in her life. Meeting Dante had done the rest. The man acted as if Cherry hung the moon. If Wade were honest with himself, he'd admit to feeling a twinge of envy for the happy couple.

"I came to take you to lunch," he explained, "but you'd already slipped out. So, I asked Ms. Persnickety here."

"Dante and I grabbed lunch at home. You should've called. I could've made other plans."

Wade turned, leaned against Gracie's desk, and crossed his arms over his chest. "You would've dropped Dante for me, huh?"

"Well, I could've—"

"He's your fiancé now, Cherry," Wade interrupted, his voice gentling. "You don't have to make excuses for wanting to spend time with him." He tossed Gracie a look over his shoulder. "Besides, it's not really a hardship to spend time with your pretty receptionist."

Cherry stepped forward and kissed him on the cheek, then leaned around him to look at Gracie. "You have my permission to drop-kick him if you want, hon. It would do him some good."

Gracie laughed, but Wade could tell it was strained. She never seemed at ease around people. Not even Cherry, and everyone got along with her. "It's fine. He was just leaving anyway. Right, Wade?"

Wade stood and stepped away from the desk. "Fine. My heart can only be stomped on so many times."

The phone rang, and he watched Gracie fairly leap for it. While she took the call, Wade said his good-byes to Cherry and moved toward the door. He was halfway to his truck when he remembered he'd forgotten to tell Cherry about the phone call he'd received from her ex-husband. The asshole suddenly had it in his head that he wanted Cherry back. The chance of that happening was about as good as finding Elvis alive and living it up in Graceland.

Wade sprinted back across the parking lot and pulled open the door, expecting to see Gracie where he'd left her behind the receptionist desk, but her seat was empty. Figuring she was taking a break, Wade started down the short hall toward Cherry's private office. A sound caught his attention, and he stopped. His gaze narrowed on the closed bathroom door at the end of the hall. He moved closer and listened harder. The noise came again, and it sounded suspiciously like a woman crying. Cherry or Gracie? Wade knocked softly. He didn't want to intrude, but the thought of either woman in tears didn't sit right with him.

"Y-Yes?"

Gracie's trembling voice floated out to him. What the hell? "Gracie, is everything all right?"

"F-Fine."

Fine my ass. In the months Gracie had been working for Cherry he'd seen her spitting mad, shy as a butterfly, and sarcastic as hell. He'd never once heard that quiver in her voice. He didn't like it one damn bit either. He wasn't going anywhere until he got to the bottom of it. As he waited, a horrible thought struck, and he froze. Had he been the cause? His teasing? He'd thought their little cat and mouse thing was all part of the game, but maybe it made Gracie more uncomfortable than she'd let on.

The door swung open, and Wade stiffened. Gracie's head was down, and she was dabbing at her eyes with a tissue. She didn't see him and smacked right into his chest, nearly knocking herself over backwards. Wade grabbed her shoulders to steady her before she had a chance to topple. Her head shot up, and her pretty green eyes filled with tears the instant their gazes clashed. Shit, that sure as hell wasn't real promising.

"I think it's time you tell me what's wrong, Gracie. And don't tell me it's nothing."

She shook her head and blew her nose as she tried to step around him. Wade blocked her path. He cupped her chin in his palm and forced her to look at him. "Is it me? Did I do this?"

She blinked a couple times, as if unsure what he meant, then she let out a hysterical laugh. "Wade, your ego is showing."

The fact that she was laughing, even while tears continued to stream down her cheeks, was further proof that something was very wrong. For the first time, Wade looked beyond the soft red hair, curvy figure, and pouty lips. He saw the dark circles under Gracie's eyes now, and they spoke volumes. She looked as if she hadn't slept in days. "Gracie, I know we may have gotten off on the wrong foot, but I can be a good listener if you want to talk."

She squared her shoulders and gently wiped her eyes in an attempt to get a handle on her emotions. "It's just a woman thing, Wade. I'm fine, really." The chimes over the door jangled, signaling a client's arrival. "I've got to get back to work. Thanks for the concern."

She brushed past him, and Wade was left staring after her, dumbfounded. His instincts were screaming at him. There was more to that crying jag than PMS. He'd bet his new truck on it.

Short of tying her to a chair and interrogating her, there wasn't a damn thing he could do. When he went out to the front, his gaze sought out hers. She smiled, and she looked as contained as ever. If it weren't for the redness in her eyes, he never would've guessed she'd been so upset. Which made him wonder just how often she wore that mask. Layers and Gracie Baron were old friends. Wade was determined to get beneath a few and find out more about the intriguing woman.

Of course, it might help if she weren't so damned stubborn.

Gracie watched through the large glass windows as Wade climbed into his truck and drove off. She let out a relieved sigh. She was smart enough to know that had Cherry's next client not shown up when he did, she would have ended up pouring out all her problems to the big, intimidating man. It would be a horrible mistake to involve someone else in the mess her life had become. It was enough she had to live it; others shouldn't be forced to as well.

She looked back at her monitor and groaned. Another e-mail from her crazy stalker. This one had a more sinister feel to it somehow. He'd threatened her before, but now it seemed there was an edge of desperation to the words on the screen.

I watch you every day, my love. Every move you make is recorded in my soul. I love the way you move. Always in such a rush and yet so graceful. You should know, though, I'm not happy about your second job. I asked you to quit, and you ignored me. This can't be allowed to continue. I've let you have your fun, but it's time you understand obedience. It's for your own good; remember that. I love you, Gracie Lynn. Nevertheless, sometimes I will need to be tough to prove to you that our love can withstand all obstacles.

Forever,
Your Admirer

Gracie shivered even as she saved the e-mail to her flash drive. She'd started saving them when she realized the man wasn't just a secret admirer; he was plain nuts. She now had over a hundred e-mails. At first it had seemed sweet. He'd been complimentary and always signed the e-mails with "your admirer." She'd never replied, but she'd felt flattered. The attention had bolstered her self-esteem. Then he'd used her first and middle name together, and it had sent cold chills down her spine.

Her middle name wasn't listed. Anywhere. Not on her driver's license, in the phone book, not even on her credit cards. Whoever had sent the e-mails had done his homework. She'd known then that ignoring them wasn't going to make the situation go away, so she'd done what any woman with a crazy e-mail fan might do; she'd gone to the police. That road had gotten her exactly nowhere. He hadn't threatened, so he'd done nothing wrong, the detective had explained. He'd instructed her to save the e-mails and contact him if the situation worsened.

That had been two weeks ago, and the e-mails hadn't let up. In fact, he'd gotten more persistent. He e-mailed every three hours now, like clockwork. Each e-mail rambled on about how much he loved her, how they'd be together soon and they'd be able to live happily ever after. Still, he was careful never to threaten her outright. She had nothing to bring to the police save for a lot of e-mails from a guy who had the hots for her.

Bile rose in her throat as she imagined what sort of person spoke like that to a complete stranger. It was like something out of a scary movie. Only in the movie the bad guy usually ended up dead and the damsel in distress would be rescued just in the nick of time.

Fear threatened to consume her when she thought of what this guy might be willing to do to keep her all to himself. An image of Wade Harrison filled her mind, and Gracie quickly banished it. She couldn't think of Wade. He would only want to help, but she refused to burden him with her problems. Besides, what would her stalker do if he suspected she desired another man? The creep hadn't done anything to harm her yet, and she knew it was partly due to the fact she kept to herself. She didn't date, didn't even go out with friends. When she wasn't at work, she was alone. The instant someone came into her life, someone as handsome and charming as Wade, things would escalate. She could very well be putting more than just herself in danger then.

The rest of the afternoon passed in a rush of clients. Gracie had been only too grateful for the distraction, as brief as it was. After the last client left, Gracie shut down the computer, then picked up the flash drive that contained all her crazy admirer's e-mails. Just as Gracie slipped it into her purse, Cherry came out of her office. "Ready to go?"

"Yep."

Cherry always insisted they leave together. More often than not, Dante would show up and escort both of them out. Gracie liked Cherry and Dante. They were good people. As if she'd conjured him, Dante opened the front door and held it for the two of them. He waited while Cherry set the alarm and locked up, then he took her hand in his. The little green monster rose up as Gracie watched them. She wondered what that kind of bond was like. That kind of all-consuming love. Would she ever know?

"I wanted to tell you now that Wade's not here that if he really ever bothers you, just say the word and I'll have a talk with him. I don't want you feeling uncomfortable, Gracie."

Gracie smiled for the first time in hours. "He doesn't bother me. Not really. I just like to give him a hard time."

"I sort of figured. Do you like him?"

Gracie stiffened, unsure how much to say. "He's attractive. The idea of going out with him is very appealing, but I don't have time for a man right now."

Cherry looked up at Dante and smiled. "Sometimes it's worth it to make time."

Gracie nodded, pretending she understood. In truth, she'd never been loved. Not the way Cherry and Dante loved. She'd had boyfriends, but hers had always been surface relationships. Deep, soul mate stuff wasn't something she knew anything about.

Once Gracie was in her car and on her way, she thought back to the day Cherry had hired her on as a receptionist. Gracie had been thrilled. The extra income meant she could help her father with his bills and still keep her own apartment. Maybe she could even get him out of debt once and for all.

Hell, who was she kidding? Her father was a drunk and a pathetic excuse for a human being. He started drinking when he woke up in the morning and didn't stop until his head hit the pillow. The only thing keeping a roof over his head was his only child working two jobs. If she didn't pay both their bills, one of them would be on the street.

As she turned a corner and started down the long, winding road to her apartment complex, her mind once again went back to Wade. God, the man was beyond delicious. His large, hard body and gorgeous brown eyes were like something out of a tough guy action movie. She'd been sucked in. He'd grinned at her, and she'd nearly fallen at his feet. His dark hair seemed forever disheveled. Models spent good money on hair products to get that tousled look, while Wade simply ran a hand through his hair. Women sighed as they watched him, longing to do the same. She knew, because she was one of those women.

The first time he'd asked her out, she'd nearly caved. Then, like an omen, a bell on her computer signaled a new e-mail message. When she recognized the e-mail address as her stalker's, the "yes" she'd been about to utter died on her tongue. She'd tried every trick in the book since to keep Wade at a distance, but, damn, the man was tenacious. She had to admit to herself that he didn't push, not really. Deep down Gracie knew if she truly meant no, he'd hear it and leave her alone. He wasn't an ass, just intuitive. He knew the attraction wasn't all on his side of the desk. He just couldn't understand why she was so reluctant to act on it. Unfortunately the truth simply wasn't something one brought up in casual conversation. *"Oh, by the way, you might become the target of a crazy man if you and I went out on a date. My stalker has this thing about having me all to his wacko self."* Yeah, that'd go over well.

As she neared the S curve a half mile from her home, Gracie pushed the maudlin thoughts out of her head and concentrated instead on simply getting home in one piece. Friday night, and she was alone. Damned pathetic. Pressing her foot down on the brake, Gracie managed the first curve and had started into the second when something slammed into her rear bumper.

Gracie automatically hit the brake. As she slowed down, her hands shook as panic started to settle over her. She glanced in the rearview mirror, but it was too dark to see more than a set of headlights behind her. She started to move her small sedan to the side of the road, her mind already on calling the police and exchanging insurance information, when another impact, harder this time, sent her car careening out of control.

"Oh, God!"

Panic turned to all-out terror as she witnessed the other vehicle speed up and smash into her yet a third time. As fear tore a scream from her throat, her car spun. Looking through the windshield, Gracie's gaze locked onto the thick woods, and the deep ravine she knew lay hidden fifty feet beyond. She clutched the wheel in a death grip and pushed the brake pedal clear to the floor, her only thought on keeping from diving into that ravine. Her car tore through weeds and brush, the world turning upside down. Suddenly, everything went black.

2

Gracie woke to a conversation that sounded way out of control. While she tried to get her eyelids to lift, she heard her father's belligerent voice, and she stilled.

"I'm her father! You have no right to keep me from seeing her."

"You can see her once you're sober. I won't have my patient stressed unnecessarily."

"Bullshit. Gracie can handle it. She's a sturdy girl."

"That may be, but I can't allow you to upset her in her condition. I will call security and have you escorted out of the hospital if you insist."

"Fine. What the hell do I care? Damn girl's nothing but trouble anyway."

Gracie waited for her father to leave before she opened her eyes. Her gaze clashed with the doctor's, and she saw sympathy there. She'd seen that look before. First on the teachers' faces during her school years and later on her boyfriends'. She hated that look.

The elderly doctor took her wrist and looked at his watch. After a moment, he smiled, kindness in his brown eyes, before writing something in her chart. "So you decided to stop playing possum, huh?"

Gracie tried to sit up and regretted the action instantly. "Ouch."

"You have a fractured wrist and lots of bruising. Thank God that's all you ended up with, considering."

She remembered then. "My car."

"Is probably totaled," he said, compassion clear in his expression. "Did you have insurance?"

"Yes. And I wasn't playing possum . . . exactly."

"Well, young lady, you're very fortunate. The outcome could have been much worse. Your seat belt and airbag saved your life. The good news is you will mend, and you can buy a new car."

"I can leave then?"

He patted her hand. "Let's wait until tomorrow. I'd like to do a few other tests to be sure everything is okay."

Damn, she hated hospitals. The last hospital she'd been to she was ten years old, and her grandma had lain there dying. Gracie had been too young to understand why her grandma couldn't just wake up and come home. After she'd passed, Gracie had been left alone with her father. Her mother had never been in the picture. She had no memories of her at all. Her father never let her forget how grateful she should be that at least he'd stuck around.

"In the meantime, there are a few people who want to see you," the doctor said, interrupting the train wreck of her thoughts. "A Cherry DuBois and Wade Harrison. Ring any bells?"

"Cherry's my boss, and Wade is . . ." She stalled out. What was Wade?

"A friend, yeah, I figured that out by the way he was carrying on in the hall. He's none too happy to be kept outside the room. He rather insisted on seeing you immediately."

She smiled despite her aches and pains. "Persistent. Yes, that's Wade."

"Would you like to see them? They're pretty anxious about the accident. I don't think Wade is going to be convinced you're alive until he sees you with his own eyes."

"Of course. Thank you." Then another thought occurred. "Wait, who told them about the accident?"

"You asked us to call your boss. Don't you remember?"

She shook her head. "I remember driving home from work, but nothing much after that."

"A hit-and-run."

Gracie tried to remember, but her mind was a blank slate. "Someone hit me then took off?"

He nodded, his eyebrows scrunching in anger. "It happens more than you'd think."

"I wish I could remember. It's so strange. I just remember getting in the car and starting out of the parking lot."

"Don't force it; you'll remember soon enough." He paused a moment, then said, "You were in shock when the paramedics brought you in, but you did ask someone to call Ms. DuBois. I believe she notified your friend and your father. Speaking of which, when your father returns would you like to see him as well?"

She knew what he was asking. Say the word, and she wouldn't have to deal with his drunkenness. She sighed, wishing she'd gain a damn backbone for once. "It's fine, doctor. I'm used to him."

"If you're sure." He stepped away from the bed and went out the door. Seconds later, Wade strode through it, his expression set in hard lines. When he looked at her, he stopped and cursed.

"Do I look that bad?"

He grunted, then closed the distance. "You look like hell."

Gee, what a charmer. "Thanks, really." She tried to smile, but it hurt too much.

"The airbag," he explained when she touched her cheek. "You have bruises all over your face from the impact. It looks like you went a few rounds with a heavyweight."

"That's about how I feel." She looked over at the cast on her wrist and groaned. "What a mess. I really didn't need this right now."

He pushed the hair out of her face and tucked it behind one ear. His touch was so gentle; it surprised her that a man so large and intimidating could be so tender.

"What happened? All I got was that it was a hit-and-run accident at a curve near your apartment. How'd you end up in some damn ravine?"

As she stared at him, a memory started to break through the fog blanketing her mind. "It wasn't an accident."

Wade frowned down at her. "Tell me what you remember."

Her heartbeat sped up as fragments of memories surfaced. "I just . . . I think someone forced me off the road on purpose."

"What makes you think that, Gracie?" he asked, his gentle tone drifting over her body in a soothing caress.

"Someone hit me from behind."

"We know that much, and it bites that he took off, but how was it a deliberate attempt to force you off the road?"

"Not once, Wade. He slammed into my car three times. I think he was trying to . . ." The e-mail from her stalker popped into her mind. His warning that she needed to learn obedience. *It's for your own good; remember that.* No, she was reading too much into his words. It was an accident. A drunk driver maybe. That had to be it, right?

Wade stroked her hair. "Gracie, is there something going on

that you're not telling me? Talk to me, honey. Let me help you."

"I don't even know where to start." Her voice broke when she admitted, "H-He's . . . I'm just so tired, Wade."

Wade's hand stopped moving. "Wait, *he?* Is this about an ex-boyfriend or something?"

"I wish it were so simple. No, he's not an ex-boyfriend. It's about . . . I have a stalker." It sounded so insane when she said it aloud.

Wade was quiet a moment, as if assessing whether she'd lost her mind when her car had gone into that spin. "Since when?" he finally asked, his voice matter-of-fact enough to calm her anxiety.

"He's been e-mailing me for about two months." She let out a breath and plucked at the bed sheet. She hadn't realized how good it would feel to confide in someone. She'd kept it to herself for so long.

Wade moved his hand away and crossed his arms over his chest. "How often does he e-mail? And does he communicate any other way? Has he approached you?"

She answered his questions in order. "He used to e-mail once a day. He's graduated to nearly every three hours. And yes, he's called. I can't swear it's him, because he never says anything, just sits there, listening. The caller ID always says 'unknown.' "

"He hasn't approached you? Have you gone to the police?"

She shook her head, regretting it when her brain seemed to rattle around inside her skull. "No, he hasn't approached me. I did go to the police, but the e-mails haven't been threatening so there wasn't a lot they could do."

Wade touched a fingertip to one of her bruises and growled low. "And you think this guy is the person who hit you?"

When he put it like that it sounded absurd. Like something

out of a movie. "I don't know what I think. I don't even know why I brought it up."

"You brought it up because you think he tried to drive you off the road. Don't negate your gut instinct, Gracie. It's trying to tell you something; listen to it." She nodded, and he went on. "I'm going to be severely pissed at you later for not telling me about this guy before. For now, you're going to do what the doctor says. After the tests, you'll rest. When you get out of here, you're coming to stay with me."

The authoritative attitude didn't sit well. She'd been taking charge of her own life since she was ten years old, after her grandmother had died, leaving her with her drunken father. Gracie wasn't about to stop now. "Forget it, Wade. I'm fine at my own apartment."

His dark espresso eyes locked onto her and held. "Yeah, I can see how fine you are. This asshole tried to kill you, damn it."

"What?"

Gracie groaned as she looked at the door. Cherry and Dante stood there. Dante had his arm around a very pale Cherry. Gracie glared at Wade and grumbled, "When I can move again without pain, I'm going to kill you. One inch at a time."

Cherry walked to the other side of the bed and took Gracie's hand. "You can threaten him later. What's this about someone trying to kill you? I thought this was a random hit-and-run accident."

Gracie filled Dante and Cherry in on everything. By the time she was finished, Cherry, the traitor, was siding with Wade. "Please, Gracie, I'd feel so much better with Wade protecting you. He's a good PI. He can find out who this guy is and put a stop to it. Let him help."

"I'm going to talk to the police again," Gracie hedged, unwilling to drag anyone else down with her. "There might be more they can do this time."

Wade rolled his eyes, as if the very idea was ludicrous. "Unless there was a witness, and I'm not seeing one at the moment, there isn't much they're going to do."

He had a point, but it still surprised her that he would suggest she not involve the police. "You don't think I should tell the police about this?"

Wade sifted his fingers through his hair, mussing it beyond repair. She ached to reach out and touch the dark strands. It drove her crazy wondering about the texture. "You should definitely make a statement," he said. "This needs to be on record. I'm just saying there might not be much they can do. On the other hand, I can do what the cops can't."

Gracie pulled her attention back to the problem. Wade managed to distract her just by being Wade. He always had. "Like what?"

"I can devote countless hours to finding out who this dickwad is and keep you safe at the same time."

Gracie was starting to see his point. All the same, she didn't want him in potential danger. The idea that something could happen to Wade caused her stomach to roll. "No, it would put you at risk. For whatever reason this guy has it in his head that I belong to him. If he learns you're helping me there's no telling what he'd do. I think the only reason he hasn't done anything drastic so far is because I'm alone. I haven't dated anyone for a long time."

"You know this by the fucking letters he sends?"

"E-mails," she corrected. "And yes. It's crazy, but he calls me his 'love' and tells me we'll be together some day."

"You're in the hospital because of this asshole," Dante said, his Italian accent thick as he glared down at her.

"Yes, but why are you in the hospital?" Cherry asked, all eyes suddenly on her. "What set him off enough to drive you off the road?"

Gracie'd known that question would pop up. "It's because I

wouldn't quit working at Serene Comfort, which he sees as some sort of den of iniquity or something. He saw that as 'disobedience.' This was his way of putting me in my place."

"Oh, God," Cherry cried.

"I'm still not quitting." Gracie clutched the sheet with her uninjured hand. "I'm sick of playing his game."

Wade spoke up then. "So, the accident was his way of letting you know who's in charge."

"Yes. Well, at least I think that was his plan."

Wade smiled, but the smile was filled with menace. She'd never seen him look so cold. "Then maybe we should push him a little harder. It could bring him out in the open."

Gracie didn't like where Wade's mind was going. "You think tempting a lunatic is a good idea?"

"I'm saying if he thinks you're no longer his love, maybe he'll get careless, make a move. Then we can catch him."

"That's the craziest thing I've ever heard. Besides, I don't have a lover and, considering he thinks of me as belonging to him, I'm pretty sure that's the one thing that would really set him off."

"You're about to come and stay with me. He'll think we're lovers. That should be enough."

He said it as if it were a foregone conclusion. "But we aren't lovers." She tried to hold on to her temper when she gritted out, "And I didn't agree to live with you, so stop putting words in my mouth."

"We'll see," he said as he stepped away from the bed. "First, you need some rest. We'll talk about all this tomorrow."

"We're done talking, Wade. I'm not moving in with you, and that's final."

Cherry and Dante both smiled. Cherry patted her hand. "Everything's going to work out fine. You'll see."

Why did she feel as if she'd lost an argument? Cherry let Gracie know she'd be back in the morning. As Dante escorted her out the door, Gracie was left alone with Wade. She looked up at him and sighed. It'd be easier to say no if he resembled a troll. With his sexy grin and rock-hard body, she could all too easily imagine relying on him to solve this mess for her. No, it'd be crazy to put him directly in the path of a stalker.

"I can see those thoughts as clearly as if they were flitting across your face. You think I should keep my nose out of it. You're worried I'll get hurt."

"Wrong. I'm worried you could get killed."

"Gracie—"

She cut him off with a hand in the air. "Look at me, Wade. This was just a warning. He's teaching me a lesson. What do you think he'll do if he suspects we're sleeping together?"

"Do you honestly believe he'll be content to keep you at a distance forever? Eventually he *will* make a move on you. The only thing I'm suggesting is that we force him to act sooner rather than later. This way we'll be ready."

"He might just lose interest." Even as she said it she knew she was deluding herself. "It's possible he'll just get tired of the game and move on. We don't know he's going to escalate, Wade."

"Do you really believe that? In your gut, do you really think this bastard is going to walk away?"

Crap, she hated to admit it, but he was right. She didn't truly believe her stalker would give up and leave her alone. Not after two months of e-mails and phone calls. The first time she defies him, she lands in the hospital. No, he wasn't going to stop. "Don't curse. It's really annoying."

"Get some rest, honey," he whispered. "We'll figure this all out in the morning."

He moved closer and leaned down. The brush of his lips over her forehead had Gracie going stiff as a statue. His lips, soft and full, felt much too good against her skin. She couldn't allow herself to imagine what they might feel like elsewhere.

That road led to disaster. When he stepped back and sat in the chair next to the bed, she frowned. "What are you doing?"

"Staying. Got a problem with that, Gracie?"

The night? He'd be able to see her while she slept. What if she snored? "You can't stay."

He stretched out his legs and crossed his arms over his chest. "I'm not leaving you alone here while some asshole has his sights set on you. I'm staying."

She tried another tactic. "You can't sleep in that chair. I'm not even sure you're allowed to stay past visiting hours. You aren't even family. Be reasonable, Wade. I'm in a hospital surrounded by people. I'm perfectly safe."

"I'm ex-military and a PI. I can sleep just fine in this chair. And hospital or not, I'm not leaving you unguarded."

What could she say to that? It was impossible to argue with a gorgeous man bent on protecting a woman with his very body. "Suit yourself, but don't blame me for the crick in your neck tomorrow."

"Sleep, Gracie. Don't worry about my neck. I've slept in worse places."

She wanted to pursue that, really she did, but she was too exhausted. Fatigue settled in around her.

Sometime in the middle of the night a nurse came in and took blood. Wade sprang to attention the instant the door creaked open. As she started to drift back off, she felt Wade's hand against hers, his thumb stroking her knuckles. The light, soothing gesture worked better than any sleeping pill on the market.

3

"She's going to be fine, Cherry," Wade whispered to keep from waking the sleeping beauty. Damn, just looking at her made him see red. Her perfect ivory complexion was now covered in bruises. The bastard would pay for hurting her. "I've already got Jonas checking into a few things for me and, as soon as Gracie's able to leave, I'm going to have her show me those e-mails. Maybe there's something there that can lead me to this guy."

"I'm worried about her. I feel responsible. Maybe if I hadn't hired her, she—"

Wade had known this was coming. "Don't even go there. This guy would still be stalking her regardless of where she worked. Which reminds me. Her other job, that office she works at, what does she do there exactly?"

"She's an administrative assistant. Why?"

"Maybe this guy works with her." Wade's gaze went back to Gracie. He remembered the tears he'd seen in her eyes the day before. Damn. He should've tried harder to get some answers then. He'd known something was wrong, but he'd let it go,

hadn't wanted to push. Well, no more. He frowned as he realized how easily the woman went to his head.

At first he'd been intrigued by the way she stood up to him.
Gracie had challenged his dominant streak something fierce.
And her cute blushes whenever he teased her turned Wade on
quicker than anything. But seeing her hurt had all his protective
instincts worked up.

Wade had never truly seen the merits of letting a woman get
too close. After all, close meant they had the power to crush
you, and he wasn't much into pain. With Gracie, everything
was different, he admitted to himself. Hell, he'd damn near beg
if it meant she'd give him just a kernel of her trust.

She started to shift around, coming awake. She tried to sit
up, and Wade saw her wince. As she opened her eyes and
looked over at him and Cherry, he saw emotion, raw and
unchecked. It broke his heart to see her so vulnerable. The Gracie he'd come to know was no victim, though. Soon, she'd be
back on her feet and driving him crazy.

"I had hoped I'd only dreamed it all." She looked over at the
cast on her wrist. "It would seem not."

Cherry smiled at her and said, "I'll go let the nurse know
you're awake."

"Thanks. The sooner the doctor checks me out, the sooner I
can get out of here. I hate hospitals."

"Doesn't everyone?"

Gracie smiled, and Wade relaxed a little. She was going to be
fine, and she wasn't leaving his sight until her stalker was behind bars. "How are you feeling?"

"Achy, but not quite as bad as yesterday." She pushed a button on the side of the bed, and it lifted her into a sitting position. "I always thought a broken bone would be horribly
painful, but I don't really feel more than a twinge unless I move
it around too much."

"You've got bruises from head to toe. And I think you might have a mark from the seat belt."

She looked down and seemed to realize how exposed she was in the light blue hospital gown. He'd tried not to look past her neck because every time he did he saw the way her full breasts filled out the top half of the flimsy thing. He felt like a complete ass for even noticing. She'd just been in an accident; the last thing she needed was him ogling her.

She pulled the sheet up higher and groaned. "I must look horrible right now."

"You're alive, Gracie," he said, as he reached up to push a wayward lock of hair off her forehead. "That's all that matters."

She nodded. "You're right." Her gaze traveled the length of him, stopping for a heart-pounding few seconds on his crotch before meeting his gaze again. "You stayed all night."

"I said I would."

"Why didn't the nurse kick you out?"

He winked. "She tried, but I can be pretty persuasive when I really want something."

She rolled her eyes and looked away. "Your ego is showing again."

"It's not ego, honey. It's my tenaciousness that kept me on guard all night."

Gracie bit her lip and fiddled with a loose thread on the sheet. "I'm sorry if I sound unappreciative. I really am glad you stayed, Wade. I don't think it was necessary, but I am glad."

He stroked her cheek with the pad of his thumb. "Wild horses couldn't drag me away." Soft as a peach, Wade thought as he dropped his hand. Her skin was so delicate; it pissed him off to see it marred. Goddamn bastard would pay for hurting Gracie. "Now, let's talk about your coming to stay with me."

"We had this discussion already."

"But we never agreed to anything."

"Fine. Then listen very closely, Wade. I am not coming to stay with you."

Wade wanted to curse. The woman was too damn stubborn. He schooled his expression and said, "I'm still going to be your shadow, Gracie. If you don't stay at my place, that's fine, but I'm not letting this asshole get to you."

"My shadow?"

"Bodyguard. As in I'm watching over you day and night until we find out who this guy is."

"I can take care of myself. This doesn't need to be your problem."

"The instant I saw those tears on your cheeks the other day it became my problem. I'm not about to walk away and leave you to deal with this by yourself. You'd better get used to having me around."

"If you insist on doing this then I'm paying you. Whatever is your usual rate."

He stiffened. "No."

"What do you mean *no?*"

He vied for control over his anger. She didn't need him acting like an overbearing dickhead right now. "I won't take your money, Gracie. You're a friend. I don't charge my friends."

She crossed her arms over her chest, her cute little nose shooting in the air. "But I'm a client like any other. What's the problem?"

"You aren't any other client, and we both know it." He planted his fists on the bed by her hips and leaned in close. Damn, he could smell her frilly scent. What the hell was it? It'd always driven him crazy trying to pinpoint the delicious aroma. Like cotton candy and vanilla bean ice cream all rolled into one. That was Gracie.

"In case you haven't been paying attention, I'm attracted to you. Hell, that's a lie. I'm not attracted to you; I'm in lust with you. This is more to me than business. And don't pretend you haven't felt the chemistry between us, because that'll just make me mad."

Her cheeks turned pink. "Okay, I've felt it. But I'm in no position to act on it right now. My life is a mess. I know you had to see my dad last night, drunk and mean as usual. I swear, Wade, if you don't take my money then I'm going to feel like I owe you, and I hate owing people. I owe you enough as it is. I'm so tired of—"

Wade cut off her ramblings with a gentle kiss. The barely-there touch sent a streak of lightning through his bloodstream. When he pulled away, Gracie was as still as a statue. "We'll work something out, honey. It's going to be okay."

She nodded, and he wanted to say more, but the door opened, and the doctor came into the room. Wade was ushered into the hall where Cherry and Dante waited.

He went straight to Cherry and wrapped his arms around her. "It's going to be okay."

"She's agreed to come stay with you?"

"I wish, but no. I am, however, going to be her bodyguard until we can figure out who this guy is and catch him."

"Thank you, Wade." Cherry pulled out of his arms and stepped back. Dante placed his hands on her shoulders from behind. Their relationship was so different than the one she'd had with Brody. There hadn't been much support or comfort in that. Brody had always been too self-absorbed to give a damn about his wife's needs. It did his heart good to see Cherry so well loved by Dante.

Thinking about Cherry's ex reminded Wade that he'd forgotten to tell Cherry about Brody's phone call the other day. "Uh, Cherry, I hate to mention this now and risk adding more stress to your day, but Brody called me."

Cherry nodded. "Yeah, I know. Unfortunately the idiot called me, too."

"I had a word with him," Dante muttered.

"A word, huh?" Wade knew better. Dante was protective as hell of Cherry. "You put the fear of God into him, didn't you?"

Cherry smiled. "I'm pretty sure we've heard the last of Brody, Wade."

"Good," Wade replied. "That's one problem solved, at least."

"I need to ask you something about Gracie," Cherry said, her eyes filled with concern. "Please don't take it the wrong way."

He didn't like the sound of that. "Shoot."

"What are your intentions toward her?"

He quirked a brow. "My intentions? What are you, her mom?"

Cherry rolled her eyes. "Of course not, but I am a friend. I don't want to see her hurt." She visibly cringed. "No more than she already is, I mean."

Wade snorted. "I don't think I've made a big secret out of the fact that I want her, Cherry. I have since she started working for you. But I'm not going to push myself down her throat either."

"She's vulnerable right now. She needs a friend more than she needs a lover. I know you can see that, Wade."

"What I see is a woman in need of my help. I'm going to give it to her. If she ends up in my bed it'll be because she wants to be there and not because she was coerced."

Cherry dragged her slim fingers through her hair, as if frustrated with him. He wasn't used to her prying into his personal life and he wasn't sure he liked it one damn bit. Especially where Gracie was concerned. He was still trying to figure that one out himself.

"I've never seen you like this. What is it about her that makes you so persistent? Is she a challenge, is that it?"

Wade's emotions were too close to the surface on this, and he snapped. "You need to back off, Cherry."

"Watch it, Harrison," Dante said, interjecting for the first time. He wrapped an arm around Cherry's middle, pulling her back against him. Dante sent him a look of warning over Cherry's head, and Wade got the message loud and clear.

"Damn it, I'm sorry. I'm pissed that she's hurt. Pissed I wasn't there to stop it. Pissed that she didn't confide in me sooner. She's been dealing with this prick for two months, and all this time she never said a word."

Cherry placed her palm against his cheek. He instantly relaxed. "She's opening up to you now, and that's all that matters. Just be careful with her. I don't think she knows how to handle all your ... attention. She's a bit innocent when it comes to men, I think."

He'd noticed that as well. The first time he'd asked her out to dinner, she'd stammered and blushed like a teenager being asked to go to prom. He'd wondered then just how experienced she was and why someone hadn't snatched her up already. When she'd turned him down, he'd tried again. Each time she'd declined he'd had the feeling she wanted to say yes, but for whatever reason couldn't allow herself. Was it because of the stalker?

Answers would come later. For now, he needed to calm Cherry's mama bear instincts. "I promise to treat her with kid gloves. Everything will be fine. You'll see."

Cherry nodded and started to speak, but the door to Gracie's room opened, and the doctor stepped out. He looked at the three of them and smiled. "She's doing fine. I'm writing up a prescription for the pain, but as soon as her paperwork is finished she can go home."

"That's great news. Thanks, Doctor Shelton."

"She will need to see an orthopedist, and she's going to need some help with that wrist, of course."

"We'll take care of it," Wade said.

"Good. I'll leave you to her."

This was it. Soon she'd be out of that sterile room and home where she belonged. And he'd be watching over her twenty-four hours a day. He only wished she'd agreed to staying with him. Adrenaline pumped through his veins as an image of Gracie, sprawled out on his bed, naked, those pretty green eyes of hers full of heat, filled his vision. Oh, yeah, he was really the noble guy helping a friend in need. Right.

He clutched the little slip of paper and watched her leave the hospital in a wheelchair, friends all around her. He hadn't wanted to hurt her, but it'd been necessary, right? She needed to learn her place. She would quit that disgusting job now. He'd had nightmares imagining her working at a place where men and women got naked and allowed a complete stranger to touch their bodies. She was too good for a place that catered to such heathens.

She smiled at something, and his heart skipped a beat. God, she was beauty personified. Even injured she was his regal princess. Her red hair, shining like a fiery halo in the sun, framed a perfect oval face. His love. His perfect Gracie Lynn.

He'd wanted to go to her after the accident, but he'd known it wasn't time. It was too soon. Their time would come; then she'd be his forever. As he started the car and began to pull out of the parking space, a movement caught his attention and he stopped, stared. The large, linebacker-looking man pushing Gracie Lynn's wheelchair stopped suddenly and leaned close. His hand rested on Gracie Lynn's shoulder. There was something in his expression, the way he looked at her, as if he had a right to her. He'd seen him before, of course. He was always coming in and out of that horrid little massage therapy office. When Gracie Lynn smiled up at the man, his skin turned clammy, and he clutched the steering wheel.

"No, no, no. She wouldn't betray me. Not my sweet love. Not my Gracie Lynn." It was nearly noon before he became aware of the tears, spilling unchecked down his cheeks.

4

_____

Gracie shifted her arm, trying to make her wrist more comfortable. It had the opposite effect, as the small movement caused pain to shoot clear to her shoulder. She winced, but tried not to let it show. She already felt ridiculous. Wade was so strong, so capable, and she had a feeling he'd be able to handle a broken wrist with his eyes closed. She looked out the windshield and saw their turn coming up. "Turn down the next road on the right."

Wade slowed and made the turn. He was being extra cautious in deference to what she'd been through, she knew. She started to tell him there was no need to worry, she was fine, but when they came to the S curve her heart skipped a beat. Images flashed in her mind. She remembered slamming her foot on the brake, her fingers clenching onto the steering wheel, and the horrible realization that she was about to crash. She'd thought for sure she was going to end up in the ravine. Instead she'd hit a big oak tree. Head on, she remembered now.

Wade slowed his black pickup truck to a crawl. "This is where it happened, huh?"

She could feel his gaze on her, but she couldn't seem to look away from the destroyed weeds and brush where her car had torn a path into the woods. "Yeah."

"It's okay, Gracie." His soothing tone calmed her nerves. "You're still in one piece; that's all that matters." He reached over and patted her on the hand.

She turned and stared at him. The tenderness in his expression melted away some of the tension. "Thank you, Wade." She paused before adding, "For everything."

"We're going to find out who this guy is, sweetheart. Soon, I promise."

He was so sure in his ability to track down her stalker and make the world a safe place again. Gracie had the feeling that if anyone could do it, Wade Harrison could. As they started moving again, she forced her mind to concentrate on her mental list of things she would need to take care of. Like checking with her neighbor, Mrs. Swinson. She needed to see if the older woman could help her out for the next few weeks while her wrist healed.

"So, do you have any friends who can come and give you a hand?"

Gracie frowned. "Do you read minds now?"

"Huh?"

"I was just sitting here thinking about that."

He smiled and kept his gaze on the road. She took a second to admire his profile. If only her life wasn't such a mess she could do more than admire. She squashed that wayward thought. "My neighbor, Mrs. Swinson. She's one of the sweetest ladies. A little nosy, but a dear."

"Think she'll be up to helping you?"

Gracie nodded. "She's sixty-three, but the woman is a dynamo. A rather loud, one-hundred-pound powerhouse actually."

He laughed. "I really need to meet this lady."

The thought made her cringe. Gracie could well imagine what Mrs. Swinson would say to a gorgeous man like Wade. She definitely wasn't afraid to speak her mind. Come to think of it, she wasn't sure she even wanted the two to meet. She didn't need Wade any more involved with her life than necessary. Gracie's mind turned to the meeting they'd had with the police detective after they'd left the hospital.

"So, what do you think the cops will turn up?"

Detective Henderson had promised to have her car looked at personally and to let her know if it appeared to have been tampered with. His attitude toward her wasn't quite so patronizing this time around. She suspected her bruised face and having her arm in a sling had forced him to take her much more seriously. Of course, Wade's commanding presence hadn't hurt either. He'd snarled and growled like a grizzly.

"I think they'll find a totaled car and not much else. That S curve is damn secluded. The chance of a witness is pretty slim."

She mulled that over in her head before saying, "He picked the ideal spot, didn't he?"

"Yeah, which makes me think he's been down this road a few times."

A chill ran down her spine. "You think he's been to my apartment?"

"Yeah, Gracie, I do."

"Oh, God, I didn't even think of it. I just assumed . . . Oh, God."

"You aren't alone now, sweetheart. I'm your shadow now, remember?"

She liked the use of the endearment. It wasn't the first time he'd called her sweetheart or honey, but it never ceased to send a little zing of excitement through her. "How do we catch him? He's like a ghost, coming and going without being seen."

"We start with the e-mails."

"What will you do with those?"

"Jonas will take care of that end. He's a whiz at computers. He might be able to figure out who's sending them. A location, anything would be better than what we have right now."

"What if it's a dead end?"

"Then we start working backwards. I'll need to know your habits, your schedule, the people you interact with on a daily basis."

Seeing where he was headed, she frowned. "You think I know this guy?"

"Maybe, or maybe he just knows *you*. It could be someone you work with or even someone you've come into contact with at the bank, grocery store. Maybe all you did was smile at him, but whatever it was he took it personally. He thinks he's part of your life now."

Frustration welled up, and she slammed her fist against the passenger window. "This is just crazy. Why me? I'm not that exciting!"

Wade reached over and patted her thigh. "Calm down. Beating up my truck won't help. Don't try to make sense of this. The guy's warped. We start with what we know. The e-mails. The way he talks to you in them. His use of your first and middle name. We'll look at each sentence and see if something rings any bells for you."

The stroke of Wade's thumb over the back of her hand soothed her. The way he talked, so methodically, made Gracie wonder if he'd seen this type of thing before. "This isn't new for you, is it?"

"Stalker cases, no. Being personally involved with the client, yes."

She shivered at his softly spoken words. Distracted by the idea of just how personal she wanted to get with Wade, she nearly missed her apartment complex. "Here! Turn here!"

Wade slammed on the brakes and swung into the parking lot before stopping and sparing her a questioning look.

"Sorry, I wasn't paying attention." *I was a little busy with thoughts of hot, sweaty sex with you.*

"Yeah, I got that. Which building?"

She pointed straight ahead. "That's mine. It's a garden apartment." She rattled off her apartment number as she unbuckled her seat belt.

He nodded and drove forward. After parking and turning off the engine, he slung an arm over the back of her seat, crowding her. "So, how's the security system?"

His nearness did things to her, wicked things. "Uh, I have a deadbolt if that's what you mean."

Wade tsked. "You live here alone and there's no security system?"

Gracie stiffened. She could see exactly where this conversation was headed. "Those things are expensive, Wade. There's no way I can afford something like that. Besides, I'm not always here alone. I have friends. Neighbors. I'm not an idiot; I do take precautions."

His gaze snagged hers. "I never said you were an idiot, sweetheart. But I think we can both agree that it's time you upgraded to a decent alarm. Especially considering you have a private entrance."

"Once I have enough money saved, yes."

"I'm getting you an alarm system."

Gracie immediately saw red. Damned arrogant man. She mentally counted to ten. Otherwise she'd end up saying something they'd both regret. "No, you aren't. I'm not a freaking charity case." He started to speak, but she wasn't quite through. "You continue to assume I'm somehow your responsibility. We aren't together, Wade. You're helping me with this stalker, and I'm grateful for it. Beyond that you don't have any right to dictate how I live my life."

His eyes narrowed, and she watched as a muscle in his jaw twitched. He leaned close, too close. She could smell his masculine scent, see his five o'clock shadow, and her pussy throbbed. "When it comes to your safety, I make the rules. Until we catch your secret admirer, you do as I say. Tell me you understand this, Gracie."

Not about to give in, Gracie crossed her arms over her chest and said, "You are not buying me a security system."

He didn't speak. Not a word. For long moments he simply stared at her. She fidgeted under his intense scrutiny. When he reached up, cupped her chin in his gentle palm, and smiled, she breathed a sigh of relief.

"You're a very independent woman, Gracie Baron."

His voice skittered along her nerve endings. No man should have a voice like that. It simply wasn't fair. "I've had to be."

He stroked her lower lip with the pad of his thumb, and Gracie swore she felt the caress along her clit. "You need to learn a few things. The first of which is that just because you allow someone to help you, it doesn't necessarily make you weak."

"You aren't just anyone, Wade. You're a man, and you've made it clear you want me."

His thumb stopped moving. "So because I want to buy you a security system, and I want you safe, that automatically means I'm going to expect things from you? Like a mistress or something?"

She hadn't meant it to come out quite like that. Damn, the man made her head spin. "No, that's not what I'm saying. Look, in my experience men don't do things unless there's something in it for them."

"Then you've been hanging out with the wrong guys, sweetheart. When we get naked and I'm buried deep inside your sexy body it'll be because we both want it. And it won't have a damn thing to do with repaying a debt either."

Gracie didn't know what to say. In fact, silence seemed like a good plan.

He shook his head and smiled, then dropped his hand. "You're quite a puzzle, Gracie."

Okay, that so didn't seem complimentary. "What does that mean?"

"You're cynical yet innocent at the same time. You look at me as if you want to eat me up, then push me away when I get too close."

Had she been doing that? Giving him mixed signals? "It was never my intention, Wade. I'm sorry if I've been a . . . tease."

The hand on the back of her seat moved to her hair. His fingers sifted and played. "Not a tease. But you are afraid of me."

She shook her head, desperate to stay on track. "No, I'm not afraid of you. It's not that."

His fingers, those talented masculine fingers, moved along the column of her neck. He kneaded and stroked, and Gracie wanted to melt against the seat and let him have at her.

"Then what, baby? You feel the sparks; I know you do. I've seen you wavering on that fence. Each time I ask you out, you're a hairsbreadth away from saying yes. Yet you deny yourself each time."

He really was a mind reader. Either that or she was just that transparent. Both options sucked. "I don't want to get into this here. Besides, I'm getting hungry." A lie, but a necessary one. Much more of his deep voice, his skillful caresses, and she'd be begging him to fuck her.

Wade released her and leaned back. "I'll let you off the hook for now. But soon we need to have this conversation."

When he opened his door, Gracie knew her days were numbered. She'd been fighting the attraction too long. The only thing left to figure out was how she would handle it once he'd had his fill of her.

5

For the millionth time, Wade reminded himself that Gracie was injured. She needed a little time. He could give that to her, he assured himself. Gracie squirmed in his arms and muttered under her breath. His cock hardened in his jeans.

"Stop squirming," he growled.

"I don't need to be carried."

Wade rolled his eyes. "You act as if I'm a wimp. Afraid I'll drop you?"

"No, I'm afraid I'm going to clobber you. I feel ridiculous. I didn't break my leg, Wade."

He grinned now. "I know, but I sort of like having you in my arms."

She looked at him with that schoolmarm expression that turned his dick to granite. "It's a sin to take advantage of a woman who is in no shape to defend herself."

He leaned down to whisper into her ear, "I never said I was choir boy, sweetheart."

She didn't say anything else. A surefire sign he was getting under her skin. Gracie only went silent when she was aroused.

He'd noticed it before. She could flay him alive with her sharp tongue, but turned on, she seemed unable to string two words together. What would she be like once he got her beneath him? Would she shout out her pleasure or purr like a cat?

"Keys?"

Gracie pulled them out of the purse she had clutched in her good hand. He watched her slip the key into the doorknob first, then use another for the deadbolt. He still couldn't believe she had some nut job hot on her tail and she hadn't invested in an alarm. Wade thought of her father, the drunken ass who'd visited her at the hospital. Didn't the man care at all about his daughter?

After unlocking both locks, she pushed the door wide. Wade crossed the threshold and entered Gracie's private domain. He'd wondered a few times what her place would look like. She seemed so straightlaced. He expected something along the lines of a doctor's office waiting room. Neat sitting arrangements and alphabetized reading material. The real thing wasn't anything like he'd expected.

The spacious living room appeared like something right out of *Country Living*. The light pine coffee table and entertainment cabinet, along with a big, fluffy, blue couch and easy chair were a nice surprise, and not at all what he'd expected. There were books, dozens of them, scattered about. The place looked lived in. He liked it. It sure as hell wasn't the neat, sterile surroundings he'd expected.

"Cozy," he said.

"Say anything negative, and I'll hurt you."

He chuckled. "I like your home, Gracie. It's warm, inviting." As he carefully sat her in the center of the couch, his gaze caught the title of one of the books on the cushion next to her. He bent and picked it up. "*Dream Lover*. Really?"

Her cheeks turned pink, and she snatched it out of his hand. "Not a word, Wade Harrison. Not one word."

Wade straightened and strode to the front door that still stood open. He closed it and turned the lock, before facing Gracie again. Making a mental note of the way she clutched onto the book, as if her life depended on it, Wade said, "Judging by that blush and the way you're holding that book, I'm thinking I may need to read it. Maybe I'll learn more about the owner."

"If you value your life you'll stay away from my books."

He tsked and crossed his arms over his chest. "Threatening violence over a silly romance novel?"

"It's not silly. I treasure my books." She smoothed her palm over the cover and smiled at it as if it were a living thing, rather than paper and ink. A spurt of jealousy shot through him. He wanted her stroking him, damn it. "They've gotten me through some pretty rough times." Her head shot up and she pointed at him. "And don't make assumptions about things you know nothing about."

Wade had meant to harass her, to get her mind off her aches and pains. And it'd worked, but he could see the signs of strain in the stiff way she sat and the lines around her mouth. The pain meds were wearing off. He hated to see Gracie in pain.

He started across the room. "Where's your kitchen?"

"Why?"

He stopped and rolled his eyes. "Don't sound so damn suspicious. I'm not going to raid your refrigerator. I want to get you a glass of water so you can take another pain pill."

"Sorry." She looked down at her lap and fiddled with the hem of her T-shirt. "I'm a little frustrated, I guess. I'm not used to feeling so helpless. Quite frankly, it sucks."

The small admission spoke volumes. Gracie didn't strike him as the type to admit weakness. He closed the distance between them and sat next to her on the couch. He cupped her chin in his palm, enjoying the feel of her satin skin way too much, and murmured, "None of us ever enjoys being helpless, honey. I should know. I've had my share of broken bones over the years and had to ask for help every time. It does suck, but that's what friends are for, to lean on when the going gets rough."

"I can't imagine you ever being helpless, Wade."

Her soft voice and the sincerity in her bright green eyes went straight to his gut. "I'm not Superman." Although in that moment she made him feel as strong as ten men. "I break just as easily as the next guy. Just ask Jonas. He and I have had to play nursemaid to each other more times than either of us care to admit."

"Jonas. He's your partner, right?"

"Yeah, you'll meet him tomorrow." He removed his hand from her chin and gave in to the need to touch her red hair. Gracie had hair of silk. Pretty red silk. "I asked him to stop by and take a look at those e-mails."

She closed her eyes and let out a breath. "I'm not used to this, Wade."

"What?" He couldn't seem to stay focused when he touched her. He removed his hand and reminded himself, once again, that she wasn't in top fighting form.

"Having people around. In my home. Messing with my things. I didn't realize how much I'd gotten used to being alone. I'm not sure that's a good thing either."

"Listen to me, honey." Once her gaze was on him, he said, "Everything's going to work out. We're going to catch this guy, and you're going to be back on your feet in no time. Right now all I want you to do is rest." She nodded, and he stood. "I'm going to get you another pain pill and order some pizza. What do you want on your half?"

"Mmm, pizza, now that sounds like heaven. That hospital food was crap. Pepperoni and green peppers on mine."

She smiled. Wade couldn't help but feel as if he could climb Mount Everest. What was it about the woman that made him want to be her hero? Christ, he needed to get a handle on his feelings toward her, whatever they were. "It's wrong to ruin a perfectly good pizza with green peppers, but your wish is my command."

"Through the doorway is the kitchen; the hallway will take you to the bedroom, office, and bathroom."

He winked. "Got it. I'll be right back."

He started out of the room, but her voice stopped him. "Bring the phone back with you. I need to call my neighbor and see if she's free to help out."

He laughed. "Getting tired of me already?"

She shook her head and looked down at her lap. "I . . . I like having you here. It's nice."

"You might not feel that way later when I start back on my campaign to buy you a new security alarm."

Her head shot up, and she opened her mouth to speak, but Wade didn't stick around to hear whatever biting remark she might have for him this time. She would be safe. With or without her compliance. That's all that mattered to him.

"You can't possibly be full already. You only ate one slice."

She would've laughed at the incredulous look on Wade's face if she hadn't been so aware of how good he looked sitting on the floor across from the coffee table, licking pizza sauce off his index finger. She had the insane urge to lean forward and do the licking for him. "I'm stuffed, trust me. I feel like I could bust."

"I ate half the pizza, and you're full off one slice?" His eyes narrowed. "Is this one of those girly things where a woman is too embarrassed to pig out in front of a man?"

She dabbed her lips with the napkin and sat back, a feeling of contentment washing over her. It'd been eons since she'd been able to relax. Really relax. It felt good. "Don't flatter yourself. I'd never choose a man over pizza; that's just wrong."

"Hmm, I'm not sure if I should be offended or not."

"Don't take it personally. Pizza and chocolate top the list of favorite indulgences for most women."

"And where do men rate?"

"Not very high, sorry."

He licked his finger again, this time more slowly, as if he knew the effect it was having on her libido. "I feel challenged to reach the top of your list, Gracie."

She had to clear the lump out of her throat before she could reply. "You could try."

He sat up straighter and murmured, "I don't try, I succeed."

"I—" The doorbell rang, interrupting her next teasing remark. Wade shot to his feet, then leaned down. When he straightened there was a small gun in his hand. Where in the world had he been hiding that? "That's probably Mrs. Swinson."

"Probably, but it pays to be careful." He went to the door and looked through the peephole, then chuckled.

"What's so funny?"

"She's a little . . . flamboyant."

The doorbell chimed again, and Wade flipped the locks and opened the door. "Mrs. Swinson?"

"Well, of course it is! Who else would I be?"

"Indeed," he said and stepped back to let the small whirlwind through.

Gracie contained a laugh. Barely. "The purple works for you, Jean." The woman was forever changing her hair color. Last week it'd been a neon shade of green. This time it was a little less blinding, thank God.

"Yeah, the green made me look sickly." She looked Gracie over and made a tsking sound. "You look like you've been hit by a truck, young lady." She plopped a large duffel bag on the floor and hobbled over to the couch. She sat next to Gracie and patted her thigh. "You may as well tell me everything. I know there must be a reason for that big hunk answering the door wielding a gun."

Gracie pointedly eyed Wade's weapon. He merely shrugged and tucked it into a hidden holster against his ankle. And why did that seem so sexy? "Uh, it's a long story, Jean."

She hopped up. "I'll get the coffee started then." She looked at Wade and pointed to the pizza and napkins strewn about. "You, make yourself useful and clean up this mess."

"Yes, ma'am."

"Ma'am? Call me that again, and I'll flatten you. It's Jean."

"Right, sorry. Wade Harrison."

She grinned and nodded. "You're trainable; I like that in a man." She was already heading for the kitchen and missed the frown Wade tossed her way.

"She's interesting."

"She grows on you."

He grunted and started cleaning up their dinner. She felt guilty sitting there while everyone else worked. She started to stand, but Wade was too quick. In a heartbeat, he was in front of her, pressing on her shoulders. "Don't piss me off by trying to get up. I will paddle your ass, Gracie."

"That's supposed to sound threatening, but right now it just sounds sort of fun."

He frowned as he crouched in front of her. "You feeling okay, honey?"

Actually, she did feel a little . . . off. "Loopy. Why do I feel loopy, Wade?"

"The meds. We should call your doctor and see about getting the dose adjusted."

"Good idea. I'll do it tomorrow. I won't need another one tonight anyway."

He tucked a strand of hair behind her ear and stood. She

watched, fascinated by his every move as he picked up the box and several used napkins. "Can I trust you to sit still while I throw the pizza out?"

She gritted her teeth against the need to do something, anything. "Yes."

"Good, I'll be right back."

Gracie slumped against the couch. "I'm not going anywhere, clearly."

6

"I should wring your neck for not telling me about all this, Gracie."

As if she hadn't heard those words before. "Get in line," Gracie muttered.

"Well, what's done is done." Jean turned her attention to Wade. "So, you're going to catch this guy, is that it?"

"Yes, I am." Wade stood at the front of the room, staring out her window, his entire demeanor on alert. Was he looking for her stalker? It gave her the willies to think he could be out there right now, watching, waiting.

"Good. What can I do?"

Wade kept his face averted as he replied, "Your only job is to help Gracie."

"It won't be the first time I've helped someone with a cast. My youngest, Brian, broke his arm when he was in the fifth grade. Jumped off a barn roof. Crazy kid. It nearly drove him crazy until it healed."

"How's he doing these days?"

Jean quirked a brow. "You mean since you dumped him?"

"I did not dump him! We had one date; that's it."

Wade slowly turned around, his brows scrunched together. "How long ago was this?"

"Last year, and it really wasn't anything. Brian is a nice guy, but the chemistry wasn't there."

Jean waved her hand in the air. "He said the same thing, but I had hopes. Four kids and not one of them have seen fit to give me grandkids yet."

Good Lord, if she'd known the woman had plans of babies and happily ever after, Gracie never would have gone out with her son in the first place. "Uh, anyway, the doctor said it's a fracture. He didn't seem to think it was too bad."

"Don't you worry; you'll get the hang of using one hand pretty quick. Just be glad it wasn't your dominant hand."

"I don't want Gracie pushing herself, though. That wrist and those bruises need time to heal."

Jean snorted. "Gracie isn't some delicate blossom, Wade. And she's not about to let a broken wrist and some bruises keep her down. You might want to coddle her, but if she doesn't want to be coddled, then nothing you say or do will change that. She's got a mind of her own."

"Don't I know it." Wade groaned as he moved away from the window and sat in the easy chair adjacent to Gracie. "I need to know your schedule, Gracie."

She hadn't even thought of how tired he must be. The only sleep he'd gotten was in that horrible chair at the hospital. "You need to go home and get some rest, Wade."

He put his elbows on his thighs and leaned closer. "Weren't you paying attention when I said I was going to be your shadow?"

She blinked. "Well, yes, but—"

"But nothing." Wade said, as if he were somehow lord and master. "I'm going to be here day and night until this guy is caught."

Gracie tucked her hair behind her ear, annoyed and too tired to fight him anymore. "You want to sleep here?"

"Where'd you think I was going to sleep?"

"At your own home, of course."

"The bad guys don't stop being bad just because the sun goes down. You need protection from this asshole, and since you won't stay at my place, I have no choice but to stay here."

She sighed. "You can be really infuriating."

"I've been told."

She shifted her arm in an attempt to alleviate the stiffness. It didn't work. "You can sleep on the couch."

Jean laughed and pointed to Wade. "If it were me, no way would you be sleeping on the couch, sugar."

Gracie's mouth dropped open. "Jean!"

Color stained Wade's cheeks as he stood. "Uh, I need to get a few things out of the trunk. Maybe Jean can help you get ready for bed before she leaves."

Once Wade was gone, Jean turned toward her, all signs of joking gone. "You're lucky to be alive, young lady."

"Yeah, I agree." Gracie couldn't even focus on the accident, not with the thought of Wade sleeping in her home rattling inside her head. He'd be a few feet away, all night long. An image of him all sprawled out on her couch, his shirt gone, jeans unbuttoned and riding low sprang to mind. She had to remind herself to breathe.

"You like him, huh?"

Jean's question tore her out of her little fantasy. "It's complicated." She didn't know what she wanted from Wade, but she had a feeling it wasn't just a quick tumble. She stood and waited for Jean to do the same. Together they walked to her bedroom.

When she entered, Jean flipped on the light, and Gracie grabbed a nightgown from the dresser drawer. She held it up, wondering what Wade would think of the plain garment. The white cotton, knee-length gown was soft and comfortable, and sleeveless, making it easier to put on over her cast. Still, it was horribly plain. She looked up and saw her reflection in the dresser mirror. Crap, coupled with the bruises all over her face she'd be lucky if he didn't run screaming.

"You know what I see?"

Gracie wasn't sure she wanted to hear Jean's next words, but she shook her head and said, "No. What?"

"I see two people dancing around each other. He's not here because you're his pal. He's here because you belong to him, and he's not about to let some freak hurt you."

"I haven't even agreed to go on a date yet! How could I possibly belong to him?"

Jean shrugged. "It's in the way he looks at you, possessive, hot. He's teetering on the edge of control, if you ask me. You could have him eating out of your hand, sweetie. So, what's the holdup?"

She threw the gown on the bed. "My life is a mess! My dad showed up at the hospital drunk. His only child is in a car accident, and he shows up drunk and starts cussing everyone out. I have a creepy stalker intent on making me his 'love.' I have to work two jobs just to keep my head above water because Dad's always drinking away his rent money. I'm just not up for more drama in my life. I need to straighten some things out before I can even think of having a relationship with a man as dominating and tense as Wade."

Jean picked up the gown and started to smooth out the wrinkles. "Take it from me, life will always be full of drama. There will always be something more pressing, always be stress. But a man like the one out there"—she pointed toward the living room—"vowing to protect you at all costs, well, they don't come around every day. Keep pushing him away, and he may just take the hint."

The idea made her heart speed up. To never know Wade's

touch, his kisses, to never feel him buried deep inside her where she so badly needed him the most, sent a shot of panic through her bloodstream. "I-I don't want to push him away."

Jean smiled. "I thought not. So, maybe tonight when you two are alone, you can show that boy what 'protect and serve' really means."

For the first time in days, Gracie laughed, so hard her bruised body protested. "I think you might just be onto something, Jean."

Wade paced the length of the living room. He should have known he wouldn't be able to sleep. All he could think about was how sweet and alluring Gracie had looked in her night-gown earlier. The oversized cotton *sheet* shouldn't have been sexy. In fact, he'd been secretly grateful she'd picked something so concealing to sleep in. He didn't need any more provocation where Gracie was concerned. Then she'd moved toward the couch and placed a sheet and a pillow on the coffee table for him, and she'd inadvertently put her body on display for him as the light from the table lamp turned the gown all but transparent. She'd turned around and smiled at him. The soft curves of her body, so close, yet so far out of his reach, had been a tempta-tion he nearly hadn't been able to ignore. Hell, he'd had to leave the room just to keep from jumping her. Wade had seen Gracie in her prim little outfits at Serene Comfort and thought her body perfect. He'd seen her in the flimsy hospital gown and knew instinctively that her full, round breasts would fill his palms; the curve of her hips would create the perfect cradle for his cock. Still, nothing could have prepared him for the eyeful he'd gotten earlier.

"Fuck," he growled. Pushing a hand through his hair, Wade fell onto the couch and wished like hell he had the right to sim-ply go to her, slip in between the sheets, and spend the rest of the night touching, tasting. He wanted to hear her cry out his name as she climaxed. He ached to strip her bare and lick every blessed inch of her.

"Don't you ever sleep?"

Wade shot off the couch so fast he ran his shin into the coffee table. He cursed and twisted around, then froze. Gracie stood in the entrance of the dark room, her fiery red hair a disheveled mess. She'd removed the sling from her injured arm and was now cradling her fractured wrist in her good hand. He stepped around the couch, closing the distance between them. "You okay?"

She winced. "I rolled over on my stomach and caught my wrist on the bedside table."

He felt like a complete shit. He'd been wallowing in unrequited lust, and she'd been in pain. "Come on, you need your sleep." He cupped her elbow and took her back to her room. Wade didn't bother with the light. He'd memorized the layout of the entire place hours ago. He led her across the room and held the covers up for her to slip beneath. He tucked her in and started out of the room, away from temptation, when Gracie's quiet voice floated over to him.

"Don't leave."

Wade looked over his shoulder, for the first time in his life unsure what to do. "You want me to stay?"

She clutched the blanket in a white-knuckled fist. "I-I've been denying myself for so long, and I'm just so tired of it. I've let him dictate my every move, Wade."

Knowing he should let her sleep, but unable to ignore the pleading in her voice, Wade covered the distance in two strides. He sat down on the bed, and their bodies touched. He had to grit his teeth against the need to pull the blanket away so he could be closer to her. The green fire in her eyes pulled at something in him, something basic and primal. Even in the dark he could make out the need in those gorgeous green eyes. He fingered one of the straps on her gown and murmured, "I've been thinking about you all night. This nightgown . . ." He wasn't sure how to put his thoughts into words. He sucked at poetic, romantic moments.

Her shoulders seem to slump. "It's shapeless and blah, I know."

"Hmm, maybe. But it's also see-through in the right light."

Her eyes grew round. "It is?"

He smiled, tracing the delicate line of her collarbone. "Every curve was on display for me earlier. It's a look that's been burned into my psyche, baby."

She bit her lower lip and looked away. "I didn't intend to entice you."

Her sweet innocence made him want to hide her away from the big, bad world, even as he imagined all the wicked things he wanted to teach her. "I know. But you need to understand something, Gracie."

"What's that?"

"Everything you do entices me," he admitted, his voice hoarse with emotion. "I see you walk, and my cock gets hard. You tear strips off my hide with your wicked tongue, and it's all I can do to keep my hands to myself."

"I've wanted you, too, Wade. Turning you down has been the hardest thing I've ever done."

He lowered his head until his lips brushed hers. "Then I propose we make up for lost time." He kissed her, careful to go slow, to be gentle, but when he licked over her bottom lip and her taste hit his tongue, everything in him shifted, changed. So soft and plump and delicious. Christ, wild horses couldn't drag him away from her now.

7

"Sweet as sunshine," Wade whispered. He let his tongue tease the seam of her lips until finally she sighed and let him in. Mint, and the warm flavor of Gracie. Hell, a man could become an addict. He lifted his head and stared down at her. Gracie's eyes were closed, and her tongue swiped over her bottom lip, as if reliving their kiss. When she started to lift her injured hand toward him, her eyes flew open, and he could see the pain there.

"I forgot about my wrist."

I should not be here. "You're in pain. I should let you get some rest, sweetheart." He had to force the words out between clenched teeth.

She quickly looked away. "You didn't like it."

He didn't have to guess at what she meant. He cupped her chin in his palm and forced her gaze back to his. "I loved it. I want more. I want all night. I'm so damn hungry for you I'm about to self combust."

She lifted her good hand and pressed it to his chest. "Then why do you want to leave?"

"Only an asshole would try something with you right now."

A spark of fire lit her eyes. "I know what I'm doing. You aren't taking advantage of me. Injured or not, I would still be lying here aching for you."

His cock leaped with joy over the bold admission so quietly uttered. Still, he tried one last time to do the right thing. "You'll be pissed at me in the morning, Gracie. When we come together I want you smiling the next day, not fretting over whether it was the right thing to do or not."

She placed her palm on his chest, directly over his heart. As if she held some sort of power over him, his heartbeat accelerated. "You aren't listening, Wade. I've wanted you from the moment you came into Serene Comfort. Even before you asked me out. I've kept my hands to myself for so long. Now, I want to know what I've been missing."

Something inside Wade snapped. Hearing the ache, the desire, in her husky voice was too much. Hell, he wasn't a damn saint. "You're sore and bruised, sweetheart, and nothing on this earth could convince me to make that ache worse." When she started to speak, to continue pleading her case most likely, he plowed on. "But I can give you a taste of what's to come."

Gracie had a sexy little smile on her lips, and her hair was like satin. The perfect red halo. It covered the pillow and gave him a perfect view of her slender, delicate neck. He might well have been a vampire in some other life because the need to taste her pulsing vein with his tongue and bite into her pale, ivory flesh there, marking her, was nearly overpowering.

Wade leaned closer and whispered, "Looking at you in this bed is turning me on right now, baby."

"Good. That means we're on the same page then."

He chuckled at her matter-of-fact tone and reached out to stroke her cheek with the tip of his index finger. "Close your eyes for me," he gently ordered.

She shook her head in denial. "I want to see you."

"And you will, but first, close your eyes."

She obeyed, and Wade's cock hardened. He wanted her total submission; nothing less would do. Not for him. He wanted to seduce her, to mesmerize her into doing as he wished. Her lashes began to flutter open, but he touched each lid with a kiss, effectively keeping them closed. "Keep them that way until I say."

She remained quiet, but her lids never lifted, thrilling the hell out of him by her sweet surrender. He caressed her hair with his fingers, stroking the silky tresses. "I love your hair, sweetheart. So soft and baby fine."

Wade trailed his hand down the silky length to smooth one finger over her neck. He touched the pulse beating wildly in her throat, and it seemed to quicken right under his fingertip. Leaning in, he inhaled her feminine fragrance. "Your scent is making me nuts. Bet you didn't know I've thought about you like this, did you, Gracie?" Her mouth fell open, tempting him. He covered it with his own, tasting both surprise and arousal. He kept it quick; otherwise he might not be able to stop until he had her under him, his dick firmly locked inside her tight pussy.

"At night, when the rest of the world is asleep, my thoughts drift to you. I imagine you lying under me, your soft body pressed against mine as I take you, fill you. I've had my fair share of hot, erotic dreams of you, sweetheart." His voice grew raspier with the fever that ran through his veins. A fever only she could cool. He knew that to be a fact, because he'd tried to date other women. None were Gracie. None had her backbone, her green eyes, her lush body.

He bent his lips to her pulse and licked the length of her protruding vein. "You want me, huh? You trust me with your body, baby?" Her jerky nod gave him exactly what he needed, her total acceptance.

"Mmm, so sweet. I want more of you too. So much more. I

want to know all your hot little buttons. The ones that cause your blood to pound through your veins and have you quivering with need. I want you begging and wriggling beneath me . . . for me."

He bent and tasted her succulent, ivory neck. It called to something primitive in him, something even he didn't recognize. He licked her soft skin and suckled, luxuriating in the little sounds coming from Gracie's pouty little mouth. Soft whimpers that he wanted to turn into cries of satisfaction. When he bit her lightly, branding her, Gracie lifted her hand to the back of his head, holding him in place, as if loath to let the moment end. Wade lifted up, forcing her to drop her hand, and stared down at her pliant body. Damn, she looked good enough to eat. "You may open your eyes now, sweet angel."

Gracie let her lids drift open, her body burning with need. When she saw the raw hunger in Wade's dark gaze, she knew it was the same for him. She wanted . . . Wade. His kisses, his caresses, his demands. Like a child being given a bite of a cookie, it wasn't enough. "The things you do to me, the way you make me feel . . . It's never been this way for me before."

"Careful, baby. I'm only a man. Words like those could get you more than you ever bargained for."

"What does that mean?"

He smiled and fingered the neckline of her nightgown. "Ah, there's that sweet touch of innocence I told you about before."

"You make me sound like a virgin. I *have* been with other men, Wade." Unable to help herself, Gracie reached out and clutched his forearm. His rough, tan skin and powerful muscles had captured her attention too many times to count. She'd only dreamed of touching, stroking. Now that she had him so close, she wasn't about to waste even a second.

"Have you ever been with a man who was into bondage? Voyeurism? Have you ever played the submissive for a dom?"

The images his words invoked had her cheeks burning with embarrassment. She couldn't speak, could only shake her head, hoping it was enough.

"That's sort of what I thought. The things I like to do with a woman, the things I want to do with you, they're very specific, Gracie."

"You want to tie me up?" Why did the idea of being at Wade's mercy intrigue her so? She should be scandalized. Instead her pussy flooded with liquid heat.

"We'll leave my *wants* for another day." The finger that had been playing with her neckline dipped beneath. The rough texture of his skin against hers had her head spinning. "Right now, the only thing that matters is you," he whispered. "I want to see this pretty body, Gracie. May I?"

"Y-Yes."

Wade removed his hand and stood. He crooked his finger at her and growled, "Come here."

Gracie tossed the blankets aside and brought her legs to the edge of the bed. As her feet touched the floor, Wade held out a hand. She placed her palm in his and let him pull her up. He raised her hand to his lips and left a soft kiss on her knuckles, before releasing her and stepping closer. He clutched fistfuls of her gown and started to tug upward. Blood rushed through Gracie's veins as she realized he would be looking at her for the first time. Her too plump body, the bruises from the crash, it'd all be on display for him.

And so would the piercings.

Damn.

When he had the material up around her waist, she stopped him with her uninjured hand against his chest. "Wait." He quirked a brow at her, clearly puzzled by the sudden change. "There's something you should know first."

His eyes softened. "You can tell me anything, baby."

"I have . . ." Her throat went dry. She swallowed and tried

again. "What I mean to say is . . ." Anxiety had her stalling out. Damn, this shouldn't be so difficult!

Wade smiled, his tone playful when he said, "Sometimes it's easier to just blurt it out. Like a bandage, just rip it off, Gracie."

"Piercings," she muttered. "I have piercings."

Wade's smile fell flat. "You have pierced ears? That's the big confession?"

"They aren't in my ears."

His gaze shot to her breasts and lingered. If it were at all possible her face heated even more. At this rate they'd have to call the fire department just to put out the blaze in her damn cheeks.

"You had your nipples pierced?" Wade's voice sounded as if he'd swallowed sandpaper.

"Years ago. I went through a rebel phase, I guess." She took a deep breath before asking, "Do you think it's strange?"

He licked his lips, his gaze still on her chest. As he started to tug her gown up, Gracie grasped one large hand in her own and halted his movements. His head snapped up, brown eyes, now nearly black, locked onto hers. "Let me see."

The quiet demand nearly did her in, but she wasn't budging. Not until she had an answer to her question. "You didn't answer me."

He licked his lips, and Gracie found herself watching, wishing, so very desperate to feel that sensual lick between her thighs. "No," he murmured, "I don't think it's strange. I think I'm about to come in my jeans right now. I think if I don't see you I'm going to die. I think my mouth is watering for a taste of you."

Gracie hadn't really expected Wade to be anything less than totally honest. It just wasn't his way. Still, the heat behind his statement scorched her and sent her into another realm. She wasn't terribly sure she was ready to deal with it. Then again, hadn't she just told the man that she was tired of not taking what she wanted? She had him in her bedroom, undressing her; this was her chance.

Gracie dropped her hand and held her breath. "O-Okay then."

Within seconds Wade had the gown over her head, the cast on her wrist barely slowing him down. After he let the material fall to the floor in a white heap, he went to work on her panties. He didn't stop until she stood before him naked. When he went back to staring at her breasts, licking his lips, Gracie smiled. Unless she was mistaken, Wade liked what he saw. The knowledge gave her the bravado to make a demand of her own.

"Undress, Wade. I want to see you too."

"In time, baby. First, a kiss."

Then he dipped his head and licked her nipple. Gracie grasped onto his head, tunneling her fingers into his thick, dark hair, and gave herself up to the man she'd only made love to in her dreams.

8

Wade couldn't believe the shy, headstrong woman with the buttoned up blouses had nipple piercings. Christ almighty. He cupped her breasts in both palms, squeezing the bountiful orbs gently before swiping his tongue over the little ring piercing one hard nipple. Enthralled by the way it shimmered in the light coming in from the hallway, he growled, "You have magnificent breasts, Gracie. Such a luscious handful. I could lick you for hours."

Large pink areolas centered by hard, berry nipples beckoned Wade to suck. Only one thing held him back. The three-inch-long mark marring the skin between her breasts and the bruises that covered her shoulders and torso. Anger at her stalker boiled to the surface and threatened to spoil what should be a sweet, beautiful moment between them. He leaned in and kissed the long mark, letting his lips linger a few seconds before lifting his head. "You should be in bed, resting. I should be horsewhipped for ever letting things get this far."

Her palm came to rest over his heart; the tender smile she gave him warmed him clear to his soul. "The bruises will fade.

The mark from the seat belt will fade. This moment, right now, it'll stay with me forever, Wade. Please, don't let him take it from me."

With only a few words from Gracie, Wade's strength scattered. It unsettled him to know she could so easily work him. Worse yet, she didn't even seem to be aware of the power she wielded. "I won't have you in pain," he gritted out. "Before we go forward I want your word that you'll do what I say. Everything I say. Are we clear, sweetheart?"

She grinned, and the playfulness of it burned a path straight to his groin. "You're the boss."

"Hmm, little temptress." With one hand he flicked and toyed with her pretty nipple, then wrapped his lips around the other, taking as much of the tender flesh into his mouth as he could. His name was a plea on her lips as she mashed her breast against his face, begging for more.

Wade was a heartbeat away from falling to his knees. His legs had turned to rubber as soon as she'd uttered the words "nipple piercings." It was a humbling thing for a man who thought he'd seen it all, done it all. When it came to sex, he'd experienced nearly everything there was to experience. So why had he been ready to explode at the sight of Gracie's creamy tits? Simple, because they belonged to the woman who'd captured his attention that first day she came to work for Cherry. One thing was certain. It would take more than a few nights to get the woman out of his system.

He didn't like the thought.

He was an independent man. He didn't relish the idea of needing any one particular woman. Variety was the spice of life. Or it had been, before he'd seen Gracie Baron in the buff. Now, Wade didn't give a damn about variety. He just wanted Gracie.

Crouching low in front of her, Wade slipped one arm behind her knees and the other beneath her neck, then lifted her, cradling her against his chest. Damn, she felt right there. She felt good. He looked down at her bed and grinned. "I like the big bed, baby. I'm going to need plenty of room for what I have in mind for you tonight."

Gracie curled against him, not saying a word. Her acceptance was like tossing gasoline on a live flame. She was giving him her complete trust, and he'd see to it that she didn't live to regret it. Wade laid her gently in the center of the bed. As he turned on the little lamp on her bedside table, drenching the room in a soft glow, Gracie groaned. "I'd rather have the light off."

He sat down next to her. "You promised to do as I say, baby."

"And you want the light on?"

"Mhmm, I want to see your pretty body." Her skin was the gentlest shade of ivory. So delicate, so easily marred. He'd need to be careful or risk adding to her bruises. And that he would never do. "Every inch of you is beautiful, Gracie."

"You don't have to say that, you know."

"You mean compliment you?" She nodded, the blush that stole over her cheeks turning his heart to mush. "It's true. From the curve of your hips, to these perfectly pierced breasts." He flicked one nipple, emphasizing his point, and smiled when she sucked in a breath. "Your nipples are the exact pink shade of bubble gum. It makes me want to pop them both into my mouth."

He dipped his head and licked at the candied confection, savoring the sweet taste of her. This moment would be etched in his brain forever. He suckled on her hardened nipple, leisurely flicking his tongue back and forth over the ring, creating a maelstrom of need inside them both. Gracie arched upward, thrusting her flesh into his voracious mouth even farther. When he gently bit down, he was forced to wrap an arm around her to keep her from wiggling and possibly hurting herself. When he released her breast, Gracie pleaded for more. He switched his attention to her other breast, taking his time, savoring the unique flavor of his little red-haired angel.

When he lifted away, slowly releasing his hold on her, Gracie's eyes were closed. His cock swelled another inch at the sight of her. Wet nipples, glistening from his ministrations, her body splayed out for his pleasure.

"Open your eyes for me, sweetheart." Slowly, her lashes fluttered open. Green fire touched him everywhere at once. He'd intended to bring her pleasure, to keep his damn pants zipped and carefully see to her needs, saving his own for when she was back in fighting form. Seeing Gracie open and aroused had the ability to kick his good intentions right out the window.

"Make love to me, Wade."

And then she just had to go and say that.

He took a few seconds to rebuild the cage around his libido before replying, "When we make love, it's going to be hard, rough, and plentiful. You're too bruised for all the things I want to do with you, sweetheart."

Her eyes widened. "But I thought—"

He placed a finger against her lips. "Do you trust me, Gracie?"

She nodded as if too overwhelmed to speak. He understood the feeling well. "Then open your legs for me," he urged. "Invite me in, baby." At first he was afraid she'd balk, too modest and innocent to expose herself so blatantly, but she only hesitated for a split second before moving her legs apart. "Wider," he ordered, unable to keep the emotion out of his voice. She shyly spread herself for him. "Good girl." Finally he could see the satiny softness of her sex. Sweet red curls covered a treasure he desperately wanted to plunder. Christ, he'd never wanted a woman the way he wanted Gracie. She made him feel things, even though she was simply lying there, staring up at him with a trusting smile that curved her pouty lips.

Wade continued to take in the delectable beauty. Gracie had a neatly trimmed bikini line, and her distended clitoris and plump nether lips were totally exposed to his view. He licked his lips, imagining her flavor on his tongue, swallowing her juices as she rode out a wild climax. "If I don't get a taste of some of that honey I'll surely die, sweet baby."

"We certainly wouldn't want that."

"Damn straight." Wade moved between her supple thighs, then lowered his head and licked her from her hot little clit on down her dewy slit. When he sank his tongue between the delicate folds of her pussy lips, Gracie's legs started to close. Wade clutched onto her thighs and held her firmly in place. "Don't move." The whispered command seemed to do the trick. Gracie relaxed, watching him as if half afraid he'd disappear. The instant her tangy flavor hit his taste buds, he'd known nothing short of a natural disaster could drag him away. He'd never sampled anything sweeter than Gracie's arousal. He inhaled her womanly scent, sucked her clit in between his teeth, and nibbled. He felt her hand against the back of his head, clutching and holding him against her. When his tongue thrust between her folds, she lost it completely and pushed against his face, undulating as he tongue-fucked her. A few more licks to her clit and she burst wide, screaming and straining against the unyielding hold his hands had on her soft thighs. He stared as she became lost in the age-old instinct to hold on to the delirious feelings of orgasm for as long as humanly possible.

Wade lifted his head and looked at the woman who was quickly stealing his sanity. She'd come too fast. "How long has it been for you, sweetheart?"

At once the glow in her cheeks disappeared, and her lax muscles stiffened. "Excuse me?"

Wade moved over her, bracing himself on his hands on either side of her head, careful not to press against her sore body. "Don't play. You know what I'm asking. How long since your last orgasm?"

She frowned up at him. "It's rude to ask that, especially after what you just did."

He dipped his head and kissed her, lingering long enough to feel her lips opening for him, letting him into the hot cavern of her mouth. Wade slipped his tongue inside and tasted the fresh flavor of her toothpaste and the spicy taste of woman. He pulled back an inch and whispered, "Answer me, sweetheart. How long?"

"Several months," she said, her breath coming in fast pants.

"Then you should get double for having to wait so long." He traveled kisses down her body, taking his time to give each bruise special attention. When his lips encountered the tender bud of her nipple, he sucked the little treat into his mouth. She started to arch into him, as if needing more, but Wade wouldn't let her, too attuned to her pain.

"Stay put before you hurt yourself."

She bit her lip, as if wanting to protest, but finally she nodded. Knowing how badly she wanted to go against him, though she was still obeying his command, sent blood rushing to his cock. Damn, she had no idea how much her acquiescence pleased him. Her submission wouldn't go unrewarded.

Wade resumed his sensual torment, licking and biting one turgid nipple, before switching to her other beautiful tit. He used his hands to plump them together and nuzzle his face into her cleavage. Languorously, Wade made his way down her body, lapping and nibbling at her rib cage until he reached her belly where he let his tongue dip into her little button. She pleaded with him, saying his name over and over. He finally caved.

Pushing her legs wide, he dipped his tongue into her hot opening. At the first contact, Gracie's good hand was in his hair, grasping handfuls and pushing his face against her. He sucked her sweet little clit into his mouth and flicked it with his tongue, before lapping at the nectar of her arousal. Gracie tried to move, as if to force his tongue deeper, trying to rush him to the finish line. Wade wouldn't be hurried; he was too aware of her injuries to allow her any leeway. He would take her there gently, or not at all.

Holding her still, Wade let his tongue tease the swollen lips of her cunt, his balls drawing up tight at the feel of her softest, most tender part so close to his cock. Hell, she might as well be wearing a chastity belt. He could fill her in an instant, true, and it'd be exactly what they both wanted, needed. But he would have her healed before letting that particular beast out of the cage. His fantasies were anything but tame, and he had a feeling Gracie would bring out the more savage side of his nature the instant his cock sank deep.

Besides, having his face buried in Gracie's swollen, wet pussy wasn't exactly a hardship. In fact, he was pretty sure he could lick her all night long and not get bored.

"Watch me," he demanded, his voice hoarse from pent-up desire. Her gaze shot to his, and he could see from her languorous expression that she was close. He placed his lips against her clit and kissed the swollen and sensitive bit of flesh. A primitive growl reverberated inside his chest at the way her body started to move against his face. He parted her with his fingers and sank his tongue deep into her dewy center once more.

"Yes! God, yes, Wade!"

Hearing her cries tore another hole in his control. The sudden burning thought of another man doing this to her had him nearly snarling. Wade had never felt such a powerful mix of tenderness and possessiveness toward a woman.

Wade began sliding his tongue in and out of her, slowly, building her pleasure little by little. He used his thumb to stroke over her soft clitoris, licking and nibbling, plying her flesh. All too quickly she screamed and clutched fistfuls of his hair, anchoring him to her as she rode out a wild climax.

Wade cupped her pussy in a protective, possessive hold and claimed, "Mmm, this is *my* hot little pussy now, Gracie." And he meant every word. He wasn't letting her go. And he sure as hell wasn't going to lose her to some asshole bent on making her his "love."

Her answer was the most wicked grin he'd ever seen on a woman. Seconds later she was asleep, her legs still spread wide, his hand still covering her mound. He moved off the bed and stared down at her. A red-haired angel, that was Gracie. Sweet one minute; fiery hot the next. She was the most potent of mixes. "Fuck," he groaned, raking his fingers through his hair. He should have known he wouldn't be able to walk away once he got her out of her clothes. Witnessing all that passion, it was akin to waving a red flag at a bull. No way in hell was he going to be able to resist going after it, again and again.

Careful not to wake her, Wade readjusted her legs to a more comfortable position, then pulled the blankets up, covering her body from his view. She stirred a little but didn't wake. The cast on her wrist caught his attention, and a kind of rage he'd never felt filled his gut. The bastard would pay for hurting her.

Wade leaned down and pressed his lips to hers, then murmured, "Sweet dreams, angel."

He flicked the light off and left her to sleep in peace. As he walked back out to the living room, the couch came into view. He sighed. "It's going to be a long ass night."

Outside the apartment, he stared at the truck he'd seen Gracie get into at the hospital. It'd been sitting in front of her place all night. He looked down at his watch. Four in the morning. Why had the man stayed all night? Gracie Lynn didn't date. He knew that. She loved him, only him. She had no need for other men. But the truck didn't move. It stayed there, taunting him. An evil specter keeping him from the woman he loved.

Sitting in the nondescript sedan, he pulled the slip of paper, so precious to him, out of his pocket and gripped it tight as he watched Gracie's front window. There weren't any lights on, only darkness. Were they in bed together? Had she let that man, that disgusting piece of filth, into her body?

He moaned. "No, no, no. She would never betray me that way." But then who was that man? She didn't have any family. He knew that; he'd checked. He knew everything about Gracie Lynn. The schools she'd attended growing up; the grandmother who'd died when she was little. That useless drunk of a father who always drained her bank account and forced her to work two jobs. Gracie Lynn was alone. Like him, she'd been waiting for the right person to fill her life with love and happiness. Soon, he would be able to take her away. She would quit her jobs and be his wife. She would be the mother to his children. She would greet him every day with a smile and take care of his house and love his children. That's the life she was meant to live.

The curtains moved suddenly, and he held his breath, waiting, hoping to see Gracie Lynn. Instead the man stood there, bare-chested, his gaze scanning the parking lot. When it landed on his car and lingered, he held his breath. Only after the curtain fell back into place, leaving him once again to his thoughts, did he manage to breathe.

Touching a finger to his cheek, he realized she'd brought him to tears. She would have to be punished. She needed to learn her place. Reaching over, he opened the dash and pulled out the razor blade he kept there for emergencies. He pushed his sleeve up, revealing the pumping vein in his wrist. As he stared at Gracie Lynn's front window, he slid the sharp, cold steel down his wrist, slitting the skin easily. Blood oozed from the fresh, shallow cut. Ten more thin lines later and peace settled over him.

Yes, she would have to pay for causing him pain.

9

It was Sunday, and Wade had woken her early. Apparently the man was a morning person. Gracie *so* wasn't. After two cups of coffee and a bagel, Gracie was clearheaded enough to place a call to her boss, Marie, at Coughlin's Furniture Manufacturing, the company where she worked when she wasn't at Serene Comfort. She'd explained to the kind, older woman about the car accident—leaving out the crazy stalker bit of course. When Marie offered to give her Monday and Tuesday off to recuperate, Gracie grabbed it with both hands, only too grateful for the break. Silently, Gracie admitted that at least part of the reason she wanted the time off was so she could spend it with Wade. Once she'd taken care of that little detail, Wade had practically dragged her out the door, explaining that they were heading to his place to meet his associate. She wasn't certain why Jonas couldn't come to her home as planned, but she was curious enough about where Wade lived to go along with the change.

Gracie still couldn't believe she'd all but begged him to make love to her the night before. Worse, she couldn't believe she'd fallen asleep on him! Her cheeks burned with mortification at the thought. What must he think of her? Surely he wasn't used to women falling asleep in his arms. The things he'd made her feel, though . . . Oh, wow. Two orgasms, and yet he'd kept his pants zipped the entire time, not once asking for anything in return. Strangely, she wished he had. She wanted to pleasure Wade. The feeling was a unique one, considering she'd never really thought much about sex. It was usually over too quickly. With Wade it wouldn't be quick; she knew that instinctively.

Now as Gracie looked out the passenger side window at the deserted city street, her eyes widened in disbelief. "This is where you live?"

"Yup." He parallel parked, then cut the engine, before turning toward her. "What do you think?"

She didn't want to be rude, but she just couldn't imagine anyone living in such a rundown old warehouse. "I think it looks like it should be bulldozed."

He winked and opened his door. "Exactly." He exited the truck and jogged around to her side and swung open her door. Cool September air floated over her skin as Wade reached in and unhooked her seat belt, then carefully helped her to the ground before grabbing her purse for her. She slung it over her shoulder, and then Wade took her hand, entwining their fingers as if they'd been doing it for years. Gracie tried not to be too obvious when she inhaled his woodsy, male scent. God, the man smelled delicious. Like a sinful piece of chocolate. She never could resist the dark, creamy confection. She tried to tug her hand out of his, but he wasn't getting the hint. "Wade," she said his name as a warning.

"You have a problem with holding my hand, Gracie?"

Actually, she liked feeling his hand, so strong and able, wrapped around hers. He made her feel safe. "Not really, but . . ." She wasn't sure what to say, how to explain her feelings. Last night he'd licked her to completion, twice. But she didn't know where she stood with him in the bright light of day. Was last night enough for him? He hadn't said anything about it all morning, and it was eating away at her self-confidence.

"I like touching you, Gracie. I like knowing you're close," he said, his voice soft and inviting, "so quit sounding so harassed and let me have my way, will you?"

A little thrill went through her. Okay, so, he wasn't through with her. Good to know. She kept her hand where it was; arguing with him would get her nowhere anyhow. The man put new meaning to the term hardheaded.

After grabbing her laptop from the floor of the truck, Wade used his elbow to shut the door and made his way up the steps. A large, dark-haired man suddenly appeared at the front door of the warehouse. Large might be the wrong word. The man was huge! Every bit as big as Wade, but somehow more . . . dangerous. Gracie tightened her hold on Wade, as if he were somehow her savior.

The stranger held the door for them to enter, his lips curving upward in a sexy grin. "Our little damsel in distress, I take it."

Wade was silent as he took her into a large living area. She was so enthralled by the sumptuous décor, so incongruent with the outside, she nearly lost track of the conversation. "Oh my, this is beautiful."

The spacious living area held only the most necessary pieces of furniture. In fact, Gracie suspected the room wasn't quite as large as it appeared. But the clever way it'd been decorated made it seem both roomy and cozy. High ceilings and white oak hardwood floors complemented the Asian-style, burgundy, L-shaped couch and matching round chairs. The steel appliances in the kitchen area added to the sleek modern style. She hadn't figured on Wade's being into interior design, and she especially hadn't expected the ugly warehouse could have such an exquisite interior. She was suddenly curious where the steel spiral staircase off to one side might lead. His bedroom? *Don't even go there, girl.*

Wade led her to the plush sofa. She sat down and pulled her purse into her lap. Both men remained standing. She felt on display with their gazes locked onto her so intently. Usually she liked to blend into the background. It made her uncomfortable to be noticed by a man. For whatever reason, she didn't really mind being the object of Wade's and Jonas's attention.

"Gracie Baron, meet Jonas Phoenix. He's a friend, as well as the other half of Phoenix-Wade Investigations."

Gracie looked up. Way up. Her heart pounded so hard she was sure the two men could hear it. "It's nice to meet you, Mr. Phoenix."

"It's Jonas, and it's definitely my pleasure. The circumstances are rather unfortunate, though."

She crossed her legs at the ankles and adjusted her skirt, more to give herself something to do than anything else. "Jonas then."

Jonas smiled as he moved to a long, oak bar that ran along one wall. "Would you like something to drink?"

"No, thank you." She watched the man help himself to a bottle of water and frowned. "Do you both live here?"

Jonas tossed a bottle to Wade before answering. "No, but our business is run out of the connecting building next door, so I tend to stop in a lot."

Wade unscrewed the top of his water and took a long drink. "But you'll be sure to knock on the interior door from now on, right?"

"Of course." Jonas winked at her. "I'm house-trained, I promise."

She was intensely curious about the two men. Private investigators—it seemed so exciting. "How did you two meet?"

"Special Forces. We ran a few ops together. Been BFFs ever since."

Wade rolled his eyes. "Christ, don't start, Jonas."

Jonas chuckled and moved to sit on the couch next to her.

Wade stayed standing, his watchful gaze making her acutely aware of her banged up face. She'd tried to cover the bruises with makeup, but there was only so much cosmetics could hide. Gracie had the insane urge to run to the bathroom and check her appearance. How annoying was that? She shouldn't even care what Wade thought of her looks. Just because he'd pleasured her the night before, that didn't mean they were a couple. He probably had no intention of even touching her again. She should be fine with that. Her life was too insane as it was. She didn't need to add a relationship to the mix. Now, if only she could convince her body, maybe she could stop craving the man for like five minutes!

"Phoenix-Wade Investigations." Gracie liked the name. The two men together made for a potent combination. She'd bet her last dollar they had plenty of female clients, too. "What exactly do you guys do?"

Wade was the first to answer. "Domestic cases mostly. Electronic surveillance."

"So, like, cheating spouses?"

Jonas spoke up from beside her. "Mostly. From time to time we take on cases that involve a little more time and attention, though."

"Like a crazy stalker?"

Jonas laid his arm on the back of the couch. There wasn't anything blatantly sexual in the way he sat, but it seemed as if he were caging her in. She shifted a little, then grimaced when her rib cage protested the movement.

"We've had our share of strange cases," he explained. "Yours isn't the first. It will, however, get our full attention."

She glanced up at Wade and noted his gaze on the arm Jonas had behind her back. She couldn't read his expression, and that served to make her even more nervous. "And why is that?"

"Don't you know, Gracie?" Jonas said, his voice dropping to a low murmur.

She shook her head, honestly confused, and a little turned on if she were being honest.

Wade moved closer and said, "Because you're special."

Gracie reached down and rubbed her cast. Her wrist was beginning to throb. She was a little bit grateful because the ache yanked her out of the sensual web Jonas and Wade so effortlessly weaved around her. She remembered the pain pills in her purse, but nixed the idea of taking one because she hadn't called the doctor about the dosage. Besides, she had a feeling she'd need a clear head if she hoped to hold her own around the two powerful men whose entire focus was now centered on her. "Why me? What makes me so special?"

Wade sat on the other side of her and placed his hand on her thigh. She felt the heat clear through her skirt. "I'll answer that one later." He looked at Jonas over her head. "Jonas, Gracie needs time to adjust."

Jonas took one last drink of his water before standing and heading toward the bar. "I need to get back to work anyway. Those bills won't pay themselves. See you two in a little while."

Gracie was genuinely confused now. "I thought we were going to go over the e-mails."

Wade stroked her thigh. His smile told her he knew exactly the effect his touch had on her. "Later for that. First, we need to get a few things straight." He paused and glanced across the room at Jonas. "Knock."

"Right." He tossed the bottle in the recycling bin and grinned back at her. "It's nice to meet you, Gracie."

"It's nice to meet you, too. And thank you for helping Wade with my . . . problem. I really appreciate it."

"We'll get this guy. Don't you worry." He left through the interior door, putting Gracie alone with Wade. Silence fell over them. His caress on her thigh didn't let up. The feel of him so close to her pussy sent her into orbit. She distracted herself by talking about her surroundings. "Your home is magnificent. I never would have expected you were into interior design."

Wade cocked his head. "I'm not. My sister is the one with the creative touch. The warehouse took a lot of time and sweat, but she was very happy with the end result."

"You have a sister?" Gracie was suddenly very alert. A chance to learn more about the man who made her body hum with pleasure was too good to pass up.

He nodded. "And a brother. Dean and Deanna are fraternal twins. Younger than me by two years."

"What do they do for a living?"

"Dean runs his own construction company. Deanna is a registered nurse. She does interior design more as a hobby. Jonas has been trying to get her to do his apartment, but she keeps giving him the cold shoulder."

"Why? Don't they get along?"

He rubbed her thigh, a little higher this time. Gracie had to swallow back the need to beg Wade to move beneath the heavy denim of her skirt. "Like brother and sister. It's more that Deanna likes to razz him. She can be a handful." Suddenly he stood and held out his hand. "Come, I want to show you something."

She squinted up at him, suspicious and a little sorry his hand was no longer teasing her to distraction. "That sounds like a line."

He chuckled. "You'll see that too, I promise. For now I have something else to show you."

She slid the strap of her purse over her shoulder, then held out her good hand and let Wade tug her to her feet. He took her to the spiral staircase that she'd been curious about earlier. She hesitated, as if aware that when she took that first step she would be accepting more than just a look at his house. She would be accepting a part of Wade that not many people got to see. How she knew that was a mystery. Gracie looked over her shoulder. "What's up there?"

He leaned down and kissed the tip of her nose, his voice deep and smooth when he said, "I promise it's not a pit of snakes. You'll like it. Trust me, sweetheart."

Trust. It wasn't something she was very good at. Still, she was beginning to trust Wade. With her life and her body. It was a scary thought. Gracie started up the stairs.

When she reached the top, she was presented with a sight that simply stunned her speechless. The room itself was huge, but what caught her eye wasn't the elegant furnishings, nor was it the floor to ceiling windows that spanned the length of one wall. What held her spellbound were the books. Tons of them. Three entire walls of shelves and all of them filled to bursting with books. Hardbacks and paperbacks alike, there were tons of them! Even if she were given an entire lifetime to spend in this one room she'd still never be able to read them all.

She walked to one wall and caught names like Dickens and Poe and Byron. Oh, how she would love to sit down in a chair and read until her eyes simply gave way to exhaustion. She never would have expected that the powerful, dangerous, ex-Special Forces turned PI would be a fan of literary art. She took in several titles and realized the man had truly excellent taste.

"Do you like it?"

Gracie dropped her purse to the floor and picked out a book at random. It looked extremely old. Careful of the fragile nature of the item she held in her palm, Gracie touched the old softened leather and gently inhaled the fragrance of aged paper and ink. She loved the smell of old books. So much history. How many people had held that same book in their palms? Cherished it as she was doing at that very moment? When she opened it her eyes lit up at one of the titles inside. Edgar Allen Poe's *The Pit and the Pendulum*. It was one of her all-time favorites! Her heart leaped when she heard a sound from directly behind her. She turned around and found herself face-to-face with Wade. The dark hunger in his gaze went straight to her blood, heating it and sending a bolt of lightning through her system. In her awe, she'd nearly forgotten he was even there. Forgotten Wade? Hell, she would've thought that was an impossibility!

Gracie held the book to her chest, as if in some feeble effort to protect it from him. Or was the book protecting her? She shook the thought from her mind, not allowing herself to guess at the answers that lay hidden there.

"Amazing, Wade. This room is absolutely amazing."

He smiled, as if pleased by her compliment. "When I saw your books, I thought maybe you'd enjoy this room." He tapped the book she still held to her chest and said, "I see you've chosen one of Poe's collected works. Very good choice. Poe is my favorite. I've read everything he's ever written dozens of times over."

His voice captivated her. As it had since the first moment he'd spoken to her. Gracie took her mind off the sound of it and concentrated on the book in her hand instead. "I love Poe, but especially this one."

He leaned down and kissed her. This time his lips pressed against hers and lingered a second before lifting away. "You can take it home if you like. In fact, help yourself to whatever appeals."

Stunned by both his generosity and the kiss, Gracie quickly shook her head. "Oh, no, Wade. I couldn't. I'd be too afraid of ruining them or losing them."

Wade laughed. "I'm not worried about it, Gracie. I saw how precious those books in your living room were to you." He eyed the book and murmured, "In fact, I think I'm a little jealous right now."

She blinked. "You are?"

"You're holding that book against your pretty breasts, protecting it as if it were a lover instead of paper and ink." His voice dropped an octave. "You have two options. Read Poe's delightfully twisted story, or let me take you to my bedroom, where I can worship those perfectly pierced nipples the way I did last night." He raised a hand to her hair and smoothed his way down to her neck. He cupped her nape in a dominating hold. "What'll it be, pretty Gracie?"

10

Gracie wasn't sure how to take this man. He was just so candid. It threw her off balance. The ache in her breasts let her know exactly what her body wanted. Just the thought of having Wade's mouth wrapped around her nipples, suckling and teasing, had her pussy throbbing and her panties soaking wet. But the man had to go and get all authoritative on her. She had two options? What if she wanted to do something else? It was damned arrogant of him to act as if he were her lord and master.

"You like it when people do what you say, don't you? You like to be in charge, having everyone obey."

He was quiet a moment, just watching her with steady, predator eyes. It was discomforting that he could be so motionless—almost as if he willed the very air around them to a halt. She shook off the fanciful notion, not willing to give in to her wayward imagination. She could ill afford to be anything but alert and on guard with Wade.

"Tell me, Gracie," he said, his voice deceptively calm, "would you be one to obey my every command?"

Immediately her back went rigid with anger. "I don't bow and cower to men. Ever!"

At once, he had the book out of her hands and his mouth inches from hers. His fingers bit into the flesh of her upper arms as he growled, "The only place I'll ever command you is in the bedroom. I don't want a damn doormat, Gracie. I want you. Full of fire and sass. The very thought of you cowering is ludicrous. You've had a stalker for the last two months, and you've yet to show any real weakness. Don't you know it's your strength that I find so appealing?"

She was too confused. Her mind was muddled from the intoxicating nearness of him. "Then why would you want to command me in the bedroom? What's that about?"

He loosened his hold, but didn't let go. She was only too glad he didn't. "It's my way. I want you to submit to me, Gracie. The way you did last night. Give yourself over to me. No reservations, no fear. You'll only find pleasure in my arms. I promise you that. Only pleasure, baby."

She was just about to cave, to give them both exactly what they so badly craved, when his manner swiftly changed. He turned and looked at the staircase, as if listening to some faint sound that only he could hear. Then suddenly he thrust her behind him and pulled out the gun he had strapped to his ankle. Then she heard it too. Footsteps on the stairs. Was that more than one set of footsteps? Her heart kicked into high gear, and she clutched onto the back of Wade's shirt.

"Yo, Wade, where are you?"

Wade cursed and lowered the gun, but he didn't put it away. "Up here," he yelled back; his voice was raw power itself. She suspected just the sound of it could have grown men going weak in the knees. All she could see was the rippling muscles of his back. The shirt covering him could barely contain the corded planes. Every nerve, every sexy, hard inch of him was at attention.

"Wade?"

He hushed her. "Stay put until I'm sure."

Could her stalker have found her here? But no, whoever had called up to them, Wade had recognized the voice. She stayed quiet and concentrated on the developing situation. Out of the silence, Gracie heard a female voice. It was seductive, with a hint of laughter. Immediately, Gracie was swamped with a nauseating amount of jealousy. Had a past lover come calling? When she'd all but made up her mind to step around Wade to find out for herself, he surprised her by moving to the side. She got her first glimpse of their visitors.

A man and a woman, both with the same dark hair and eyes as Wade's. The woman had a flowing mass of shiny chocolate brown hair. More vibrant and beautiful than it had a right to be. She was flawlessly built, too, with curves in all the right places. She was every bit as tall as Wade, Gracie noted. Gracie suddenly felt even more frumpy and battered than ever. The man at the other woman's side smiled with mischief. He looked like a younger version of Wade. Was this the brother and sister then?

Her head started to pound. Gracie touched her fingers to her temples and rubbed, closing her eyes as she did—trying in vain to be rid of the headache. Instantly Wade was there, touching her face with light, soft caresses. "What is it, Gracie?"

"I'm getting a headache." She peeked up at him with one eye and grumbled, "It's no big deal, really."

Wade put the safety back on the small revolver and shoved it in his ankle holster before saying, "I don't care to see you in pain."

Gracie closed her one open eye again, unsure what to say. Wade pulled her fingers down, replacing them with his own. He massaged and pushed at all the right spots, softly whispering, willing her to relax. Who was she to bitch? The man had the magic touch. She folded her arms over her chest and let

Wade have his way. Soon, she felt better. He'd reduced the headache to barely a throb. She touched her forehead and couldn't help wondering what else the talented man had up his sleeve.

"Thank you."

He leaned down and kissed her forehead, then murmured, "You're welcome."

Someone cleared his or her throat, and Gracie felt her cheeks heat. She'd nearly forgotten they weren't alone. Wade had the ability to block out the rest of the world.

She saw them standing at the entrance to the library. The woman still looked classy and beautiful. The man who so closely resembled Wade still had a grin on his face.

"Aren't you going to introduce us, bro?"

Wade's arm came around her waist and pulled her in tight in a possessive hold that spoke volumes. "Gracie, this is the brother and sister I told you about earlier." Wade glared at Dean and said, "Your timing sucks."

Gracie crossed the room and stuck her hand out. "It's nice to meet you both. Wade was just telling me about you."

Dean was the first to step forward. "It's a pleasure to meet you, Gracie." To her utter astonishment, he bowed over her hand and left a light kiss on her knuckles. She heard Wade say Dean's name, as if in warning. Dean only bobbed his eyebrows at her and said, "He can be sort of touchy."

She smiled at his playfulness. Dean was just as big and muscular as Wade, and a bit more intense. Although he didn't send her heart racing the way Wade did. The woman merely shoved Dean to the side and gave her own introductions. "Deanna. Nice meeting you, Gracie."

"It's nice to meet you too. Wade was telling me that you're the genius who decorated his home. It's beautiful."

She waved the compliment away. "Eh, it's a hobby. I enjoy it, but it's not something I want to get paid to do."

"It seems to me you could make good money, though."

"Yeah, but then I'd have to kiss up to people and put up with their ridiculous tastes. No, thanks."

Gracie laughed. "I do see your point."

"And now that you've all met, how about you scram so Gracie and I can get back to doing what we were doing before you barged in. Again. Without knocking."

"We knocked. You just didn't hear us."

"I would've heard."

Dean glanced at her, then back at Wade. "I'm thinking you were distracted."

"Whatever. Did you two actually want something or are you just here to harass me?"

Deanna spoke up this time, her frown of disapproval obvious. "You said we'd go check out that apartment together for Mom. Remember?"

He raked a hand through his hair. "Shit. I forgot about that."

Dean shoved his hands in his pockets and in a sarcastic tone, he said, "Yeah, we figured that out all by ourselves." He flicked a glance to Wade's ankle. "What's with the hardware? Something up?"

"Stalker. Jonas and I have it covered."

"That why she has the bruises and the broken wrist?"

Wade stiffened. "That happened before we were brought in, smart-ass."

"Ah, I see." Dean started back toward the stairs, his grin once again in place. "Well, we'll let you get back to protecting and serving."

Again Gracie blushed. Damn, she hated when she did that. It was a big, flashing sign that stated: Look at me! I'm embarrassed!

"Do you two mind checking out that apartment without me?"

Deanna spoke up this time. "Don't sweat it."

"Thanks. I'll make it up to you."

"Dinner at the Squeeze," Dean was quick to say.

Wade rolled his eyes. "You would pick that place."

Curious, Gracie asked, "What's the Squeeze?"

"Only one of the most expensive seafood restaurants around," Wade grumbled.

Gracie suddenly felt selfish, and terribly guilty. She was keeping him from his family, and that wasn't right. "You could always go with them. I'm sure I'll be fine here alone for a while. Besides, Jonas is right next door."

Wade's expression tightened, his eyes glittering with anger. "You trying to get rid of me, Gracie?"

"Of course not! But your family needs you right now. Besides, I doubt my stalker knows where you live, Wade. I'm sure I'll be fine."

"No."

His tone brooked no argument, which immediately pissed her off. "No?"

He crossed his arms over his chest. "No. I'm not leaving you unprotected. And I'm not leaving you in Jonas's care either, so get that notion out of your head right now."

"You're being incredibly stubborn. Again." She heard Dean chuckle, and she glared over at him. "Do you have something to add?"

He held up both hands, palms out. "We were just leaving. We'll, uh, call you later, Wade."

Dean started down the stairs, but Deanna hung back. Wade passed a hand over his face and sighed. "Was there something else, sis?"

The beautiful woman, whom she'd been so jealous of moments earlier, gave her an admiring look before turning her attention to Wade. "I like her. She's got backbone."

Gracie was stunned and admittedly flattered. Her supposed backbone fairly melted, however, when Wade looked down at her and murmured, "That's what I've been trying to tell her."

"Just don't screw it up."

Wade's gaze shot to his sister's. "Gee, thanks for the vote of confidence."

She blew him a kiss, then disappeared down the stairs. And Gracie was once again alone in the library with Wade.

"Where were we?" he whispered. "Ah, yes. We never finished our conversation. Will you give me obedience in the bedroom, Gracie? Will you submit to me?"

There was a small part of her that wanted to argue. To shoot him down for even daring to ask such a thing. But there was a much bigger part aching to do exactly what Wade wanted. A tiny battle waged inside of her, but it was an unfair fight. "Yes."

"You won't regret it, sweetheart." His voice had changed, lowering to a velvety whisper.

Gracie felt him caressing her arms. His strokes were so gentle, like a butterfly's wings. He so easily kept her off balance. One minute demanding; the next caressing. "Wade?"

"I'm hungry," he murmured.

All at once, his face transformed. His eyes heated and darkened; his mouth curved up in a predatory smile. "I want another taste of your pretty body. I've been thinking of nothing else since last night."

"I fell asleep on you."

"Yes, you did. And I'm glad."

"You are?"

"Yes. Had you been awake I wouldn't have had the strength to hold back. I would've taken you, Gracie. Hard. Do you know what I'm saying?"

"Y-Yes."

"I'm not a gentle man, baby. I want you in fifty different, dirty ways. I want my cock buried in your tight little cunt. I want to suck and toy with the rings in your nipples. I didn't sleep for thinking about all the ways I wanted to fuck you."

"I'm not a child, Wade. You don't have to hold back. I want those things, and I'm not as sore today, not like yesterday. It's going to kill me if you don't stay this time."

"I'm not going anywhere, Gracie. But I won't hurt you, so we may have to alter things a bit this first time."

Gracie placed her palm against his chest, directly over his heart. "You'd never hurt me." She knew it in her bones.

"Only pleasure," he reiterated, and then he bent toward her and touched her lips with his own. Tasting and licking. Nibbling and enticing her mouth to open for him. She whimpered and sagged against him.

He caught her tight against his chest and sank his tongue into her mouth. For the first time in her life, Gracie submitted fully to a man.

11

Wade watched Gracie drift into his kiss. Christ, he loved watching the expressions chase across her face. She had no idea how much passion she exhibited when she let herself go. He'd been going crazy since his first glimpse of her body. Being with her all morning and not being able to have another taste of her had been pure hell. She'd been on fire last night and now he would finally feel all that scorching heat wrapped around his cock.

He dipped his knees and, as gingerly as possible, lifted her into his arms. She wrapped her arms around his neck, and he could feel the hard cast covering her wrist against the back of his head. It was a reminder of how fragile she was right now. He'd need to take care or risk hurting her.

He took her to his bedroom, the place he'd so badly ached to have her since the instant she'd looked up at him with that sweet smile at Serene Comfort. He placed her on his king-size bed. She opened her eyes and watched him. Excitement brewed in the pretty green depths, but so did uncertainty. He stepped back and reached down to unhook his ankle harness. He placed it and the gun on his end table before flicking on the little lamp. The soft light bathed the room in a gentle glow. He drank in the sight of Gracie—from her fiery red hair to the curves so strategically concealed by the oversized blouse and long skirt she wore. She might think she was fooling people with the conservative clothes, but he'd seen the sexy hourglass figure beneath the miles of material. So had his brother Dean. It'd pissed him off to witness the lust in his brother's eyes. Any other man would've gotten a fist in his face for kissing Gracie's knuckles. Her body was his to kiss. His own personal playground. It didn't matter that the gesture was only meant as a greeting. He'd still wanted to rip into Dean.

Wade unclipped his cell phone and sent a quick "do not disturb" text to Jonas, then set the device on the table next to his gun. "Now, where were we? . . ." Wade whispered, as he knelt on the bed and kissed her. He didn't stop until he felt her relaxing. He loved kissing Gracie. She had an untamed and untutored mouth that made a man insane with need. The innocent feel of her soft, plump lips drew the beast out in him. The slow, shy way she opened for his invasion. It was fucking addicting. He wanted to drink in her freshness. Keep her bound to his bed forever.

Taking her mouth wasn't enough, though. Would never be enough. He needed the flavor of her pussy on his tongue. He wanted to sip at her every morning, lick her to completion for lunch, and sink his tongue deep for dinner. He willed his dick to relax, but it wasn't much into doing as commanded. Slowly, she tipped her head to one side, exposing the throbbing vein in her ivory neck. Her skin beckoned to him, tempting him beyond reason. He licked a leisurely path downward, taking little sweeping tastes of her lips, her chin, until finally he was hovering over that very spot that was driving him into a whirlpool of frenzied need.

"When my cock sinks deep into your hot, little pussy, baby,

you're going to hug me tight, aren't you?" Wade whispered to her and felt her begin to nod in agreement, as if unable to form the actual words. Normally so headstrong and defiant, yet now she could've been a virgin the way she peeked at him through her lashes. So innocent, yet so eager. Wade licked the silky length of her neck, feeling her pulse jump and speed up. He lifted slightly and spoke again, this time putting more emphasis into his demand. "Tell me you want this. That you trust me with your pleasure. Let me hear the words, sweet angel."

He could see her trying to speak, but nothing came out, only a slight murmur of sound in the quiet room. He cupped her chin in his palm and stroked her lower lip with the pad of his thumb. "Do I really need to repeat myself, Gracie?"

"You make me breathless," she admitted, her voice shaky, husky. "I can't think straight when you kiss me, touch me."

"Do you think it's any different for me?" Damn, if only she knew the power she held over him with nothing more than a smile. And her courage. It amazed him to realize all she'd been through, and she had yet to fold under the pressure. Two jobs, a drunken ass for a father, and some warped asshole taunting her day and night. Her fortitude astounded him.

Wade felt himself becoming even more aroused, his jeans too constricting. He forced himself not to rip them off his body. He needed the barrier between them or he'd never hold out. Somehow Wade managed to tamp down on his desires. So sweet, her body would hug his perfectly. Their lovemaking would be that much sweeter if she were completely engulfed with pleasure. He wanted to watch her beg for him, watch her buck in wild abandonment.

Ruthlessly, Wade pushed aside his mounting lust and lay down on the bed next to her. He touched his teeth to her neck. Biting down gently, he felt Gracie's body shudder in reaction. She began to twitch and rub against him, and he knew she was on the brink of a climax. Son of a bitch, he hadn't even gotten to the good part yet! He suckled her skin, letting her rub her body along the length of his. Allowing her to enjoy the experience as much as possible. The taste of her smooth skin, so much like cream, tore at his control. She would wear his mark. It was strange, the need to see it there. To know he'd been the one to put it there. He'd never needed that sort of confirmation of ownership before. It was downright primal the way he felt about Gracie.

Wade almost lost control, sucking too hard. Gracie moaned his name, pleading to be taken. She grabbed onto his forearm, her nails digging into his skin. Out of the corner of his eye he could see her spreading her legs, all but inviting him in. Fuck, it was sheer torment not being able to drive his cock into her!

He removed his mouth and carefully lifted his head, caressing the purplish mark with his gaze. "You'll have a hickey. Do you mind?"

"The only thing I mind is that we're both still dressed."

He chuckled. "Such a demanding little thing."

His lips lightly touched her cheek before he started on the buttons on her blouse. Within seconds he had her naked, the pretty rings piercing her breasts beckoning to be licked. "I fucking love your nipple rings, Gracie." He dipped his head and sucked one turgid peak into his mouth.

"Oh, God! That feels so good. I missed your touch, Wade."

He flicked her nipple with his tongue once more before using his hands to cup and plump her tits together. Wade groaned as he nuzzled the pillowy softness of her breasts. He squeezed both with his hands, first kissing one then licking the other, relishing their fullness. He nestled his face in the valley between, and she whimpered. Wade inhaled her sweet scent, deliberately driving himself mad. She was a powerful mix of heat and aroused woman.

He didn't think he could wait another second to be inside of her. He reminded himself that his goal wasn't to rut, but to give

Gracie as much pleasure as possible. He wanted to give her something she couldn't get with any other man. If he pleased her well enough, she'd stick around. And she'd want him, again and again, the way he wanted her.

Wade's palm traveled down her body, coasting over the bruises on her torso before reaching her tiny bud. "Mmm, look what I found." She moaned, and he watched her twist and thrash as his fingers continued their torture. "Be still. I don't want you hurting yourself."

"I can't. It's impossible to stay still when you do that, Wade."

He ground his teeth against the need clawing at him. "Then I'll stop. I won't have you reinjuring yourself."

"Don't stop. I swear I'll try to stay still. Just, please, don't stop."

He heard the desperation in her voice. He felt the same wild drive as she. Still he pushed for a more solid answer. "You'll tell me if there's pain?"

"I promise I'll tell you," she breathed out.

Wade knew it wasn't going to get any better than that. He'd just have to watch her closely for any signs of discomfort. She'd been hurt enough; he'd not be adding to her pain. In fact . . . "You remember I mentioned to you about having very *specific* ideas?"

Her gaze widened, and he felt her stiffen. She slowly nodded.

Reaching over, Wade pulled a pair of handcuffs out of his end table drawer and held them up for her to see. "I want to handcuff you to the bed. Will you let me?"

"Um, I've never—"

He flicked her nose. "I figured that out by the look of horror on your face, baby. But you trust me with your body, remember?"

"Yes, I remember."

"I'd cut off my own hand before I'd ever harm you, sweet angel."

Her gaze softened as she looked him over from head to toe. Smiling now, she said, "On one condition."

Damn, she was way too quick with the game. "A condition, Gracie? I thought we agreed you'd submit to me."

"It's a small favor. You wouldn't begrudge me that, would you?"

The little minx. She knew he would do whatever she asked. "What's the favor?"

"I want you naked."

"That's the favor? I need to be undressed or you won't allow me to use the cuffs?"

She nodded, a grin lighting up her entire face. It turned his heart to mush to see her dropping her defenses with him. "You drive a hard bargain, but I suppose the payoff is worth disrobing."

"Thank you." Gracie touched her lips against the warmth of Wade's mouth. Heaven. It had to be heaven; nothing else could feel so good, so right. She let herself flow with the desire that coursed through her body. Nibbling and licking at him, playing the way she'd wanted for so long. Taking her time, she built his excitement before allowing him entrance to her mouth.

Wade's probing tongue arrogantly pushed its way into the soft opening and took her on a ride. Her breasts tingled and ached. She felt her nipples harden in anticipation of his ministrations. But he seemed content to linger on her mouth, taking his time to explore every tiny recess. She pushed against him, shamelessly, telling him without words how desperate she was to feel him, skin to skin. Wade continued to tease and torture. She wanted more. Everything. Now.

Deciding to move him along a little faster, she let one of her hands drift down his back, caressing the muscled firmness of his buttocks through his jeans. She heard him emit a low growl.

A warning, she knew. Feminine satisfaction welled up. Lazily, Gracie moved her hand over his hip until she cupped his hard cock. Grasping him through the unforgiving material, she squeezed and pumped, slowly massaging his length. Wade broke the kiss on a curse and slid off the bed. Standing over her, his gaze snaring hers in a sensual trap, he stripped out of his clothes with quick efficiency. Gracie watched him unabashedly bare himself for her, and one thought kept skittering through her mind. This man—this flawlessly constructed man—was hers. At least for tonight, he was all hers. She would damn well make the most of every second they spent together. Because if there was one thing she knew, it was that life was unpredictable and tomorrow could bring all sorts of trouble. Today was for them alone.

"I intended to give you the slow loving you deserve, baby. But damn if you don't go straight to my head. I can't seem to muster an ounce of self-discipline with you."

Gracie rose to a seated position and smiled, hoping to look tempting, alluring. She wasn't certain she pulled it off; she'd never tried to look alluring before. "I don't want slow and easy. I want you wild, and every bit as eager as me."

Not waiting for an answer, she let her uninjured hand slide over her stomach and rib cage to her aching breasts. She squeezed one soft orb and plucked at the ring piercing the nipple. Wade's gaze darkened, nearly black with desire.

"Fuck, you're playing a dangerous game, Gracie."

"I've been playing it safe for too long. I'm tired of safe." While his eyes roamed pleasingly over her bare body, she slowly, deliberately trailed her fingers downward. When Gracie reached her swollen clitoris, she let out a sigh. Sliding her index finger back and forth, she teased herself to a fever pitch. "Come closer to me," she whispered, her voice husky with arousal.

Without a word, Wade stepped forward. The movement put her mouth in direct line with his jutting cock. God, the man was big. The sheer size of him had her pussy wet and throbbing. She needed him filling her, taking away the cold and replacing it with blazing hot passion. With the same finger she'd used to caress her clit, Gracie touched the tip of his fat cock, enthralled when a pearl of moisture emerged. Her gaze shot to his.

"Lick it up, sweet angel."

Yes, good idea, she thought. Angling her head, Gracie took him into her mouth. She could only manage a few inches; his cock was much bigger than that of any man she'd ever been with. She swirled her tongue around the bulbous head and tightened her lips. Wade cursed and grabbed the back of her head.

"Little tease. Suck harder," he ordered.

Gracie kept her eyes trained on his and took another inch into her mouth.

"Gracie."

Her name, thickly garbled, was all that emerged from his lips. His fingers burrowed into her hair as if he was afraid she'd disappear if he didn't hold on. Loving him this way somehow seemed even more intimate than intercourse. Being able to bring such a powerful man as Wade to climax with just a lick of her tongue stimulated the very core of her femininity.

Gracie lifted her hand and cupped his sac, squeezing gently. Wade's eyes shut, and he threw his head back on a groan. Gracie allowed her hand and tongue and lips to play for another minute before sliding her mouth off him. She gave a loving kiss to his tip, then sat back. Later he could come in her mouth. She'd swallow every salty drop, too. For now, she needed him to be inside of her, fucking her.

Wade cupped the sides of her head in his strong hands and leaned close. "I can't decide whether to fuck your mouth or fuck your pussy."

Gracie smiled and tried to lighten the mood. "How about my pussy. First."

He didn't smile; if anything he grew even more intense, as if ready to pounce. "You'll drink my come," he said, his gravelly voice unyielding, "after I bury my cock in this lovely little cunt. The thought of spurting my come all over your tongue, your teeth, down your throat . . . Christ, what you do to me."

He grasped onto her waist and moved her to the center of the bed, then placed first one knee then the other on the mattress, and crawled toward her. "You need to be tied to the headboard."

Butterflies flitted through her stomach at the reminder of the handcuffs. She'd hoped he'd forgotten about that little detail. When he picked them up and attached one to her good wrist and snapped the other over one of the iron bars that made up the headboard, she shuddered.

"Lay your other hand above your head, out of the way. I don't want to accidentally hurt it."

She did as he said, but curiosity over just how bound she was had her wiggling experimentally at the handcuffs.

Wade stroked her cheek with his fingers and whispered, "You can't loosen them, sweet angel. Only I can. Trust me?"

Trust a man? She'd never had reason to trust a man before. Not any of the few men she'd slept with; not even her own father. Wade wasn't like any other man she'd ever known. He was good, deep down hero-type good. She knew he'd never bring her harm. She took a deep breath and nodded.

He smiled and moved on top of her, keeping his weight on his forearms. "Knowing you're willing to submit to me, to let me be in charge, it does things to me, Gracie. I want to love you, for hours. Just love this pretty, curvy body and take you clear to the moon. Then when you come back down to earth I want to do it all over again."

Gracie felt his words clear to her soul. If she wasn't careful she was going to fall. Head over heels, madly, deeply in love with Wade Harrison. And that was the scariest thing of all.

12

Wade slipped down her body and kissed her belly. Her body was so attuned to his touch; she came alive in an instant. As he made his way between her legs, she groaned. "What are you doing?"

"You got to taste me; now it's my turn."

He pushed her legs wide and stroked a finger over her labia. Oh, hell, that felt good. "I-I thought we were going to make love."

"Hush now. Let me play with this soft little pussy for a bit." As he glided his tongue in between the swollen lips of her sex, Gracie gave in and let him have his way. When his mouth leisurely licked up and down between her swollen folds, Gracie lost all reason, bucking against his face.

"Oh, yes! Please, Wade," she pleaded. He hummed against her wet clit, wrapped his arms around her hips, and clutched her bottom. She melted. She tried to wriggle free, aching to open her thighs for him, to give him better access, but he held firm.

"Be still," he growled an instant before he sank his tongue

deep, in and out, tongue-fucking her. He laved at her, as if starved for her flavor. Tremors built inside her core when his talented mouth found her clitoris. He suckled the little bud, then took it between his teeth and flicked it with his tongue. Lightning streaked through her bloodstream, and she came totally undone. Clutching the railing, Gracie held on tight as Wade stabbed her pussy with his tongue over and over. Her climax crashed over her, wave after wave, hitting her like a wild thunderstorm. She shouted his name and tightened her thighs around his head in a desperate bid to hold on to the sensations bombarding her body for as long as possible. Only after the last little spasm abated did Wade release her legs and lift his head.

"Your cunt is the juiciest fucking fruit. I want to eat you for hours, baby." He placed a delicate kiss to her clit, then rose above her. With both of his muscular arms caging her in, Wade whispered, "Are you on the pill?"

It took her a moment to process his words, her body still humming with pleasure. When she felt she could speak clearly, she answered, "Yes. And I'm clean. I just had a checkup last month."

"Same here. I want to go bareback. Do you mind?"

She yearned to feel him without any barriers. Just Wade, sinking deep and sending them both to the moon, as he'd promised. "I want that, very much."

"Good girl," he growled. "Now, wrap those sexy legs around me."

She obeyed, her arousal already at full peak. Without another word, Wade placed his cock at her entrance. Slowly, as if afraid of hurting her, he slipped in a mere inch. It wasn't enough, not nearly. She pushed her hips off the bed. The little move caused another inch to fill her. "More, now. Don't tease me, Wade."

"Goddamn," he bit out between clenched teeth. Without warning he impaled her in one smooth movement. Gracie shouted Wade's name as her inner muscles stretched to accommodate the width and length of his cock.

"Like a hot little fist wrapped tight around my cock," he murmured against the shell of her ear. "So damn perfect."

They fit together as if God had fashioned them that way. One for the other. The notion should have sent fear through her; she didn't want to need anyone, much less a man. With Wade, everything changed. The instant he pushed inside her body, she knew nothing would ever be the same again.

Riding on a sea of emotion, Gracie let herself go. She began moving her hips in little circles, drawing out their pleasure— aware of each stroke of skin, each time her body clutched around him. Wade's lips found their way over her cheeks, her eyelids, like a blind man committing each piece of her to memory by the simple touch of his mouth. When one hand journeyed between their bodies and found the tiny nub of her desire, she moaned loud and long. As her need mounted, her movements became more frantic, driving him farther into her until there was no separating them. She forgot about her bruises, her stalker; all her troubles simply melted away. Nothing mattered except this moment with Wade.

"Look at me, beautiful." As their gazes clashed, Wade took her clit between his thumb and forefinger and pinched the bundle of nerves. She arched off the bed, coming apart, breaking into a thousand glorious shards. "Now, Gracie," he ground out. He thrust deep, then pulled all the way out and slammed into her once more. Hard, fast strokes that had them both sweating and moaning.

"Wade." His name, nothing more. She wasn't capable of more in that instant.

"Mine," he said, his voice as dark and dangerous as the man himself. She could only hold on for the ride as Wade pushed her past pleasure, past contentment to a place she'd never known before. Raw, untamed, it was as if he were staking a claim.

Wrapping one arm beneath her bottom, Wade pulled her in tighter, anchoring them together. In all his untamed and natural beauty, he slid his cock outward, then shoved balls deep inside her pussy. "You burn me up, Gracie."

Watching the dark fires in his eyes burn out of control sent her blood rushing through her veins. Gracie lifted her head and flicked his chest muscles with the tip of her tongue.

"Bite me. Show me some of that fire, pretty baby."

Gracie licked one nipple, then swirled her tongue around it. She felt his fingers digging into the flesh of her ass, his heart hammering in his chest. She closed her eyes and let instinct take over. His scent was power itself. He pushed his chest against her face, and Gracie opened her mouth and bit down.

"Shit!"

His curse came a second before he began to pound into her pussy. Gracie bit him again, tasting the intoxicating flavor that was pure Wade. Squeezing her thighs tore another string of curses from him. She suckled his nipple and felt a sense of feminine satisfaction when Wade growled, "God, baby, I'm going to lose it if you don't stop."

The muscles in his neck were straining, and his sinewy arms were anchoring her to him, effectively keeping her in place, forcing her to submit. "Come in me, Wade. Now. Let me feel you filling me." That was all it took. He drove into her fast and hard, pumping like a man gone mad. One last thrust, and he was there, pouring every ounce of his hot seed inside of her pussy.

Gracie let her legs fall to the bed, her chest rising and falling as if she'd run a marathon. Wade unlocked the handcuffs, but stayed inside her, staring down at her with fathomless eyes. Suddenly unsure of herself, Gracie looked away.

He cupped her chin and brought her gaze back to his. "You rock my world, Fiery Angel."

Gracie smiled. Well, okay then.

* * *

"Tell me about your parents."

Wade felt Gracie stiffen against him. Shit, he'd known opening that can of worms would ruin the mood, but he was intensely curious about her. Gracie was so closed up, holding everything inside. It was time she learned that she could trust him with more than just her body.

"We just made love, and you want to chat about my mom and dad?"

It probably wasn't the right time, but he couldn't stop the curiosity. He wanted to know what had made her the independent woman she'd become. The woman he'd been lusting after like some lovesick fool. "Got a problem with that, Gracie?"

She shrugged, as if it didn't matter one way or the other. Had Wade not been so attuned to Gracie, he would've missed the slight tensing of muscles. "What do you want to know?"

Ah, so she thought to make him play twenty questions. "Everything. And don't give me an outline either. I want to know the good, the bad, and the ugly, Gracie."

She started to get up, probably wanting distance between them now. He tightened his arm around her, keeping her cuddled up next to his body. He wasn't about to let her go. No way in hell. "Where are you going?"

She glared at him. "Isn't Jonas coming over soon? I thought he was going over those e-mails today."

"He's waiting for my text message." She started to speak, but he stopped her with a finger to her lips. "I know you didn't have it easy growing up. I have a fair idea why, too. But I want to hear it from you, baby. You don't have to hide anything from me."

She frowned, and Wade thought it was adorable. "I'm not hiding anything."

"It makes you uncomfortable, though," he pushed. He wouldn't allow any barriers between them.

She sighed and relaxed against him. "It's not a pretty picture, Wade. No white picket fences. No cookies and milk waiting for me when I got off the school bus either. My mom was never in the picture. I have no memories of her at all. My grandmother helped raise me, and she was very kind. But she was sick a lot, and she could only do so much. She died when I was ten years old. That left me alone with Dad."

The sadness in her voice tore a hole in his heart. "And he's an alcoholic," Wade inserted, remembering the belligerent ass who'd shown up at the hospital. How could such an obnoxious fool raise someone as sweet and loving as Gracie? It boggled his mind. He ached for the little girl who had no one to love her, to read stories to her at bedtime. No mother to play dress up with or look up to. He could still remember Deanna playing with his mother's makeup and toddling around on heels five sizes too big for her tiny six-year-old feet. What had it been like for Gracie?

"Dad was manageable," she said, her voice soft, faraway, as if caught in the past. "When Grandma was alive, Dad was actually kind to me. She would get on him, and he'd stay sober about half the time. Grandma tried to shield me from his . . . bad days."

He coasted his hand down her back, soothing her the only way he could. "When she died the drinking got worse?"

"Yeah. He'd go on binges, be gone for days at a time. I did okay, though. Grandma taught me how to take care of myself. By the time I was seven I could cook, do laundry, mop, and do dishes. She even showed me how to balance the checkbook. Now that I look back, I think she was trying to prepare me. I think she knew she wasn't going to be around forever, and she wanted to do the best she could by me. It was her daughter who left, after all. I think she felt guilty for having raised such a selfish person in the first place."

Wade reached down and pulled Gracie's thigh over his. He

needed her close. He needed her to know she wasn't alone. Never again. "It sounds to me like your grandmother loved you. I don't think it was all out of guilt. Some of it, but not all."

She placed her injured wrist on his chest, her fingers playing with his chest hair. He didn't think she was even aware of what she was doing; her mind wasn't in the present. "No. You're right. I'm not being fair. She did love me. She used to pray every night that Mom would come back. That Dad would get better. She always believed his drinking was a sickness. She couldn't admit the truth, not even to herself."

"The truth?"

"Yeah. Grandma couldn't bring herself to admit that Dad would never get better. That he liked wallowing in self-pity. He enjoyed making me feel guilty for ever having been born. As if it were my fault his wife left him."

If he'd known what she'd gone through, Wade would've beaten the shit out of the asshole at the hospital. He wanted to make him pay for hurting Gracie. "We all make our own choices. He and your mom, they made their beds; they have only themselves to blame. But that doesn't explain why you choose to keep bailing him out. Why not let him deal with the consequences of his actions?" Silence greeted him. Several seconds stretched by before Wade asked, "Gracie?"

"He's the only family I have. I don't expect you to understand. I'm not even sure I do. But, I don't know, I guess I'm not quite ready to give that up yet, Wade."

The sadness in her was heartbreaking. He'd thought he could handle anything after serving in the army. He and Jonas had seen some bad shit during their tour, but nothing had prepared him for Gracie's unshed tears. And that's exactly what it was, he knew with sudden clarity. Hell, he wondered if she'd ever allowed herself to cry. Always so strong, so cool and collected. It killed him to see her like that. He wanted her blazing hot again. Moaning and writhing beneath him. The way she'd been before he'd opened his big mouth and touched the wounds of her childhood.

"Are you sore?"

She blushed and shook her head.

His cock hardened. "Are you sure?"

"Yes."

Her voice, so warm and sexy—the sound of it never failed to send his blood pumping hot in his veins. "I want you again."

Her gaze snared his as she said, "Then take me, Wade."

Without waiting another second, Wade slipped his hand between her thighs and delved his middle finger into her pussy, which was already wet. "You're ready, aren't you?"

"I always feel . . . ready when you're around."

Fuck, he didn't need that image in his head. "You have no idea what that does to me, sweetheart."

His thumb slid over her swollen clitoris, and he added a second finger inside her, fucking her with slow, gentle strokes. Wade heard her moan, her pussy tightening around his fingers. Gracie closed her eyes, as if reveling in the delicious torture. Christ, how he ached for his cock to feel that soft squeeze!

"You're so tight, baby. Tight and wet and silky soft." All thought fled as Gracie began moving her hips, finding her own rhythm. Suddenly he needed her taste on his tongue. Wade pulled his fingers free, then licked the slick juices off each one. "Tangy and sweet. But not enough." He turned her to her back, then moved down the bed. He let his gaze travel up her body until he was staring into eyes the color of emeralds. "Is this my pussy, Gracie?"

She flung her head back and clutched the sheet with her uninjured hand. "Wade, please."

He gripped her hip, refusing to be swayed. "Say it, angel."

"Yes, it's yours!"

"Good girl," he growled, and then he put his mouth against her slick opening and kissed her. Her hips shot off the bed, and

Wade was forced to wrap his hands around her thighs to hold her in place as he teased her delicate flesh with his tongue. Gracie plunged her fingers into his hair and shouted out her climax. Goddamn, it came on so fast; Wade hadn't been prepared. It staggered him to know how easily she let herself go with him. Gracie so willingly gave him her pleasure, with no reservations, no inhibitions. She was one hundred percent real, and she was the most beautiful creature he'd ever seen.

Wade kept his mouth against her pussy until the spasms subsided, then he slowly slid his index finger into her wet heat and wiggled. She moaned and gripped his hair in a stinging hold. He pulled his finger out and touched the slippery digit to her lips, then demanded, "Taste yourself for me." Mesmerized, Wade watched as Gracie sucked his finger into the dark cavern of her mouth. She closed her eyes and lapped up every drop. "Mmm, see how sweet you are?" Not waiting for an answer, he pried her hand out of his hair and brought himself over her body. He braced himself on his hands, placed at either side of her head, before positioning his cock at her cleft. "Open your eyes. I want you watching."

Gracie's eyelids fluttered open.

Unable to help himself, Wade leaned down and kissed her lightly. He slid his tongue over her chin to her throat, tasting her erratic pulse. Their passion mingled in the air around them. Wade made a leisurely path farther down her body until he reached one pretty nipple. He licked it before nipping it with his teeth. His name breathed past her lips. Succumbing to the needs rioting inside him, he opened wide and sucked the pretty raspberry bud into his mouth. He tasted perspiration, as well as the addicting flavor of Gracie. This time when he lifted his head she had a smile on her face.

"What's with the pretty smile, Gracie?"

"It's you."

He cocked his head to the side, confused. "What's me?"

"The way you treat me, with such gentle care. You're so attuned to every breath I take; every little move I make, you seem to notice. As if I matter. As if . . ."

She cut herself off, but he had a feeling he knew where she'd been headed with her little confession. "As if I care, you mean?"

She nodded.

"I wouldn't be here if I didn't, little red," he murmured. "I wouldn't do *this* if I didn't care." Wade hooked her legs over his arms and glided his cock slowly into her tight cunt. It was just the smallest amount, but he watched closely as she chewed at her lower lip and clenched her eyes tight, giving away just the tiniest bit of uneasiness. Discomfort from their earlier loving or fear over the fact that he cared about her? He didn't know, but he did intend to find out.

He let go of her thighs and leaned down to lick at the wound she was causing on her lip, then very slowly pulled out of her. She whimpered. "You want me back, baby? Filling you, loving you?"

"Yes! Please, don't stop."

"Are you sore?"

"No, I swear it."

She wrapped her legs around him and tried to pull him back, but he wasn't budging. Not without some answers first. "Then why the frown?"

"You scare me, Wade."

That hadn't been at all what he'd expected to hear. "I'd never hurt you, Gracie."

She shook her head. "No, I mean, the way you make me feel scares me. I have no defenses when it comes to you."

"Don't you think it's the same for me? You could ask me to rob a bank, and I'd probably do it. You have me wrapped, little Gracie."

She tried to speak, probably to deny his admission, but he

stopped her with a hard kiss. The time for words was over. He needed to show her the effect she had on him. He kept his mouth on hers as he touched her swollen pussy lips with the tip of his cock. When he started rocking his hips back and forth, Gracie wrapped her arms around his head and sank into the heat of the moment. Wade licked the seam of her lips and growled low and deep when she opened for him. He controlled his every motion, licking at the inner recesses of her mouth, even as he waited for her tight pussy to open for his intimate invasion. It wasn't easy, not when all he really wanted was to thrust, hard and fast and deep. To fuck her the way he'd always imagined. But for Gracie, he would bring nothing but sweet pleasure.

He lifted a bare inch, her breath hot and sweet against his mouth. "You're so fucking tight, Gracie, and you feel so damned good hugging my cock." He kissed his way over her face and to her neck where he found that same jumping vein that he now craved. He bit down. Gracie groaned and started moving her hips, thrusting against his lower body, but he was bigger and a whole lot stronger. Wade held her down, keeping her from hurting herself.

"No, baby. Soft and sweet this time," he whispered as he continued his assault on her tempting pulse.

He had to grit his teeth against the tempting sounds of her eager cries. "Shh, Gracie. You're tender, and I could hurt you." To his horror, he saw a tear trickle down her temple. He kissed it away. "Next time you can get on top and ride my cock. I'll let you run the show, I promise."

Her eyes lit up. "Really?"

He smiled at her excitement. "Yeah, really."

She capitulated finally, relaxing her flexing hips. "You said you liked to be in charge. You'd better not be lying, Wade."

"Never, baby," he swore, as he resumed his slow, torturous movements. He took his time, wanting to make it as pleasurable as possible. He feasted at her gorgeous tits, intent on build-ing her passion. "I'm buying you a chain for these rings. And you'll wear it for me, won't you, baby?"

"Yes."

"Fuck," he growled. He could so easily imagine it there. A slim bit of gold hanging between her round tits. "Would you wear it underneath your blouse? To work?"

"Do you want me to?"

"Son of a bitch." No one but them would know that she wore his chain. That her tits were tied together by the jewelry he'd bought her. "Never thought I'd say this, but I'm going to really enjoy picking out jewelry."

She smiled, and his world seemed suddenly brighter, warmer. That was Gracie. Light and heat and passion. God, it was fuck-ing beautiful.

Wade thrilled when her inner muscles relaxed for him, and he moved farther into her. Watching for any sign of pain, Wade pushed deeper, filling her completely. Now their bodies were fused together, moving in unison. He braced himself on his el-bows and watched the expressions chase across her face. Desire turned to blazing passion. With a gentle rocking motion, Wade made love to her. And that's exactly what it was—love. He'd never needed to be slow with a woman, never wanted to coax forth an orgasm with tender thrusts. Looking down at Gracie, her sweat-soaked red hair, the tenderness shining in her green eyes, Wade knew this moment would forever be etched into his soul. When he reached between their bodies and flicked her lit-tle button, her back arched, and her little moans turned to cries of ecstasy. He followed right behind her, filling her with his hot come.

He very nearly collapsed on top of her, but the thought of how sore she must be kept his muscles from going lax. He wanted to comfort her. Give her nothing but sweet memories.

Sliding out of her boneless body, Wade went to the master

bath and turned on the water to begin filling the tub. He looked around and realized he didn't have any bubble bath. Shit. He grabbed a bottle of shampoo and dumped a good portion into the water. Bubbles started to appear. Satisfied, he went back out to Gracie. Her eyes were closed, and she had a dreamy smile on her lips. His body burned at the sight of her in his bed, so replete and at ease. As he bent down and wrapped his arms around her back and behind her knees, her eyes popped open.

"Time for a bath, sweetheart," he explained. He took her to the bathroom and set her on her feet. She swayed a little, but caught herself.

Gracie looked around, then stared at the rising water in the Jacuzzi-style tub. "Does that thing have those massaging jets?"

Wade reached over and flipped a switch. The jets kicked on, and Gracie grinned up at him. "I'm really going to enjoy this."

He swatted her ass, and she yelped. "I plan on seeing that you do."

She wrapped her arms around her middle, as if nervous all of a sudden. "Uh, you are?"

"Yep." He winked at the heat filling her cheeks. "Just consider me your own personal bath toy. You can rub me all over your sexy body or just let me lie there in the bubbles while you wash. Either way, I'll be as happy as a clam. Besides, you'll need help if you want to keep the cast dry."

She laughed, and her arms loosened a fraction. "You're so outrageous."

Unable to help himself, Wade leaned close and whispered, "You have no idea, baby." Then he kissed her.

13

Wade watched her sleep. Damn, she'd been out for hours. After their bath, Gracie had called the doctor about the pain medicine. He'd instructed her to take half a pill, which seemed to do the trick. Wade had tucked Gracie back into bed, then quickly slapped together a couple of ham-and-cheese sandwiches for the two of them. The instant Gracie had finished hers off, she'd started sawing logs.

Now, with her round bottom cradling his dick, he had to bite back a groan. He wanted to fuck her there. She'd be so damned tight. He wanted to see his come dribbling out of the tight pucker of her ass.

Shit, he wanted her again! His cock was as hard as a hammer. He'd always enjoyed sex, but he'd never been so damned hungry for a woman before.

As Gracie blissfully slept, unaware of the turmoil she caused simply by being Gracie, Wade had the terrifying feeling that he'd still want her fifty years from now. A few times between her supple thighs should have been enough to ease his need. At the very least quell the urge for a few hours. All it'd done was addict him further. He'd been such an idiot to think he could have sex with Gracie Baron and walk away unscathed. She lay beside him like Sleeping Beauty, so serene and at peace, and he had the insane urge to keep her that way. To slay all her dragons and make all her dreams come true.

Wade turned her to her back, then slid his tongue over her plump lower lip, knowing the instant she woke. He pulled back and watched her eyes flutter open. "Hi," he murmured.

She pushed her hair off her forehead. "Hi."

"Jonas will be here in a few minutes. We need to get up and get dressed."

"Oh, of course." She bit her lip and looked away.

He cupped her chin and tugged her face back to his. "Don't be embarrassed."

She shrugged. "This feels like the awkward morning after."

"It's actually ten o'clock at night, not morning, and there's nothing awkward about what we did. Now, if you had stood on your head while I licked your pretty pussy, then I could understand your feeling a little awkward."

She laughed and slapped his forearm, which was still wrapped tight around her middle. This time when her gaze met his it was filled with joy. "How do you do that?"

He flicked the tip of her nose. "Do what?"

"Make me feel so at ease. I've never been good around the opposite sex. I've always been too shy, and I usually end up saying something or doing something completely embarrassing."

"First, I'm glad you're shy around *other* men. Let's keep it that way. Second, the only thing you need to be around me is you."

She cupped his cheek in her palm. "I can do that."

"Good." He kissed her, keeping it quick and light, lest he get distracted, then scooted off the bed. He held out a hand, and she took it willingly. He looked down her body and hummed his approval. "You are a sight, pretty Gracie."

She looked down at herself and grimaced. "My bruises are turning all sorts of shades. Not exactly sexy, Wade."

"All I see is pierced nipples that I want to lick. Swollen pussy lips that I want to suck on. And"—he turned her around—"a sexy ass that I desperately want to fuck."

"Wade." His name, nothing more.

He turned her toward him again and cocked his head to the side. "And how do you always do *that?*"

"Do what?"

"Say my name. All you do is say 'Wade,' and I know that you're turned on."

"How can you tell just from a single word?"

"I can see it on your face; hear it in your breathless voice. And, I can smell the delicious scent of your arousal, Gracie."

"Oh."

He winked and stepped back, away from temptation. He slid open a dresser drawer and pulled out a pair of worn, cotton shorts and an old T-shirt from his army days. "Here." He handed them to her. "You can wear these."

She didn't take them. Instead, she crossed her arms over her chest and said, "I could just put my own clothes back on."

"Uh-uh. I'd much rather see you in my clothes." He pulled her arms away from her body and started to dress her. "Raise your arms over your head for me, sweetheart." When she did, he was careful not to hurt her as he slipped the T-shirt over her cast. After pulling it down, hiding the allure of her gorgeous breasts, Wade knelt down and started on her shorts. To distract himself from the fact that her soft pussy was within kissing distance, he asked, "How's the wrist feeling? Need another half a pill?"

Gracie placed her hands on his shoulders for support. "I think it might be time for another. It's a little sore."

As he tugged the shorts up her calves, he sent her a hard glare. "How sore?"

She took over tugging the shorts on once they reached her thighs. Dressed now, she stepped back. "Just a twinge, really."

She was lying to him; he could see it in the way she frowned and bit her lower lip. "You're more than a little sore." He stood and closed the distance between them. "You should have said something earlier."

Her chin went up in the air. Damn, she was adorable. If she was going for intimidating, it wasn't working for shit. "Well, I'm saying something now."

He heard a knock on the front door. "Ah, saved by the knock." Wade grabbed her hand; entwining their fingers seemed as natural as breathing. "Come on; let's get those pills, then we can get to work on those e-mails."

"What's Jonas going to do with them?"

When they were halfway down the stairs, Jonas knocked again. Impatient bastard. "He'll try to track down the IP address. I would do it myself, but computers boggle my mind. I'm lucky to get the damn thing turned on."

When they reached the living room, Gracie looked up at him and grinned. "So, Jonas is the brains, and you're the muscle, huh?"

She was tweaking him, and he loved it. The wall was coming down. He cupped her chin in his palm, more because he wanted an excuse to touch her than anything else, and growled, "Be good."

She rose on her toes and murmured, "Or what?"

Wade started to tell her, but Jonas's fist against the door interrupted him. What had he been thinking texting Jonas? He could still be wrapped around Gracie, all warm and cozy.

In two long strides, Wade crossed the room and flung the door wide. "Will you stop it already! I heard you the first time, damn it."

Jonas pushed his way in. Some things never changed. "Hell, took you long enough."

Wade reached over and flipped on the light. "A little fucking patience would do you good."

Jonas's face split into a grin when he saw Gracie standing in the middle of the room. Wade watched him rake his gaze over her body, slowly. When he seemed fixated on her chest, Wade pushed him, hard, ready to gouge the lecher's eyes out. Jonas stumbled, but wasn't dismayed. He started toward Gracie. To what? Hug her? Flirt? No way in hell. Wade moved around him, cutting him off and effectively blocking Jonas's view of Gracie's sweet tits. "Gracie, can you grab your computer and boot it up for me?"

"Sure."

After Gracie turned around, Jonas flipped him off and whispered, "Killjoy."

Wade felt a headache coming on. "Let's remember why you're here."

Jonas waved a hand in the air. "IP address. Stalker. Yeah, yeah."

Gracie moved past them and went to the kitchen table. Wade stared, transfixed by her precise movements. Her fiery red hair was all mussed and looking sexier than ever. The voluptuous curves of her ass beckoned him to reach out and squeeze. She sat the laptop on the oak tabletop, then pulled out a chair and sat down. He noted the way she used only her right hand. Already she was getting used to doing things one-handed. Then he remembered the pain pills. He looked around the room for her purse but came up short. "Where's your purse?"

"Oh, I think it might be upstairs in the library."

He smiled when her cheeks started to turn pink. "Be right back."

He took the steps two at a time, not willing to leave Jonas

alone with Gracie any longer than necessary. He hadn't liked the look on his friend's face when he'd stared at her breasts. Wade didn't think Gracie's piercings were visible through the thin cotton T, but damn, he should have given her a sweatshirt to wear instead.

Wade located Gracie's purse on the chair next to the bookshelf. She must have put it there after she'd placed the call to the doctor. Christ, he wanted Jonas gone. Wade wanted Gracie beneath him again. First things first. If they could find out more information about Gracie's stalker, then maybe they could track the prick down. Gracie would finally feel safe.

Safety trumped his hard-on.

When Wade came back into the kitchen he found Jonas leaning over Gracie's shoulder with one hand beside her on the table, practically caging her in. Wade ground his teeth and just barely kept himself from leaping. He handed Gracie her purse. "Do me a favor, babe."

She looked up at him and smiled. "Yeah?"

Wade stopped, stared. God, she was beautiful when she smiled like that. It lit her entire face. "Grab a bottle of water from the refrigerator and take half a pill before that wrist gets any worse."

She rolled her eyes. "Yes, doctor." Not giving him a chance to reply, she looked over at Jonas and said, "Once it's booted up just hit the e-mail icon, and it'll pop up. You'll see a folder called 'Admirer.' I've stored all his e-mails in there. Any new ones that come in will go in there as well." She vacated the chair and turned to Wade. "Mind if I use your restroom?"

Wade cupped the back of her head and hauled her in for a quick, hard kiss. "Use the one upstairs. And take your time." He wanted to have a word or two with Jonas, and he didn't want Gracie overhearing.

"Thanks," she said, her voice a little shaky. She picked up her purse and reached into the fridge for the water, then headed back up the stairs. Once she was out of sight, Wade grabbed Jonas by the front of the shirt. "What the fuck are you doing?"

Jonas quirked a brow, and his lips twitched. "Uh, I thought I was here to track down a stalker. What did you think I was doing?"

"Flirting with Gracie. And you can wipe that innocent look off your damn face, I know you too well."

Jonas grinned, as if he weren't in danger of dying at any moment. "She is a pretty little thing. All those curves. Mmm, makes a man want to reach out and touch."

Stepping closer, Wade bit out, "She's off-limits. Touch her, flirt with her, hell, look at her wrong, and I'll make it so you're the one with the broken bones. Got that?"

A frown replaced the shit-eating grin. "You're awfully damn touchy about this one. What's your problem?"

"This one? Hell, Jonas, she's not a damn poodle. She's a woman, and she's been through hell. Give her some fucking breathing room."

"Like you are, you mean?"

Wade released him and watched as Jonas went about straightening his shirt. What the hell was wrong with him? He'd never had the urge to hit Jonas before. But then again he'd never been so jealous over a woman either. It was damned unsettling. "What's that supposed to mean?"

Jonas took the seat Gracie had occupied and started going to work on her computer. "You're panting after her like a bull who's just spotted the pretty red flag."

Wade watched as Jonas pulled up Gracie's e-mail. He hit a few more buttons and e-mail started to download. He'd connected her computer to their wireless network apparently. It pissed him off that Jonas knew how to do shit like that. It wasn't that Wade couldn't; he'd just never wanted to learn. It had seemed easier to let Jonas handle that end of things. Now, he wished he could be the one touching Gracie's computer. There was something strangely intimate about it. Jonas was touching something of Gracie's. Keys that her fingers had stroked. Now Jonas was touching those same keys. Jealousy. A damned ugly emotion. "I'm not panting. You just worry about finding this prick."

Jonas started to flip through the folder Gracie had told them about. Wade pulled up a chair and started reading. After the first two e-mails, Gracie reappeared. He looked up and saw the embarrassment. As if somehow she'd brought this all on. Like it was her fault some asshole had set his sights on her. He wrapped an arm around her waist and tugged until she was sitting on his lap. Ah, now that was much better. "You have nothing to be ashamed of, baby. This guy is messed up. If it weren't you, it'd be some other woman." And then, because he couldn't help himself, he kissed her.

Wade pried her lips open with his tongue, too eager to wait a minute longer to taste her sweet flavor. He needed her, ached for her like no other. She opened willingly. Her body was pliant under his seeking hands. Her slender arms wrapped around his neck, and his strong hands wrapped around her waist. His tongue dueled with hers. Sucking and savoring her sweetness. He heard someone cough and remembered then they weren't alone. Gracie pulled back, ending the kiss. The hunger in her gaze had him wishing Jonas would just disappear.

"E-mails," Jonas reminded him.

Wade willed his raging hard-on down and gritted out, "Right."

14

Gracie wanted Wade with a desperation she'd never before felt. It was insane the way he could so easily light her on fire. A look, a touch, a simple smile, and she went up in flames. She'd always been too embarrassed to kiss a man when others were around. Public displays of affection weren't her thing. And yet, had Jonas stayed silent, she knew she would have gone on kissing Wade for as long as possible.

To get her mind off the erection pressing into her bottom, she pointed to the laptop and asked, "So, how does this work exactly?"

Jonas tapped the screen. "Every e-mail has an IP address. I'm going take that address and feed it into an IP tracer site."

Confused and distracted by the way Wade kept drawing little circles on her thigh with his middle finger, Gracie asked, "A what?"

Jonas crossed his arms and sat back. "There are tons of on-line sites where you can simply input the address, and they'll tell you a general location of the user. They'll even tell you what operating system the person is using, and let you know who the person's Internet service provider is."

Intrigued now, Gracie sat up straighter. "Wow, I had no idea that was possible."

Jonas grinned. "It's not a big deal. Anyone can do it." He looked back at the computer screen, his smile turning into a scowl. "But I'm not feeling real confident."

"Why?"

"This guy doesn't strike me as an idiot. Sick, but not stupid. I'm betting he's using some sort of spoofing software."

"English, Jonas," Wade growled.

"Spoofing software is a utility that masks the person's IP address. If he's using that then the e-mails are useless."

Gracie didn't want to think negatively. She wanted this over too badly for that. "Who comes up with this stuff?"

"Unfortunately, there are a lot of people on the Net with something to hide. A company can make quite a profit off them. Now, hackers are a whole different breed. They don't need the software to hide their IP addresses."

Gracie placed her hand over Wade's to stop the caressing. Getting turned on and not being able to do anything about it wasn't her idea of a good time. "They don't?"

Jonas looked at her hand and winked, as if he knew what she was feeling. Thankfully he didn't comment. She wasn't sure how she would've handled it if he had. "Nope. A hacker will just find an IP address of a trusted host, and then they'll modify the packet headers. It'll look as if it's coming from a legitimate source."

Wade cursed. "Tricky bastards."

She couldn't agree more. "We can still bring the e-mails to the police, though, right? I mean, maybe they could track down the right Internet service provider."

Jonas shook his head. "They'd have to get a court order first in order to get the ISP to hand over their records. And since our boy hasn't technically done anything wrong, I highly doubt they're going to go to those lengths."

"Nothing wrong? Have you seen her, Jonas?"

Jonas held up a hand. "Don't get so damn testy. I'm not saying this asshole doesn't deserve a bullet for the shit he's put Gracie through, but he's not exactly a terrorist here. In the grand scheme of things, a stalker is pretty fucking low on the list."

To diffuse the rising tension she could feel brewing between the two men, Gracie leaned back against Wade's chest and said, "You both curse way too much."

Wade wrapped an arm around her waist. "I've been told."

"Then maybe you should clean it up a bit, Mr. Harrison."

He smiled down at her and her heart did a little flip. "What's my incentive?"

It wasn't so much the question as the heated promise behind it. "What do you want?"

"A kiss every time I curb my tongue," he quickly said.

She liked the idea, way too much. "And if you don't manage to curb your tongue?"

He cocked his head to the side. "Huh?"

"You should be punished, don't you think?"

"You can spank me. How's that sound?"

Jonas cleared his throat. "Uh, does this include me too?"

She laughed. Wade didn't. "Find your own woman, Phoenix."

Jonas tsked. "Always a black cloud."

"So, back to the e-mails," Gracie said. They could work out the details of their little bargain later. When they were alone.

Jonas sat up and started tapping the keys. "Right."

Silence descended over them. Gracie could feel the tension in the air. They were all hoping her stalker had made it easy for them.

Several minutes later, Jonas was scowling at the computer screen. "Judging by the first fifty—and for the record this guy must seriously have nothing else to do—it's pretty obvious he's masking his IP. The e-mails are a dead end." He looked over at her, his gaze filled with regret. "Sorry."

"It's not over yet."

Wade's determination renewed her fast waning strength. "What do you mean?"

"We still have his words. We can learn a lot just by reading his e-mails. The way he talks to you, the terms he uses. There might be something there that'll give us a clue as to where he's met you."

"Do you do anything else online?" Jonas asked. "Any social networking sites you belong to?"

"I blog if that's what you mean." Realization dawned. "You think he reads my blog or maybe comments?"

Jonas turned his attention back to her computer. "It's a possibility. What's the blog address?"

She bit her lower lip before replying, "Uh, I'd rather not say."

Both men were suddenly staring at her. Wade spoke first. "Why?"

Like a kid in the principal's office, Gracie felt like squirming. "It's personal. Like a diary. I feel . . . exposed."

Wade cupped her chin, forcing her gaze to his. "Whether it's personal or not, this guy could be one of your readers. In fact, I'm betting he is. We need to see it, baby. Trust us."

"I do, it's just . . ." She couldn't put into words how important her blog was to her. She used it to stay sane. Her problems with her dad, the stress of working two jobs. Her love life, for crying out loud! She'd mentioned Wade even. She hadn't used his name, of course, but she'd certainly expounded on his many attributes. She'd confessed that she'd desperately wanted to take him up on his offer of a date. Most of her readers, women who had come across her blog because of one of the books Gracie had posted a review of, had encouraged her to go for it even. It would be too weird if he read those posts and put two and two together.

"We're not out to embarrass you. Whatever you talk about

on your blog, it's your business. We just want to help, that's all."

She didn't believe that for a second. Oh, he definitely wanted to help. He'd made no bones about the fact that he intended to find the guy harassing her and put a stop to it. But he was also curious. "You and I both know you'd read all the posts. Don't lie."

"Fine, I'm interested in you. It's not a crime, Gracie. Still, you can trust me with your private thoughts. I won't hold them against you, sweetheart."

Trust—there it was again. Clearly she sucked at trusting men. Worse, she sucked at relationships with men. Her experiences with past lovers had all been surface relationships. She'd never felt deeply about any of them. Wade would have nothing less. "I'll agree to show you the blog, but only you." She turned to Jonas and said, "It's nothing personal, but some of the things I discuss on there are very private. And, well, I just—"

"It's none of my business; I get it." He reached over and patted her thigh. "Don't worry, you aren't hurting my feelings."

She breathed a sigh of relief. "Thanks for understanding."

He shoved his chair back and stood. "But I am hungry. If this is going to take a while, I'm thinking I should order some pizza."

Wade kissed the top of her head. "Sounds good to me. Pepperoni and green peppers again?"

Her stomach growled. There was nothing quite like a hand-tossed. "No, how about just pepperoni, extra."

Wade smiled. "Ah, going without the green this time, good choice. Do you like mushrooms?"

Gracie stuck her tongue out. "Ew. I hate those slimy things."

"You're killing me here." Wade looked up at Jonas. "Order a medium with extra pep and a large with pep and mushroom."

Jonas nodded. "Will do. I'll pick it up; give you time to look at the blog." He headed toward the front door. With his hand on the knob, he shot Wade a look over his shoulder. "Do I need to do the whole knocking thing again?"

Wade laughed. "No, it's okay."

"Good."

Jonas strode out the door, and she could hear the lock slide into place. She stared at the laptop sitting on the table, knowing she was going to have to show Wade her blog. Her deepest, darkest secrets would be there for him to read. Thinking about it had her wishing she could disappear.

"Now, about that blog."

Gracie groaned. "You aren't going to let up, are you?"

"Have I yet?"

True, he hadn't once given up on her. Not when she'd denied his request of a date and not when she'd told him about her stalker. Some men would have taken it all in then run the other way, not willing to get involved with a woman with so much baggage. Wade wasn't intimidated so easily, though.

"It's called Gracie's Ramblings." She pulled the laptop close and typed in the address. When her header popped up, she wanted to slink under the table.

"Interesting image you've got there, Gracie."

"Shut up." Her cheeks heated as she stared at the hot, shirtless cowboy covering the top of the screen. "It was an impulse, that's all."

He chuckled. "I'll bet." The hand he had wrapped around her middle started a slow path down her body. "Maybe I should buy myself a cowboy hat."

She slapped his forearm. "Concentrate."

His hand didn't stop moving until it was covering her pussy. Nuzzling her neck, Wade whispered, "How can I with you sitting on my lap?"

Gracie relaxed against him, the blog forgotten. "What about Jonas?"

He slipped his hand beneath the waistband of the shorts

he'd loaned her. Warm, calloused fingers touched her clit, and she moaned. "We've got time. Spread your legs for me, baby."

"W-Why?"

"I want to play with my pretty pussy."

Gracie moved her legs apart, giving him better access to her body. "Oh, God, this is so crazy."

A finger glided between her pussy lips. "No, this is necessary."

"Necessary?" Her voice sounded as if she'd run a marathon. His effect on her was potent.

Slowly, as if savoring every inch of her, Wade pushed his finger deep. "Yeah. If I don't touch you, I'll die. And that would really suck."

She didn't laugh as he no doubt intended. Hell, it was all she could do to hold on as he teased and played with her; already he knew exactly how to touch her, how much pressure to use to elicit a moan, or several moans. The man was a very fast learner.

When a second finger joined the first, she cried out, all sense of modesty gone. All she wanted, all she craved was Wade and the things he could do with his hands, mouth, cock. He pressed his lower body upward, showing her just how much he wanted her.

"Wade, I need you," she admitted, too eager to feel his cock stretching and filling her.

"Later for that, sweetheart," he murmured against her ear. "Right now just feel."

His fingers continued their gentle torment. Sliding in and out, fucking her with a maddening tempo designed to drive her to the very brink, but never beyond. "Please, Wade!"

His other hand cupped her breast and squeezed. "Soon, little angel."

Wade stroked the curls of her mound. It seemed so wicked to make out in his kitchen. Jonas could walk in at any moment. She didn't care. All her concentration was on Wade, his powerful body beneath her, surrounding her. His hot breath against her neck sent a shiver down her spine. She could smell the potent mixture of his aftershave and his desire.

Wade cupped her chin and brought her head back until he was staring directly into her half-closed eyes. "Is this my pussy, Gracie?" He skimmed his thumb over her clitoris. "I want to own it. I want to hear you say it belongs to me, only me."

She wanted to speak, needed to answer him, but his touch was electric. Only Wade had the power to make her burn so completely.

Three fingers thrust between the swollen folds of her pussy, and she lost control. She pushed into his hand, seeking more, needing everything.

"Mmm, you're so pretty like this, baby. Excited and hungry to be fucked. Later, I'm going to show you what it's like to have this little ass filled with my cock. For now, I want you coming for me. I want your cream soaking my fingers."

Gracie clutched onto his arm, her fingers digging into his flesh. "Please, faster, Wade." The carnal images his words evoked ripped through her mind like some forbidden film. She ached for everything he had to give.

"Like this?" His strokes increased, driving all rational thought from her mind.

"Yes!"

His smile fluttered against her cheek. She felt his male triumph. He knew she was helpless with him. It grated on her, but she couldn't think why. All she really cared about was the feel of Wade's long, thick fingers filling her. His thumb flicking her clit, and the hand tugging at the ring in her nipple. He was everywhere at once, driving out everything except the way he made her body hum with pleasure. Intense, hot, eager. It'd never been that way for her before. Not with any other man. With Wade, a mere touch sent her blood pressure into the danger zone.

A few more pumping strokes and she was there, soaring into the air. Wade covered her mouth with his and drank in her moans of pleasure. Only after the last little quiver died away did Wade release her mouth and pull his fingers free. He brought the wet digits to his lips and licked each one clean. His dark smile promised things. Wild, taboo things.

"You taste like warm, sweet cream."

She blushed. "Um, thanks, I guess."

"Hmm." He dipped his head and kissed her, a tender peck, nothing more. When he lifted his head the intensity in his gaze had changed. The smoldering passion was still there, as was the hard-on prodding her butt cheeks, but there seemed to be satisfaction there as well. Strange, considering he hadn't gotten to come. "I could take the edge off for you, too. If you want."

He shook his head and started rubbing her lower back. The soothing motion had Gracie cuddling closer. "Jonas will be here any minute. Besides, when I get naked I'm going to want more than a few quick minutes in the kitchen."

"Oh." She didn't know what else to say, so she didn't say anything.

"Anyway, I want to read your blog."

Where had that come from? She could barely breathe, her body was still vibrating, and he wanted to read her rambling posts? "How can you even think of that right now?"

"I'm always thinking of your stalker, Gracie. I won't stop until we catch the bastard."

His conviction made her feel protected. "You cursed."

"You can spank me later."

"I—" She didn't get to finish what she was going to say because her cell phone started tinkling. She sat up and reached for her purse. She pulled the phone out of a side pocket and checked caller ID. "Crap."

Wade stiffened, his arm tightening around her middle. "Who is it?"

"My father." The satisfying aftereffects of her orgasm vanished.

"What does he want?"

"God only knows."

Gracie flipped her phone open. "Hi, Dad." She tried to sound chipper, but the instant she heard the slurring words on the other end her heart sank. Her father was drunk. "Slow down; I can't understand you." His next words were crystal clear. Gracie froze.

Wade's arms tightened around her. "Baby, what is it?"

Pulling the phone away from her ear, Gracie looked at Wade. She blinked a couple of times, hoping it was just a bad dream and it would go away. "Dad's at my apartment."

"And?"

Gracie squeezed her eyes shut, praying she'd wake up and find herself in Wade's cozy bed, his protective arms surrounding her. Of course, it wasn't to be. In her experience prayers were rarely answered. She opened her eyes and said, "My home has been broken into."

Wade straightened in the chair, and if his arms hadn't been around her she would've fallen. "What the hell?"

She threw her hands in the air. "Dad's there now. H-He says the place is trashed." Her voice quivered as she imagined her things ruined.

Wade took the phone out of her hands and brought it to his ear. "Mr. Baron, I need you to hang up and call the police." She could hear her father cursing. "Just do it!" Wade shouted and slammed the phone onto the table. He cupped her cheek. "I should've insisted on that damn security system. I'm sorry, sweetheart."

Gracie refused to allow Wade to take responsibility for the actions of some psycho. She shook her head, denying his words. "No, Wade, this is not your fault." Another thought occurred. "What if I'd been there?"

Wade raked a hand through his hair. "My guess is he knew you weren't and wanted to send you a message."

What had started as a mere nuisance was turning her life upside down. It was enough to make a perfectly rational person commit murder. "What kind of message is he trying to send? First, he runs me off the road; now this. God, Wade, this is insane!"

"Shh, it's going to be okay. We do need to get over there, though, and talk to the police. We'll need to make statements. And I want to call Detective Henderson. He should be informed."

Gracie heard the door open. Jonas strode through, a smile on his handsome face. "You have no idea how hard it was not to dig into this pizza." He looked at them, and the smile disappeared. "What happened?"

Wade spoke first. "Gracie's apartment's been broken into. According to her father, the place is trashed. He's calling the police now."

"Jesus, this guy isn't working with a full deck is he?"

"No." Wade lifted her off his lap and lightly tapped her cast. "Do you need help getting dressed?"

She shook her head. "I think I've got it."

He nodded. "I'm going to call the detective then. We'll eat on the way."

Bile rose at the thought of food. "I'm suddenly not hungry. Go figure." She turned and went up the stairs, legs shaking with each step. When would it end? She was so tired of being at the mercy of some nameless, faceless asshole. He knew everything about her, apparently had no problem getting into her apartment, and yet she could walk up to him on the street and say hello and not even know it. A ghost. He was a deranged ghost.

15

Everything she owned was destroyed. Her furniture was shredded, the cheap, store-bought artwork she'd hung on her walls ripped right out of their frames. They littered the floor as if they held no more importance than garbage. And her books, her precious paperbacks that had given her countless hours of enjoyment over the years, appeared to have been sliced into pieces. He'd cut up her books. *My God, what sort of person did something like this?* The rage he must have been in to do this much damage . . . She shivered at the thought. There didn't appear to be a single thing left to salvage. Nothing had been left untouched. She stared from the front of the room, unable to move any farther. She couldn't bring herself to see what he'd done to her bedroom. Her skin crawled as she imagined him riffling through her clothes, her private things.

"Wade." Her voice sounded far away, as if she were floating outside her own body.

"Right here, sweetheart."

The calm tone quieted her fears as nothing else could. The

arm he had wrapped around her shoulder kept her from sinking to the carpet. "I checked every room. He's gone. Judging by the scratch marks on your doorknob, and the fact that none of your windows are broken, I think he picked your lock." He paused, then asked, "Do you want to see the rest of it?"

"I don't think I can, Wade."

"I'll be right here, baby."

As they started toward the kitchen, her dad suddenly appeared at her front door. "Where the hell have you been?"

Wade released her and stepped forward, his stance protective and ready for battle. "She's been with me, Mr. Baron. And you should be damned grateful too. If she'd been home when this had taken place, she could've been hurt."

Her father sneered as he looked at Wade. "Who the hell are you?"

His words weren't slurred, but she could tell all the same that he'd been drinking. His clothes were wrinkled, and he looked as if it'd been a good week since he'd last showered. Had he left her wrecked apartment to go drink? God, probably. Humiliation suffused her. She should be used to her father embarrassing her. Hell, she'd definitely experienced it enough times. Just once she wished he could've been sober. That she was like any other daughter and could run into her dad's loving arms and feel secure. That was the stuff of fairy tales, though, and her life had never been a fairy tale.

Gracie placed her hand on Wade's forearm, hoping to stop the train wreck of a conversation before it had a chance to gain momentum. "Dad, this is Wade Harrison. He's a private investigator. He's been helping me with a problem I've been having."

Her father pointed a finger at Wade, his gaze narrowing. "What do you need a private investigator for? Are you in some sort of trouble, Gracie?"

Wade snorted and crossed his arms over his chest. "What was your first clue? The car accident that landed her in the hospital or the fact that someone broke into her place and destroyed nearly everything?"

Her dad stepped forward. His wobbling gait didn't escape her notice. "I don't think I care for your tone."

"I don't much give a shit. Right now, all that matters is your daughter's safety. Or are you too drunk to give a damn?"

"You son of a bitch!" Before she could intervene again, her father launched himself at Wade, arms flailing. Of course, Wade was bigger, stronger, and sober. Her father didn't stand a chance. Wade caught one flying fist in his hand, then slung her father around and pulled both his arms behind his back. Her father cursed, spittle dribbling down his chin. Wade held firm. "Calm down, Mr. Baron. The police will be here any minute. Do you really want them to see you like this?"

That seemed to do the trick. After her father stopped struggling, Wade released him. He stumbled but caught himself and turned around. His bloodshot eyes shot daggers at them both, but he stayed silent. Ah, self-preservation. It was the only thing that ever registered with Quinn Baron. Gracie knew she shouldn't care one way or the other. Her father had always been a selfish man. Still, her heart broke a little bit every time she had to witness him in such a state.

As if sensing her inner turmoil, Wade reached down and took her uninjured hand in his and gave a gentle squeeze. "You did call the police like I asked, right, Mr. Baron?"

"I haven't had the chance, damn it." He waved a hand in the air. "I've been a little preoccupied trying to make sense of this mess."

Wade cursed under his breath as he pulled out his cell phone. Gracie knew her father was lying. More likely he'd forgotten to place the call entirely. After Wade reported the break-in and shoved his phone back onto his hip, Gracie spoke up. "Dad, do you really want to be around to answer questions when the police get here?"

Her father shot her a look of disapproval. "You'll mind your tongue with me, girl. I won't be taking any of your sass."

Gracie sighed. She'd get nowhere with him, not until he sobered. That was the only time he was even remotely reasonable. Unfortunately those moments were pretty few. "Look, it's been a really trying few days. How about I call you a cab? Tomorrow I can fill you in on everything that's been going on. Okay?"

"Fine." His gaze darted to Wade, then back to her. "There is one other thing."

Here it comes. "What is it?"

"They've threatened to shut off the electricity again," he grumbled. "I don't seem to have enough in the bank to cover the bill."

Gracie wasn't sure she had the money to cover it, but to get him out of there, she said, "I'll take care of it."

"Gracie," Wade said, his voice a warning in itself.

She knew what he was about to say. He didn't like it that her father used her. Truth be told, she wasn't all that crazy about it either. But there was still a thread there, that family connection. Quinn Baron was the only family she had, and she simply couldn't ignore him. Even if it were the best thing for the both of them.

"It's okay, Wade. Just let it go for now. The police will be here, and I just don't have it in me to worry about electric bills at the moment."

Wade stayed silent, though she could tell he wanted to protest. Instead he flipped open his cell phone again and called for a cab for her father. In that moment Gracie knew the truth. She was falling for Wade Harrison, PI and all-around good guy. It was both scary and exhilarating. When she heard sirens off in the distance, she put thoughts of her dad, of love, and of family obligations out of her mind. She looked toward the kitchen. "How bad is it?"

Her father shook his head. "It's not like in here. The bedroom is the worst. Just a few things broken in the kitchen. There's something you'll want to see, though."

She followed him, noticing for the first time the way her father slumped. As if in pain? She sighed. The drinking was killing him. How could he not see that? Probably the same reason he couldn't see that it had all but killed her love for him. He would have to actually give a damn first.

With Wade close behind, a hand on her shoulder for support, Gracie walked into the kitchen. Right in the center of her round oak table sat a single black rose in a black vase. She shivered at the sight. There was a card attached, but she couldn't bring herself to move closer to the ominous thing. Wrapping her arms around herself, she stared at it as if it would reach out and take hold of her. When would it end? How far was he willing to go?

Gracie didn't think she wanted to know the answer.

Wade tugged Gracie around until she faced him. Damn, she was as white as a sheet. "Come here, baby," he murmured, coaxing her closer. When her arms snaked around his waist, he could feel her trembling. "He's just a man. We'll catch him, angel. I promise you."

Gracie looked up at him, then turned and stared at the table where the flower still sat like a bad omen.

"Come on. You need to sit down."

She shook her head. "I'm fine."

Bullshit. "No, you aren't." Wade heard someone honk, and he realized it was the cab. He took out his wallet and pulled out a few bills, then shoved them at Gracie's father.

"Uh, I guess I'd better go," her father said, his voice a little steadier as he took the cash. "Call me tomorrow, Gracie."

She nodded, but didn't speak. Wade suspected it was all starting to really sink in. The shock was wearing off. Damn, what he wouldn't do to get his hands on the bastard tormenting her. He wanted to tear him apart, slowly. He wanted it to hurt for a good long time before death finally came.

He took her to one of the kitchen chairs and helped her sit, and then he crouched down. "I'm sorry, baby. I should have insisted on that security system. At the very least I should have been keeping an eye on this place."

"No, it's not your fault, Wade. None of it. Besides, you were protecting me. You can't be in two places at once."

He wouldn't let her make excuses for him. Wade cupped her cheek in his palm. "I could've had Jonas here, Gracie. I was a little too intent on getting you into bed. Everything else sort of fell to the wayside."

She smiled, and as usual the brilliance of it lit him up like a freaking Christmas tree. "I'm not sure if you noticed, but I was pretty intent on that, too."

They both fell silent. Wade stood and strode across the room, then started opening drawers. "Do you have a pair of tongs or something that I can use to pick up the card?"

"Um, the third drawer down, I think."

Wade pulled it open and found a pair of red-handled tongs among a bunch of other kitchen utensils. Grabbing them, he went back to the table and used them to pluck the card out of the vase. He had the insane urge to throw the entire thing into the damn trash, but it was evidence, and he couldn't destroy evidence. There could be a fingerprint. He highly doubted it, but there was still a chance, and he clung to it. It took a few tries to get the card out of its envelope. Once the card was free, Wade read it to himself first.

"What does it say?" She straightened her spine, as if bracing herself for yet another impact.

Instead of repeating the words aloud, Wade handed her the tongs. The whole situation was putting him into a dangerous rage. "I'm usually a pretty patient man, but this asshole is really pissing me off."

You've betrayed me, Gracie Lynn. I can't let your slutty be-
havior continue. I'll see you soon, my love.
Forever, Your Admirer

Wade watched the look of disgust come over Gracie's face. Nothing in his life had ever been more difficult than standing around, helpless, while his woman was being tormented. When she started to shake uncontrollably, Wade took one long stride, then reached out and snagged the tongs holding the card out of her hand and placed both gently on the table, before pulling Gracie into the safe cocoon of his arms. They held each other tight. "I will find him," he vowed, "and he'll pay for all of it." The bastard's days were numbered.

"I thought I was braced for the worst, but the words on the card . . . Wade, he's crazy." She had her face buried in his T-shirt, causing her words to sound garbled.

"Crazy, but he'll make a mistake, and we'll get him." The implications of the words on the card said it all. He'd seen him and Gracie together. And it'd pushed him to act out. Wade knew that would be the way to find him.

"God, he was in here. All over my apartment." Suddenly, Gracie jerked out of Wade's embrace and ran to the trash. She threw up so hard Wade's gut clenched. He went to her. Placing his palm on her back, Wade soothed her as best he could as he held her hair back with his other hand. He murmured soft words to her and finally her spasms eased. She raised her head to look at him. "Sorry."

"Don't. You have nothing to be sorry for, baby." Gracie seemed to pull herself together then. Walking over to the sink, she reached up and grabbed a paper towel from its holder, and yanked. As she went about cleaning herself up, Wade heard the sirens again, close. "The police are here."

Gracie went back to the table and leaned down to look at the card. "The way he says Gracie Lynn . . . It's starting to seem familiar. Like I've heard it before. But . . ." She broke off then as if contemplating something.

"But what, honey?" Wade urged.

She looked up at him, a frown marring her pretty face. "I told you before I've never used my middle name. But I could swear someone called me Gracie Lynn recently. I wish I could remember."

"You will. Give it time."

She sighed and tossed her hair over her shoulder. "I'm so tired of his having the upper hand."

"Me too. But he's losing his composure. This sort of de-struction was done in one hell of a rage."

"And you think we can get him to make a mistake if he sees us together again?"

"Yeah, I do. Now, about your staying with me." A loud knock interrupted them. Instinct had Wade moving between her and the doorway.

"It's the police."

He nodded, hearing the exhaustion in her voice. "Stay here. I'll let them in."

She plopped down onto the chair. "It's going to be a really long night."

Unable to help himself, Wade closed the distance between them. Leaning down, he placed a gentle kiss on her forehead. "A few hours, and then you'll be back in my bed, snuggled under the covers and driving me to distraction."

She smiled. "Thank you for being here. For making me feel safe and for . . . everything."

He winked. "There's more of that *everything* to come, sweetheart."

16

Gracie heard voices coming from the other room. She took a deep breath and left the kitchen. God, the sight of all her things destroyed tore a hole in her heart all over again. She looked toward the front door where two uniformed police officers stood talking to Wade. It had taken them long enough to arrive. The police station wasn't that far away. Clearly, the local law enforcement wasn't all it was cracked up to be. When one of the officers noticed her, they all turned and stared. She wrapped her arms around herself and tried on a smile. It fell flat. In a few strides, Wade was across the room. He pulled her into his strong arms, comforting her. Once again she found herself wishing the world would just go away. It would be so nice to live the rest of her days in Wade's protective embrace. Pushing against Wade's broad chest, Gracie forced herself to deal with reality. The sooner she got this over with, the sooner she could begin the arduous task of sifting through her ruined belongings.

She walked over to the two officers and gave one of them

138 / Anne Rainey

her hand in greeting. She spoke to the two in a calm voice, or she hoped it sounded calm. "Gracie Baron, thanks for coming."

"Ms. Baron. I'm Officer Andrews, and this is my partner Officer Delaney. We'd like to ask you a few questions about the break-in."

As Officer Andrews spoke, Gracie heard a hint of a Southern accent. He was older than his partner; his salt-and-pepper hair matched a mustache that needed to be trimmed in a bad way. His tall muscular build seemed in total contrast with his smooth, gentle voice.

"Of course. We should go into the kitchen. The furniture in here is pretty much ruined." She showed them to the back of the apartment and waited as they both took a seat. "Would anyone like something to drink? I could make a pot of coffee."

"No, thank you, Ms. Baron," Officer Delaney said. He gestured to the chair across from him. "Please, have a seat, and we'll get started." There was something in the tone of his voice and the way he looked at her. He wasn't nearly as friendly as his partner. In fact, she'd say he was even a little hostile. And where was Detective Henderson?

Wade waited for her to sit, before taking the chair next to her.

"Didn't you say you called Detective Henderson?"

He reached over and took her hand. "Yeah, but I got voice mail. I'm sure he'll call us soon."

Wade's attention turned to Officer Delaney. "Gracie's been dealing with a stalker for the past two months. At first it was just e-mails. It escalated to phone calls shortly after. Hang ups, never a voice. The other night Gracie was run off the road. You can see the bruises and the broken wrist. Tonight this."

"How do you know all these incidences are related? The break-in could be completely random."

Wade's expression hardened. "Did the living room look like the work of a random B and E? Her things are destroyed.

That's rage, not someone looking for quick cash. Never mind the fact that he or she left the television and stereo." Wade pointed to the flower and the card. "Then there's that."

Officer Andrews pulled out a pen and used it to drag the card across the table. He frowned, then his gaze landed on Gracie. "This has been going on for two months? Did you report it to the police?"

"I've filed reports, twice. Detective Henderson has been looking into the hit-and-run." A knock on the door interrupted whatever Officer Andrews was about to say. Gracie started to stand, but Wade was quicker. "Stay put." She nodded and glanced across the table to the two officers. They both stood with Wade, and the three of them went out to the living room. A few minutes later Detective Henderson appeared, Wade and the officers behind him.

"Detective."

"Ms. Baron. I would say it's nice to see you again, but . . ."

She smiled despite the seriousness of the situation. "Thank you for coming."

Wade crossed his arms over his chest, his feet braced apart as he looked at the detective. "I'm sure you're aware of just how terrifying this has been for Ms. Baron. It's not bad enough this guy put her in the hospital, but now he's been in her home."

"And from the looks of things he was in quite a state when he was here. You weren't home, I take it?"

Her cheeks heated when she admitted, "No, I was with Wade."

He nodded. "Damn good thing you were, if you ask me. Under the circumstances, you've sure handled this well. A lot of women wouldn't be so calm."

Gracie folded her hands in her lap. "You should have seen me a few minutes ago. I wasn't so calm then."

Wade placed his hands on her shoulders and squeezed. "You had every right to get upset, sweetheart."

Gracie looked at Wade. A little thrill ran down her spine as she noticed the admiration in his dark gaze. "Thank you." She hadn't expected him to come to her defense so quickly. However, this was one time she was glad she had a man to speak up for her. Wow, she really wasn't feeling herself.

Detective Henderson took out a notepad and a pen. "Let's start at the beginning. You were gone, and when you came home your apartment looked like this?"

"My dad called. He'd stopped by and found the door unlocked and the place in shambles."

"And it doesn't appear the perpetrator took anything?" This time Officer Delaney spoke.

Before Gracie could answer, Wade effectively stopped her with a look. He turned to address the young officer himself. "We haven't gotten a chance to go through everything, but nothing seems to have been taken. I think the asshole picked her lock. No windows were broken."

"Does your lease allow for pets? It might give you some peace of mind to have a dog around," Detective Henderson said.

She shook her head. "I thought of that, but I'm afraid no pets allowed."

He frowned. "Do you have somewhere you can stay for a while?"

"She'll be staying with me until this guy is caught," Wade stated, as if it'd already been decided.

All three men stared at Wade while they digested that little tidbit of information. Gracie wanted to kick him for his high-handedness. She would've too, if not for the relief swamping her at the idea that she wouldn't have to stay in the apartment. She couldn't imagine ever staying there again. The very idea made her queasy. She felt violated. And she hadn't even gotten a look at her bedroom.

The detective took a pair of plastic gloves from his inside

breast pocket. After putting them on, he picked up the note. One eyebrow arched upward. "I've been going through the copies of those e-mails you showed me, and I've noticed he calls you Gracie Lynn." He tucked the note in a plastic bag and sealed it. "In the note too. You have no idea who this guy could be? A coworker maybe or an ex-boyfriend?"

Gracie had asked herself that same question a hundred times; she still had no answers. "I can't think of a single person who would do this. And no one calls me by my middle name."

"He's obviously becoming more and more violent toward you, Ms. Baron. Breaking into your home tells me he's damned confident he won't get caught."

"Or he just doesn't give a damn if he is," Wade growled.

Detective Henderson tucked the note into his pocket. "Either way, you aren't safe alone. We can have an officer keep an eye on your apartment."

Gracie pushed a hand through her hair. "I'm not sure it's necessary. Not anymore. He's already ruined everything anyway. And I won't be staying here. So what's the point?"

The detective cringed. "Yeah, the damage is done. But his next step could be to harm you personally."

"He'll have to go through me first," Wade said, his voice as hard as steel.

The detective nodded approvingly. "We'll need you to come down to the station and give us a statement." He pointed to the vase and said, "In the meantime maybe we can get some fingerprints. Something to indicate who this guy is."

Gracie wasn't holding her breath on that one. So far her lunatic admirer had proven damned resourceful when it came to hiding his identity; she doubted he would make a mistake now. But she kept her thoughts to herself. "I just need to call my neighbor. She'll worry if she sees police in my apartment."

The doorbell rang, and Gracie frowned as she glanced at the clock. It was two in the morning. "Who could that be?"

"I'll check," Wade said.

Curious, Gracie followed him out of the kitchen, but when he looked out the front window and cursed, her curiosity increased. "Who is it, Wade?"

"Jean," he said, with a definite grimace.

Gracie smiled. Knowing Jean had come over to check on her took some of the chill away. Gracie closed the distance and nudged Wade aside and opened the door. Jean stood on her doorstep, her hair up in rollers. The rainbow-colored robe she wore should have looked garish on her, but somehow Jean pulled it off.

"What on earth is going on? I saw the police car and—" She stopped talking, and her eyes grew as round as quarters. "Oh, my Lord! What happened here?"

"My stalker decided to pay me a little visit."

"Oh, no!" Jean looked her over from head to toe. "Are you okay, dear? Did he hurt you?"

"I'm fine. I wasn't even here."

She peeked around her shoulders, her gaze glomming onto Wade. "You were with the big hunk, I take it?"

Gracie nearly laughed. It was either that or cry. And she was so done with the tears. "Yes, I was with Wade." She moved to let Jean enter, then closed the door behind her. "I'm glad you're here. I was going to call you. Wade and I need to go to the police station. I didn't want you seeing the squad car out front and getting worried."

"When did this happen? I didn't even hear anything."

"I'm not sure. Earlier in the evening sometime." Another thought occurred. "Jean, I'm not sure it's safe for you to be alone right now, especially considering you live right next door. Can you stay with Brian for a little while? Just until this is all sorted out."

She nodded. "Yeah, that's not a bad idea." She adjusted her

robe, as if to cover herself better. "You'll be staying with Wade then?"

She couldn't help it; she blushed. "Uh, yeah."

"Good." Jean pointed to Wade, a stern look on her thin, wrinkled face. "You'll take care of her, or you'll answer to me."

Wade shoved his hands in his pockets. "Yes, ma'am."

"Do you need anything, Gracie?"

Grateful for the offer, Gracie hugged her friend close and said, "Thanks for asking, Jean, but I'll be fine."

Jean patted her on the back and told her everything would work out. Emotion clogged Gracie's throat. Is this what it felt like to have a mother's love? She didn't know, but she did know she was grateful for Jean. Knowing the woman cared made all the difference in the world. In that moment Gracie realized how lucky she was to have friends concerned about her, offering their support. Her gaze caught on Wade's. He watched her, tenderness softening his harsh features.

Her stalker might have destroyed a few pieces of cheap furniture, but he definitely hadn't hurt the things that truly mattered. If only she could keep it that way.

17

Wade didn't know what he had expected, but it hadn't been Jean in rollers and a bright rainbow-colored robe. The woman had the oddest fashion sense of anyone he'd ever known. And the way she bossed him around, she didn't seem to realize he wasn't one of her children. And why the hell was he putting up with it? Before he could get a word of greeting out of his mouth, she'd started issuing orders. His temples started throbbing. Damn, would this night never end?

Nothing had gone according to plan. He'd hoped to get Gracie away from the scene of the destruction as soon as possible. It pissed him off to see her so upset. If he were honest with himself, he'd admit that he wouldn't feel comfortable until he had Gracie back in his home. He wanted to hold her, to know she was safe. Once they were both rested, he'd wake her, slowly, and make love to her for several hours. He was ready to explore every inch of her sweet tight body all over again. To know she was alive and safe. And his. His dick swelled with the tantalizing image.

Wade put a stop to his train of thought and closed the front door. When he turned around and saw Jean enveloping Gracie in a tight embrace, he knew it was exactly what Gracie had needed in that moment. A caring friend.

"Hate to interrupt here," Detective Henderson said, "but I have a few questions."

Jean and Gracie both turned. The detective stood with the officers on the other side of the room. Gracie wrapped her arm around Jean. "Detective, this is my neighbor, Jean Swinson. Jean, this is the detective who's been helping me. Officers Andrews and Delaney responded to the 911 call."

"Ms. Swinson, did you hear or see anything out of the ordinary tonight?"

Jean rolled her eyes and planted her hands on her hips. "Of course not. Don't you think I'd have done something about it if I had?"

Wade hid his smile. Damned if it wasn't nice having a break from Jean's sharp tongue. He should feel bad for the detective, but he was still pissed over the way the man had handled Gracie's concerns when she'd first filed the complaint.

"I see. Which unit is yours?"

"I'm to the right. Directly next to Gracie."

The detective quirked a brow. "And there weren't any unusual noises?"

"Well, truth be told, I had my earphones in for most of the night. Music is the only way I can get any sleep. So, no, I didn't hear anything." She looked at Gracie, her eyes full of regret. "I'm so sorry, dear. I should have been more alert."

Gracie hugged the smaller woman close. "This isn't your fault, Jean," she soothed. "If you had heard something, you might've come to check it out. And I don't even want to think what this guy would've done if you'd interrupted his temper tantrum."

For a change Jean stayed silent. Wade reached out and cupped Gracie's nape. "We need to get to the station."

Gracie nodded, but kept her worried gaze on Jean. "Call Brian. I won't feel comfortable until I know you're safe."

Jean waved a hand in the air. "Don't fret over me, dear. I've been taking care of myself for a long time now." She hugged Gracie and made her promise to call, then left. Wade waited, watching in silence along with the detective and the two officers as Gracie took another look around the room. The sadness in her eyes when her gaze lingered on her torn up books was unmistakable. "I never looked through the bedroom," she said, her voice quivering a little. Anyone else might not have detected it, but Wade knew Gracie too well to miss it.

He kissed the top of her head. "I saw it, sweetheart. It's pretty bad. Maybe tomorrow"—he stopped himself and checked his watch—"later today actually, will be soon enough to start going through everything."

"Yeah. I guess it's a good thing I have renter's insurance, huh?"

He smiled down at her. "You don't worry about any of that for now. Everything's going to be okay, baby."

"Thanks, Wade. I'm ready to look at the bedroom now. Might as well get it over with."

He nodded and followed close behind as they went down the hall. When they entered he heard Gracie gasp. "Oh, God."

"Yeah," Wade snarled, pissed all over again.

Gracie moved around the room, picking up various articles of clothing, all destroyed. The dresser mirror was shattered. Makeup and hair accessories were scattered everywhere. And there were more destroyed books. She picked up a cover that had been torn off and cursed. "I thought I was prepared. No one could prepare for this."

Wade stayed silent, waiting for her to absorb it all. When she dropped the cover and turned toward him with haunted eyes, Wade knew a whole different sort of hell. In that moment, Wade made a promise to himself to help her replace every single book she'd lost. It didn't matter how long it took. Then he'd find the bastard and make him pay for causing Gracie so much grief.

"I don't want to be here anymore," Gracie said. "Tomorrow is going to be a really long day."

Wade stepped away from the doorway and waited for her to step through it before following her down the hall to the living room. Her back was straight, head held high, and Wade's respect for her grew. Or was it something deeper? He had a feeling he was falling for the red-haired beauty. The thought should have sent him into a panic. Wade wasn't the sort of man for happily ever afters and white picket fences. That he could so easily picture exactly that with Gracie was damn telling.

Imagining waking to her snuggled up against him in bed every morning sent his blood racing through his veins. Knowing she seemed to be slipping inside his heart made him even more desperate to get her stalker behind bars. The quicker it was settled, the quicker he could start concentrating on more pleasant things. Like convincing Gracie that he was good for more than protection.

Gracie woke to light streaming through the large window across from Wade's bed. She blinked and looked to her left. She was alone. A note sat on Wade's pillow. She frowned. Wondering what he was up to, Gracie picked up the slip of paper.

You looked so pretty I didn't have it in me to wake you. Take a long bath, and when you're ready, come downstairs. I have a treat for you.
Sweet kisses, Wade

Her heart began to race. She sat up and pushed the covers aside. Immediately she spotted a lovely emerald green blouse and a pair of jeans draped across the overstuffed, black chair across from the bed. "He bought me clothes?"

Rubbing the sleep out of her eyes, Gracie glanced down at her fractured wrist. It only throbbed a little. "Thank God for that at least." She stood and crossed the room. As Gracie picked up the blouse, she eyed the label. It was her size. Careful not to wrinkle the delicate satiny material, Gracie placed it back on the chair before checking out the jeans. She didn't know how he did it, but both items were her size. How he'd managed to purchase new clothes for her while she slept was a mystery she hoped to solve soon. Then a rotten thought invaded her mind. Did he already have them on hand? From a previous girlfriend maybe? The idea made her stomach roll.

Dressed in one of Wade's soft cotton Ts, Gracie left the clothes behind and headed for the bathroom. First a hot shower, then she'd get some answers. As she entered the smaller room, she flipped on the light. The first thing she noticed was a black bra and a pair of matching panties draped over the towel rack. More satin. The slip of paper perched precariously on top of the sensual set caught her eye. Gracie bit her lip and moved forward. Picking up the note, she realized her heart was beating faster. At this rate she'd go into cardiac arrest, for crying out loud!

The note was folded in half. She counted to ten and opened it.

You're too suspicious, Gracie. The clothes are not from another woman. I told Deanna about the break-in; she bought you the clothes. See you downstairs, my Fiery Angel. P.S. The plastic bag and rubber band on the counter is for the cast.

Gracie smiled as she noticed the bag. Wade had a way of doing that to her. She had a madman on her tail, her apartment was in shambles, and yet she couldn't stop grinning. And all because of a few words written on a slip of paper.

As she turned on the water and adjusted the temperature, her mind glommed onto the nickname he'd given her. Fiery Angel. She liked it. It was sexy and tough. Like a kick-ass heroine in one of the romance books she loved to read. It was much better than the way her last boyfriend had described her. He said she was boring and predictable. She snorted. "What a jerk."

Careful to cover her cast with the bag, Gracie stepped into the shower and shoved thoughts of her ex out of her mind. Letting the hot water soothe her aching body, she glanced down and noted that the bruises from the accident were lighter this morning. The yellow and green marks made her look sickly, but they were finally starting to go away. As ugly as they were, it was a wonder they hadn't deterred Wade from making love to her. Instead of cringing at the sight, he'd looked at her as if she were the most beautiful woman in the world. She'd never truly felt beautiful. Adequate, nice looking, but never a raving beauty. He'd seen her at her worst, and yet he hadn't been able to keep his hands off her. It wasn't just the sex, though, she admitted; it was as if Wade saw in her more than a good time. She'd thought their time together would be about mutual desire, chemistry, and sating each other's needs, wants. But with the morning came renewal. She felt refreshed and ready to see where things between them would lead. Did Wade want more than a few nights? What would he do once her stalker was caught? Would he move on?

Odd how quickly Wade had managed to get under her skin. Her other relationships had always been about comfort and companionship. Deep feelings weren't part of the equation. With Wade she had a need to know everything about him. His deepest, darkest secrets. His life in the army. His childhood. The man simply fascinated her. Was this love? Sadly, Gracie wasn't sure, as she had absolutely nothing with which to compare this. All her past lovers, as few as they were, seemed so two-dimensional all of a sudden. Wade was her strong, dark-haired protector. And he made her feel alive. Sexy and wild. Heck, even treasured. She'd known him such a short amount of time. What kind of woman fell in love so quickly? If that's what this even was, as she still wasn't ready to put a label on it.

Gracie finished showering and shut off the water. She pushed the curtain aside and came face-to-face with the man she'd been thinking so hard about. She bit her lip and grabbed the towel he held out for her, then attempted to ignore the way his black T-shirt stretched to accommodate his yummy chest.

"I thought you might need some help buttoning the blouse."

"Oh, of course. Thank you." Gracie stepped out of the tub and started drying off. A wave of shyness swept over her when she caught Wade watching the towel's progress over her body. Why, after everything they'd shared, would she feel so self-conscious? There wasn't a single inch of skin on her body that Wade hadn't explored. And yet her hands were shaking.

He grinned and stepped closer. "Plus, I was beginning to miss you. Figured if I was ever going to get my good morning kiss, I'd better come after it myself."

Gracie's head shot up. The dark promise in Wade's gaze took her breath away. She dropped the towel and before she knew it, Wade had her in his arms, her damp body pressed tightly against denim and cotton. His lips teased at first, then grew more demanding. She wrapped her arms around his neck and sank into his kiss. He groaned. She became aware of his warm palms against the bare flesh of her bottom, squeezing and kneading. His thumb caressed the flesh between, and her body vibrated with need. Gracie whimpered, and Wade lifted his head, his gaze zeroing in on her breasts. Or more specifically, the rings in her nipples.

"I ordered a chain for you."

She couldn't think, could barely breath. "A what?"

He flicked one nipple and licked his lips. "A chain. A pretty gold chain for you to wear with your nipple rings."

"Oh."

"Priority mail."

She grinned and shook her head. "You're obsessed with piercings."

He placed a light kiss to her temple and growled, "With you. I'm obsessed with you, baby."

Her heart did a little cartwheel at the heated confession. "I'm pretty fond of you, too." Boy was that an understatement!

"Good. Now, let's go eat lunch."

"Lunch?"

He picked up the black bra and handed it over. "It's one in the afternoon."

"I had no idea."

"You needed the rest." He pointed to the cast. "Feel any better?"

She nodded as she took off the bag and rubber band, and wrestled with the bra. "Much better. Just wish it wasn't so awkward all the time."

Wade sighed. "I'll never understand why women wear bras to start with. They look uncomfortable as hell."

"They're not that bad."

"Turn around so I can fasten the damn thing for you."

She refused to let go. Suddenly it seemed important to do this one small task alone. "I can do it, Wade. I need to get used to doing things with this cast."

He crossed his arms over his chest as he watched her struggle. "Is it so hard to ask for help from me, Gracie?"

She tried the two small hooks once more, but failed to get them both attached. "No, it's just that I'm not used to people offering, I guess."

He moved around her and helped fasten the contrary hook.

When she turned to tell him thanks, he placed his finger over her lips and murmured, "If you thank me, I'll spank you. Knowing I haven't been able to catch your stalker, that he broke into your home and trashed your things and I wasn't able to stop him makes me feel as fucking useless as tits on a bull. The least I can do is fasten your bra."

His severe expression shredded her. She wouldn't allow him to blame himself, not for any of it. She cupped his cheeks in her palms and closed the distance between them. "It's not your fault I refused to let you buy the security alarm. And it's not your fault I didn't confide in you before the accident. You tried to get me talk to you; I refused. I'm so used to taking care of myself. Relying on someone isn't second nature to me." She paused before adding, "There's only one man to blame for all this, and he's not in this room."

A muscle in his jaw jumped, and his gaze turned icy. "When I get my hands on him, I'm going to make him pay. I'm about done with his being one step ahead all the time. It's time to step things up."

She wasn't sure she liked the sound of that. "How?"

He patted her bottom and moved back a few steps. "We'll talk about that after you eat." Wade picked up the blouse and said, "Now, put this on before I forget my good intentions and lay you out on the tile and have my wicked way with you."

She held out her arms and let him help her with the sleeves. She pulled it over her shoulders, and immediately he went to work on the pearl buttons. As she watched him carefully work his way up from the bottom something occurred to her. "You cussed."

He smiled, but didn't take his eyes off the buttons. "I know."

"The deal was that if you cussed I got to spank you."

"Yep."

After the last button was in place he stood up straighter. She could see the wicked gleam in his dark eyes, and she knew. "You did it on purpose."

He chuckled. "Never been spanked by a woman before. Call me curious."

Liquid heat pooled between her thighs. Wade Harrison at her mercy. Mmm, now that was a delicious thought.

18

He'd made cannelloni, only her favorite Italian dish ever. Could he be more perfect? "This is the best I've ever had. I had no idea you could cook."

"My mom always had a thing about equality. She made sure Dean and I could cook, do laundry, and mend our own clothes. She also saw to it that Deanna could work on her own car as well as any mechanic. Drove my sister crazy; she hates getting dirty. The woman is a neat freak."

Gracie liked his mother already. "What did your dad think of this philosophy?"

Wade swallowed another bite of his cannelloni before replying, "Dad thought Mom hung the moon. He would've done anything for her."

She took a sip of her iced tea and thought of how nice it would've been to grow up with siblings and two loving parents. "It sounds like a pretty great childhood."

After finishing off his last bite, Wade sat back in his chair. The black T-shirt he wore only seemed to enhance his powerful chest and hard abs. "Dad owned his own landscaping business.

He made a good living with it. Mom was a nurse. She retired last year, after Dad died."

Gracie immediately felt bad for prying. She reached across the table and covered his hand with hers. "I'm so sorry."

Wade turned his hand palm up and entwined their fingers. "That's okay. I've dealt with my grief. It was a little harder on Mom and Deanna. I think both of them walked around in a daze those first few months."

"How did he die?" she asked, then quickly added, "if you don't mind my asking."

"A brain aneurism. He didn't suffer. I'm grateful for that. The hard part lately has been talking Mom into selling the house. She rattles around in that big two-story. We want her to have something smaller, to be close to other people so she won't feel so alone."

She remembered Wade's brother and sister coming over the day before, and guilt assailed her. "The apartment you were supposed to look at for your mom. Oh, Wade, I'm so sorry. You should have gone with them."

He shrugged. "It's okay. Deanna told me it's a dump. Back to the drawing board. We need to find something soon, though, because Mom has someone interested in the house."

Gracie thought of her own place and said, "What about my apartment complex? It's a nice neighborhood. Er, until this whole nasty business with my stalker, I mean. Before this all started I never had a single problem there."

His thumb stroked over her knuckles, and Gracie nearly lost track of the conversation. "Not a bad idea. I'll let Deanna know. She's been sort of heading up this project. She's a little protective of Mom. So far Deanna has nixed every apartment we've looked at for one reason or another. I'm starting to think she's not ready to let go. She grew up in that house. It's hard to move on."

She understood, all too well. She'd hated when her father

had sold her grandmother's small house. It wasn't anything grand, but it was her grandma's and that made it special to Gracie. "All her memories of your dad are tied to that house."

He smiled, but it didn't quite reach his eyes. "Yeah, pretty much."

She had a feeling he was covering his own grief. "What about you? Are you ready to move on?"

A subtle tightening of his fingers on hers was the only indication that Gracie had struck a chord. "It'll be hard, but I'll always have Dad in my heart. It's Mom I'm worried about. The more she stays out there, the more she becomes a hermit. I'm afraid she's withdrawing."

"She won't."

"You sound pretty sure of that."

"She has you, Dean, and Deanna. She has something to live for. Maybe she just needs to feel needed again."

He sat up straighter, giving her his full attention. "What do you mean?"

Gracie wasn't in familiar territory. After all, what did she know about families? "Well, I don't know her, but she's a mother, and she used to be a nurse. It seems like she's the caregiver type. Maybe if she thought someone needed her again it would help."

He frowned and released her. "Her kids need her. She's our mother."

Gracie tucked a wayward lock of hair behind her ear and attempted to explain. "Her kids are grown, on their own and thriving. Her husband is gone. Her job is finished. That's a lot to take in, Wade. Maybe she just needs a new purpose."

He studied her, not speaking. Gracie was terribly afraid she'd overstepped the bounds of their relationship.

"I see what you mean," he said at last. "Still, I have no idea what would make her feel needed."

Gracie stood and brought their plates to the sink, mulling

over the idea. When she turned around and leaned against the counter, she said, "There's always charity work. She's a nurse; maybe she could be of some use at the women's shelter downtown. The way you talk about her, I think she'd make a great counselor."

Wade left his chair and came toward her. He tucked his hands in the front pockets of his jeans, his expression pensive. "Helping women who've been in abusive relationships?"

"Think about it for a second. From what you tell me, she has a great sense of self-worth. A lot of women could really benefit from talking with a woman like that."

He smiled, then took her face between his large hands. "You're amazing." He dipped his head and kissed her. It was light and fleeting, and she wanted so much more. "I'm going to talk to Mom about this. I think she'll love the idea."

"I'm glad I could help." Gracie didn't say it aloud, but she was grateful that she could do something for him for a change.

His finger feathered over her bottom lip. Gracie melted. "You make me lose my mind," she softly admitted. "I can't seem to think straight around you." He touched his lips to hers again. Soft, coasting back and forth with barely-there strokes. When his tongue darted out, a shiver of excitement raced the length of her spine. He was doing it to her once more. To be in his presence was to be a living, breathing flame of desire and need. When he pulled back and stared at her, a frown marring his brow, Gracie worried she'd somehow disappointed him.

"I want to take you somewhere today."

Gracie thought of her destroyed apartment and wanted to groan. She had a ton to do. For once in her life, Gracie didn't want to be the responsible one. "Where do you want to take me?"

Wade winked, and her bones liquefied. "I want to take you to the shooting range. I want to show you how to handle a gun."

His life as a PI fascinated her, but she wasn't comfortable with guns. "I'm not sure that's such a good idea."

"I have a .38 caliber Ruger. It will be a nice size for you. Easy to handle. Give it a try, baby. Please?"

"This is because of my stalker."

His expression hardened. "Damn straight. To tell the truth, I'd rather you were licensed to carry, but until we can get that taken care of, I'd feel better if you at least knew a little more about guns." He glanced down at her cast and frowned. "You can't shoot, not with your wrist fractured, but I can show you a few things."

She pushed out of his arms and moved away from the sink. "It's not going to come to that, Wade. It won't." Even as she said the words, she knew she was fooling herself.

He took a step toward her. She took a step away. He sighed and pushed his fingers through his thick, dark hair. "Hopefully not, but I want you safe, Gracie. That's my first priority here."

She could feel herself caving, and it pushed her frustration level to an all-time high. "You're very pushy, do you know that?"

"Determined, baby, just determined," Wade growled, as he came closer. Gracie moved away. He chuckled and stalked her around the kitchen. "I will catch you, and when I do I'll have to punish you."

Gracie had no idea what he had in mind, but knowing Wade it would be the sort of punishment she'd only read about in her romance books—and secretly craved. "Stay away from me, you perv." She darted toward the stairs and heard him coming up behind her. She was going to let him catch her, but that didn't mean she had to make it easy on him.

"Never."

Gracie heard the dark, sexy tone and felt hot breath against her ear. As she reached the first step leading to the upstairs loft, Gracie glanced around her shoulder and yelped when she came face-to-face with an extremely turned on dark-haired hunk. Her hunk. He grinned and wrapped his hands around her waist, lifting her easily into the air. "Time for your punishment, sweetheart."

She laughed as he cradled her in his arms and took her up the stairs. "Think you're man enough, do you?"

"You're my woman," he murmured. "I'll always see to your wants, your needs."

She wrapped her arms around his neck, but as his words sank in, she tensed. The first thing that popped into her mind came tumbling out of her mouth. "Why would you say that? It's only been a few days, Wade."

His gaze on her intensified; his arms tightened a fraction. "I don't give a damn. You're mine."

She frowned, unable to think straight. His heat and woodsy male scent filled her senses, blocking out all rational thought. "Don't, Wade. It's too much, too fast."

He stopped on the upstairs landing and stared down at her. "Don't you know that time doesn't matter? I've dated other women, Gracie. Some of those relationships went on for several years at a time. I've never felt the type of connection with any of them that I feel with you." He paused, and Gracie held her breath, afraid of what he might say next. "Can you honestly tell me this is just sex to you? That you don't feel something for me?"

Gracie had no words. Only feelings. In truth, she felt too much. Gracie was terrified she was falling in love with Wade. "It's not just sex," she admitted, her voice not quite steady. "I've been attracted to you for a long time, but somewhere along the line, I admit, it became more." His lips curved upward, a sure sign she'd just given the devil his due. Gracie smacked his chest. "Don't smile. I'm not saying that's a good thing. I don't know how to trust a man. What's more, relationships boggle me."

"This is new territory for me, too. We can figure it out together. Just know that the instant you took that nightgown off in your apartment and showed me those pretty piercings, you became mine."

Gracie wanted to hear him tell her he loved her. That his heart, his soul, belonged to her. At the same time, a part of her wasn't ready for that monumental step. She was very much afraid she might never be ready. For now, Gracie vowed, she would enjoy the beauty of having Wade want her as badly as she wanted him.

Once Gracie and Wade were in his room, their lips met again. Gracie's fears drifted away. All that mattered was Wade and this moment.

It was an hour's drive to the shooting range, and by the time they arrived Gracie was nervous as hell. How had she let him talk her into handling a gun? Wade parked his truck and turned off the engine. He wrapped an arm around her shoulders, and as always his strength calmed her. It was a little scary how easily he did that.

"Ready?"

Gracie looked out the windshield at the large, tan building that housed the shooting range. It was intimidating as hell. "Not really."

He squeezed her shoulder. "It's going to be fine. Trust me."

"If you say so." She kept her reservations to herself as she unbuckled her seat belt and turned toward him.

"I do." Gently, Wade kissed her; the tender brush of his lips nearly had her forgetting where they were. Nearly. He opened his door and stepped out, and Gracie distracted herself by watching him make his way around the front of the truck. His powerful body the stuff of fantasies. Her mind flashed back to the hour they'd spent in his bed after lunch. He'd teased her to a fever pitch, then very skillfully showed her just how stimulating a spanking could be. Already she wanted him to do it again.

Now, dressed in a black T-shirt, a black leather jacket, and a pair of worn jeans, Wade looked good enough to eat. Damn, would she ever get enough of him? The way he affected her, it was downright mind-blowing. She'd never been so starved for a man before, and yet just watching Wade walk had her pussy creaming.

Wade pulled her door open and wrapped his hands around her waist, helping her to the ground. She waited as he pushed the seat up and took out a large black case tucked behind. She wasn't sure she wanted to know what it contained.

They both signed in, but Gracie also had to fill out some paperwork since she wasn't a member. She noticed how well Wade knew his way around the place. He spoke to the guys working there as if they were old friends. After paying, Wade opened the large black bag he carried and brought out two sets of safety goggles and earmuffs. He handed one set to her. "Put those on."

Gracie didn't have to be asked twice. After they both had the protective gear in place, Wade pushed open a door that led outside. Confused, Gracie grabbed his arm. He arched a brow and mouthed the word "what." She pointed to his earmuffs. He got the message and pulled them away from his head. Gracie did the same. "What's wrong, baby? Still having second thoughts?"

"No, but why are we going outside? I thought we'd be shooting inside."

He nodded. "We will, but first I wanted to get some quick practice in using the rifle. I'm a little rusty."

She so didn't like the sound of that. "Rusty as in shoot a toe off rusty?"

He laughed. "Have a little faith, sweetheart."

Faith, trust, what was the difference? She was terrible at both. She placed the earmuffs back over her ears and nodded.

He winked and led the way outside. "The range sits in a valley," he yelled in order to be heard over the earmuffs. "The hills provide protection when shooting at the targets." He took her over to a long, narrow table where several people, men and women both, were already practicing.

Wade handed her a long scope, but Gracie had no idea what to do with the thing.

As if understanding her predicament, Wade shouted, "The target is four hundred yards away. You'll need that if you want to see where the bullet hits."

Gracie held the scope to her right eye and waited.

Wade loaded the rifle with bullets that were obscenely long as he took up position behind the table. He placed the gun on something that looked like a beanbag. After adjusting the bag a few times while he stared down the scope on the top of the rifle, Wade pulled the trigger.

Gracie jumped.

Wade looked up at her and frowned. "I should have warned you," he yelled. "Even with the ear protection it can be startling."

Gracie waited for her heart to stop sprinting before yelling, "I thought I was ready for it since other guns are going off, but I guess not."

Wade reached out and stroked her arm, soothing her frazzled nerves instantly. "Look into your spotting scope, sweetheart."

Gracie put it to her eye. It took her a second, but she finally found Wade's target. "Wow, you're good," she called out. The bullet hadn't hit the center but the next ring out. She raised her eyes to his to find him grinning down at her. "What?"

Wade placed his palm beneath her chin and gently tugged her toward him. "I am *very* good."

He'd said the words close to her ear, his hot breath fanning the flames of her desire. When he touched his lips to hers, disarming her completely, she had to force herself not to lean into his body. Ah, if only they were alone. Unfortunately they weren't. As she glanced around she noticed a few of the women checking Wade out. From head to toe. The twinge of jealousy skating down her spine took her by surprise.

She pulled away, and Wade's eyebrows shot up in silent inquiry.

She indicated their very public surroundings with a wave of her hand. "Behave," she mouthed. Not exactly the reason she'd pulled back, but he didn't have to know that.

He didn't speak, simply stroked his thumb back and forth over her bottom lip. Gracie was hard-pressed to keep from moaning. When Wade resumed target practice, Gracie sighed in relief. Much more of his feathery touches, and she would've been dragging him off to his truck.

The remainder of their time outside was spent in silence. Gracie was suitably impressed with Wade's marksmanship. She should've known he would handle a rifle like a pro. After all, the man was damn good with his hands. Careful and precise. And while she wasn't a gun enthusiast, she could see Wade took it all very seriously. He took his time, shooting the gun repeatedly.

By the time they made their way to the indoor range, Gracie wasn't nearly as nervous. Maybe it was because Wade made her feel safe, or maybe it was because the .38 caliber Ruger was so much smaller than the daunting rifle he'd used. She didn't know. Either way, handling the small gun wasn't nearly as difficult as she'd expected.

Wade carefully walked her through the entire process. He demonstrated everything from where the safety was to how to load the clip. He showed her how to chamber a round and shoot. He even instructed her on how to check to see if the gun was loaded. She couldn't do much with her cast, of course, but simply becoming familiar with the firearm, the weight and feel, was one step closer to feeling less vulnerable. Somehow Wade had known that Gracie needed that small measure of comfort.

How was it possible he knew her so well in such a short time? She'd spent her entire life carefully keeping men at arm's length. Without her even realizing it, Gracie had somehow let Wade around her defenses. He made her want more. A deeper connection. A life full of love and laughter . . . with him.

And that sent fear through her like nothing else.

19

"I can't believe you called *everyone* to help clean, Wade. You really shouldn't have done that."

"The more help we can get, the faster it'll go." Wade picked up one of her torn books and carefully placed it on the pile with the rest of them. He wasn't throwing them out, not until he had a chance to write down the title and author of each book destroyed. "Besides, that's what friends are for. To lend a hand when needed. Might as well get used to it, Gracie."

Wade watched Gracie stare out the front window. He followed her line of sight and noticed Cherry and Dante pulling into Gracie's apartment complex. Wade went to the door and opened it for them.

"Cherry's my friend," Gracie said, her voice a little too shaky for his peace of mind, "but your brother and sister and Jonas, they've only just met me." She turned to him. "Why would they want to help clean up this mess?"

She was truly baffled, and it broke his heart. He closed the distance between them and took hold of her shoulders and noticed that her eyes were filled with tears. How she managed to keep them from falling down her cheeks was beyond him. The woman had strength and pride in spades. "Because you're a sweet, loving, gentle person, sweetheart." She started to speak, but he wouldn't hear more protests. "You didn't deserve what this asshole did to you. Stop acting as if you have to bear this burden alone. You aren't alone, not anymore."

"He's right."

They both turned. Cherry stood in the doorway, her arms full of cleaning supplies. He could've kissed her right then and there. "You aren't alone. Besides we both know you'd do it for any one of us."

Gracie nodded. "Of course I would."

Cherry grinned. "Good, it's settled then. Where do I start?"

Dante came through the door then, carrying several empty boxes. "I thought Gracie might want to store any valuables that managed to escape the destruction. Until this is all over with, I mean."

Gracie pushed a lock of hair behind her ear and said, "I didn't even think of that. Good idea."

"Come on, you can start on the kitchen." Wade led Cherry to the other room. "Most of the dishes are broken. Be careful where you step."

Cherry dropped her supplies on the table and glanced around. "Wow, he really did a number on this place, huh?"

Wade felt his anger rise. The son of a bitch would pay. "Her bedroom is even worse. Panties, nightgowns, makeup, it's all ruined."

Cherry visibly shuddered. "I can't imagine how she must feel. It's such a horrible invasion of privacy."

"Once things are in order, she'll feel better." He hoped like hell that was the case anyway.

Cherry cocked her head to the side, no doubt seeing more than he wanted her to see. Their long-standing friendship meant they could read each other like a book most of the time. "How are you holding up?"

He clenched his fists at his sides, feet braced shoulder-width apart. "I want the bastard, Cherry. Dead or alive, it doesn't matter."

"Careful," she warned. "The soldier in you is showing through."

"If this was an op, I would make sure he never hurt another woman again. He would simply disappear, and Gracie would be safe."

Cherry stepped forward and placed her hand on his forearm. He figured the gesture was meant to soothe him, but the only thing that would do that was seeing Gracie's stalker behind bars . . . or dead. Preferably the latter. "This isn't an op, though. You aren't in the army anymore, Wade. You have to play this right. Let the police do their job."

"They haven't done shit so far. I'm tired of them dicking around. He's out there somewhere, watching her, waiting. What will he do next, Cherry?"

"It won't matter, because you'll be there. You wouldn't let anything happen to her."

Her conviction brought him down a notch. "Damn straight. He won't come within a hundred feet of her."

"You really care about her that much?"

Wade pushed his hands in his pockets. Suddenly he felt like a little kid again, shy and uncertain. "I care."

"She's lucky to have you in her corner, Wade. You're a good man."

He smiled. "So you no longer think I'm taking advantage of her?"

She rolled her eyes and waved a hand in the air. "Gracie can take care of herself. I was stupid to think otherwise."

He denied that with a shake of his head. "She's more vulnerable than you think. This has really taken a toll. I'm worried about her, Cherry."

"She's not had the easiest life, Wade. She's withstood a lot. And now she has someone standing with her. That's more than she's ever had before."

"Thanks, Cherry. Your friendship means a lot, to both of us."

"You've been there for me too, Wade. I'm glad to repay the favor."

"Wade?" He turned at the sound of Gracie's soft voice. "I hate to interrupt, but your brother and sister are here. Jonas too."

Wade strode across the kitchen and took Gracie in his arms, needing the connection to keep his sanity. If he let go of his control now, he wouldn't stop until the sick asshole was in the ground. "In a few hours your apartment will be livable once again. Once it is, we're going to start the process of making it safe."

She groaned. "A security system."

"Yep. Jonas is going to install it, along with a few other little gadgets. You won't be staying here, though. Not until this is all over. If you have a problem with that, we may as well deal with it now."

She shook her head and looked up at him. "I don't want to be here. Not now that he's . . . touched everything. All I want is to get it cleaned up. Soon my lease will be up, and then I'm leaving here for good."

"Leaving?"

She pushed out of his arms; that determined look she always got when she was readying for battle came over her face. "I'll find a new apartment. I can't stay here now."

"You could move in with me. Make it permanent." Damn, he liked that idea. A lot.

Gracie bit her lip and glanced quickly at Cherry. "We should talk about this later, Wade."

He heard Jonas arguing with Deanna in the other room and wanted to curse. "You're right. We've got things to do here." He could tell she was relieved, maybe a little too relieved. His chest tightened. Didn't she like the idea of living with him? Was he moving too fast? A commotion in the other room splintered his thoughts.

Taking Gracie's hand in his, Wade steered them out of the kitchen. "Come on. We'd better separate my sister from Jonas before she hurts him."

"They don't get along?"

"More like she purposely tries to rile him. She gets a kick out of driving the man crazy. I never could figure those two out."

As they entered the living room he spotted the pair of antagonists immediately. Jonas looked ready to spit nails, and Deanna was grinning like the cat that had just spied the canary. "What's the problem with you two this time?"

"Your sister is the devil; that's what the problem is."

Deanna laughed, and even Wade had to admit that it sounded just a little evil. "You just aren't used to women telling you no," she said.

Wade stepped forward, his gaze locking on Jonas. "What the hell did you ask her?"

Jonas crossed his arms over his chest and started to speak, but Deanna talked right over him. "He asked me on a date. I turned him down."

Wade saw red. "You aren't dating my sister, Phoenix. So forget it."

Dean, who'd been deep in conversation on his cell phone, chose that moment to end the call. "You have the hots for Dee?"

Jonas held his hands up, as if in surrender. It wouldn't do him any good, because Wade was going to kill him. "Did you two miss the part where she turned me down?"

"I heard," Wade growled, "but why'd you ask in the first place?"

Deanna stepped in front of Jonas, her protective stance shocking everyone in the room to silence. The heat in Jonas's eyes as he stared at the back of Deanna's head was unmistakable. Forget death, Wade would castrate him instead.

"You act like I'm some ugly, little troll." Deanna pointed a finger first at Wade, then at Dean. "Did it ever occur to you two morons that maybe I'm a big girl and can speak for myself?"

"No," Dean and Wade said in unison.

Deanna stepped forward, her anger palpable. "Well, guess what? I'll date whomever I choose. Neither of you have any say in it whatsoever."

Wade tried for calm. The last thing he wanted was Deanna with her back up. She gave *stubborn* new meaning when she set her mind to something. "You're our baby sister, honey," Wade said, his voice gentle. "Jonas knows he shouldn't have asked you out."

"What you really mean is that he shouldn't have thought of me as a woman."

Great, now he'd hurt her feelings. Wade felt like he'd fallen down the damn rabbit hole. "That's not the way I meant it. He's my partner and my friend, which makes you off-limits. There's a code here." Wade glared at Jonas. "Tell her you know that, Phoenix."

Jonas slumped. His entire demeanor baffled Wade. He'd never seen his friend so defeated before. "Yeah, sisters are off-limits."

Deanna swung around. "You're taking their side?"

Jonas reached toward her. Deanna moved out of reach. His

gaze hardened. "I'm not taking anyone's side, Deanna. But Wade's right. If I had a sister ... Well, let's just say I see your brother's point."

Deanna was quiet a moment; everyone in the room seemed to hold his or her breath. "Then I was right to turn you down," she said, her voice not quite as firm as before. Wade didn't like that. Deanna was a fighter. She'd always had the backbone to go against anyone and win. Right now she looked ... crushed. The whole situation was bizarre as hell.

Crazier still, Jonas paled. The man Wade had watched take down drug lords in foreign countries without so much as breaking a sweat looked visibly shaken. "Deanna, don't."

Deanna waved a hand in the air. "Never mind. At any rate, we're not here to debate my personal life. We're here to help Gracie get her apartment back in order. I say we get to it." With that, she headed for the kitchen.

Jonas watched her until she disappeared, then he cursed and walked out the front door. Wade looked over at his brother, wondering what the hell they'd just done. Dean just shook his head, every bit as confused.

A soft, feminine hand touched his forearm. Wade knew that hand. He cherished that hand. Looking over, he saw Gracie smiling up at him. "Sorry about the family drama. Things aren't usually this ... weird."

She quirked a brow at him. "Uh, family drama is something I'm quite used to, Wade."

He knew Gracie was referring to her father, but all he could think about was the look on his sister's face. "I don't think I handled this very well."

"She's your sister; she'll forgive you. But can I give you some advice?"

He pulled her into his arms, soft curves fitting against him. Damn, he wished they were back at his place. "I'll take anything I can get right now."

Gracie leaned back a few inches, her gaze caressing his face. "Deanna seems like an intelligent woman to me. If she chooses Jonas, then maybe you should trust her judgment."

Women and their logic. "I've seen him with women, Gracie. He's not exactly the boy next door." Wade left out the part that they'd even shared women. Jonas with Deanna? His stomach turned just thinking about it.

"She strikes me as the type who can handle it, though. If it even comes to that. In the meantime, it could put a wedge between you and your sister if you try to stand in her way."

He mulled that over and came to one conclusion. "If she wants him, then I'll step back. But if he pushes her, even a little, there'll be hell to pay." Wade couldn't make any promises where Dean was concerned, though, and his brother tended to be damned protective of his twin.

Gracie came up on her tiptoes and pressed her lips to his. Wade growled low at the contact. Cupping the back of her head, he held her still, reveling in her sweet flavor. The satiny softness of her lower lip beckoned him to bite. He heeded the call and nibbled on her a moment before pushing his way into her mouth. Their tongues played, and Wade's cock hardened to the point of pain. Gracie was the first to pull back. "We need to save the rest of that for later, when we're alone."

"Mmm, I'm going to make you beg for me, baby."

"I'm pretty sure I've already done that, darling."

Wade groaned as he watched her walk away, the sway of her hips a thing of beauty. He looked at the mess around him. Hours. It'd be hours before he could get her in his bed. One more thing to lay at her stalker's feet.

His Gracie Lynn wasn't supposed to have friends. She had her loser father, and she had him. He knew everything about her. The people she worked with, the books she read, the few brief relationships she'd had with men. But as he sat in his car across from her apartment, he watched a tall brunette walk out her front door carrying trash to the Dumpster. He frowned. Where had they all come from? And she wasn't learning from the lesson he'd tried so hard to teach her, either. She should be begging his forgiveness by now. Trying to get back into his good graces. Instead she was surrounded by friends, and they were helping her clean up the bits and pieces his outburst had created.

He thought over the previous night for the hundredth time. He hadn't meant to lose his temper. He'd only been trying to show her that he wouldn't tolerate her slutty behavior. She'd caused him pain, and he couldn't allow that. The instant he'd seen her leaving with that big oaf, something had snapped inside him.

At first he'd been exhilarated to be inside her apartment. Touching things she'd touched. He'd spent time in her bed, letting himself imagine what it would be like when he finally had her all to himself. He'd savored the release that visual had afforded him. But then he'd remembered the other man, standing at her window, bare chested. He'd gotten angry all over again. As he went through her dresser and saw all the silky panties, he'd started picturing her wearing them for the stranger. Her beautiful body encased in silk for another man. Something in his mind had snapped. It had scared him a little. He'd literally floated outside himself, watching as his body had moved through the rooms, destroying the things Gracie Lynn treasured.

"It was necessary," he reminded himself. For her, for his perfect Gracie Lynn, he would do whatever it took to save her from herself. She would thank him for showing her the way. He knew that in his gut. Love wasn't always easy, but theirs was beautiful and timeless. And worth the extra effort of preserving it. Besides, the fates were on his side. He hadn't known she wouldn't be returning. He'd taken a huge risk staying so long, chancing getting caught. Yes, the fates had approved of his lesson, and they'd made sure he'd had enough time to do it right.

Gracie Lynn belonged to him. No other had a right to touch her. She was his love, perfect and sweet. That man, the one stuck to her like glue, he was the real problem. He was corrupting his sweet Gracie Lynn. Turning her into a whore.

"I can't let it continue." He watched, mere feet away, as another of her friends carried more trash to the Dumpster. "Soon, my love," he promised, as he took the worn scrap of paper out of his hoodie pocket and clutched it close to his heart. "Soon."

20

After cleaning her apartment, they'd all gone out for a late dinner. For the first time in months, Gracie had been able to relax and enjoy being among friends. She'd gotten to know Wade's brother and sister better. It was inevitable that she found herself comparing Wade and Dean. Both men had short, dark hair and the same dark brown eyes, but Wade was somewhat taller and a little less intense. Dean was every bit as muscular, but maybe rougher around the edges. He was friendly enough, but Gracie couldn't help feeling there was something dangerous about him. Deanna, on the other hand, had been full of questions. It seemed the woman was intensely curious about the new woman in her brother's life. When they'd gotten onto the topic of interior design, however, her entire demeanor changed, became more animated. It had been the perfect change of topic. Being the center of attention wasn't Gracie's forte.

At first she'd been wracked with nerves. Having Wade's siblings' approval was important to her, which was crazy. Who knew if she'd even see them again? Gracie's mind snapped back to that moment in her kitchen, when Wade had asked her to move in with him, to make her stay a permanent one. She liked the idea way too much. Living with a man was a big step, especially when she'd only spent a few days with said man. Gracie still wasn't sure if he would get bored with her once her stalker was caught. And had his offer been a spur of the moment thing, one he'd later regret?

Her nervousness came back full force as she stood in the middle of his bedroom watching Wade from across the room. He leaned against the doorframe, his entire body relaxed, as if he had all the time in the world. But his quiet intensity was doing a number on her. He was acting so strangely. He'd been silent on the drive back to his place. She was about ready to jump out of her own skin.

"Shouldn't we be looking through my blog posts? You said there might be a clue there, that maybe he reads and comments."

He nodded. "And those e-mails as well. We need to read through them carefully, see if anything clicks with you. But there will be time for that tomorrow. I've got something else in mind right now."

"You do?"

He nodded. Gracie watched with fascination as Wade's sexy mouth tilted sideways. "Yes, I do."

Gracie was about done with this new game of his. She crossed her arms over her chest and said, "Care to fill me in then?"

Without answering, Wade moved away from the doorway, his long strides eating up the distance between them. When he came to stand behind her, her pulse began to beat out a wild rhythm.

"Look to your left, Gracie."

Curious, she did as he asked. Their reflection in the dresser mirror filled her vision. Fascinated, Gracie watched Wade's gaze wander the length of her. Her flesh tingled to life as if he'd physically stroked her. "You're so handsome, Wade. Every inch of you. I saw women staring at you at the shooting range, you know," she admitted. "It made me crazy."

His gaze heated. "Jealous?"

Gracie bit her lip and nodded. "I've never been the jealous type. I'm not sure I like it one bit."

Wade stroked a finger down her cheek, his voice dropping an octave. "I know the feeling, sweetheart. If I could keep you locked away so other men could never look at you, I think I would."

"You would?"

"Mmm, I know what they're thinking when they see you, because I'm thinking the same things."

"Things?" Gracie asked. Suddenly it became imperative that Wade explain, in great detail, what sort of things he thought when he looked at her the way he was looking at her now.

"Did you know that when we were cleaning today I caught Dean watching you a few times?"

That wasn't what she'd wanted to hear. "No. I didn't even notice."

"It wasn't in a weird, creepy way, but I could tell he was curious about you." He stroked her arm, leaving goose bumps everywhere he touched. "A man sees this body, and he wants to know it, baby. Men want to view it up close, with nothing in the way to hamper the glorious sight."

Her gaze never veered from his in the mirror as she asked, "Is that the way you felt when you asked me out, Wade?"

He moved closer, until his body pressed tight against hers. She could feel his hard cock prodding her buttocks, and her panties grew damp. "The first time I saw you I wanted to strip you bare. You bewitched me, Gracie."

"Is that why you asked me to live with you?" Gracie hadn't meant to ask, but since it was out, she was glad. She needed to know the reason behind his offer.

"I asked you to live with me because I enjoy being with you. You're an intelligent, kind, beautiful, hardworking woman. And it's the first time I've ever asked a woman to move in."

Her gaze widened. "Really?"

"I told you before that what I feel for you is different. It's more, deeper, and I want us to have the time to explore it. To see where it might lead."

"There's never been a man in my life who treated me the way you do. I'm so far out of my comfort zone, and it's scary, Wade."

Wade turned her toward him, his gaze searching hers. "Relationships are hard for you, I know. But don't you think I'm worth the effort? That we're worth the effort?"

She could see the hurt her words had evoked, and it tore at her. Wade was so strong and able, as if bullets really could bounce off him. It baffled her that she could cause him even an ounce of pain.

Reaching up, Gracie cupped his cheeks in her palms and spoke from the heart. "When you smile, I lose my ability to think straight. All you have to do is look at me, and my heart speeds up. You're such an enigma, Wade. You have a collection of books that would have any librarian worth her salt creaming in her panties, and yet you handle a rifle so well it makes me wonder how you learned such a skill. You're a soldier, my very own hero, and the only man capable of making me want to scream with frustration one minute and melt with pleasure in the next."

He gripped her shoulders and growled, "Then that's a yes? You'll move in with me?"

Gracie couldn't help it, she grinned. He was so tenacious. "That's a 'let's wait and see what happens' after we catch the freak stalking me."

"Fine. But in the meantime, I want you."

In a flash, her body went up in flames at the sudden possessiveness in his voice. Geez, she loved hearing that tone from him. So aggressive. So male. It was hot.

"Wade," she said, too breathless to say more.

"Off with the blouse and bra, my Fiery Angel. He brushed the back of his hand down her breast and murmured, "I want to see the soft pink of your succulent nipples. And those pretty piercings, I miss them."

Gracie surprised herself when she began to do as Wade commanded. She was powerless against the pleasure that she knew awaited her. With his sharp brown gaze holding her captive, she slowly, temptingly stripped to the waist.

Wade's right hand moved, and then the left, until he cupped and massaged both of her breasts. He flicked his thumbs over the pierced buds, then pulled both aching swells upward for a long, lazy lick.

His tongue swept back and forth over one tight peak, while his fingers played with the other. As he pulled back, Gracie watched through half-opened eyes as his tongue moved downward to her belly. He growled something unintelligible an instant before his tongue darted out and toyed with the small indentation. Gracie pushed against him, on fire already.

Oh, God, she was suddenly aching with need. Her entire body yearned. "That feels so good, Wade."

"I'll give you more," he growled. "Much more. But first I want you on your knees."

Her body trembled at the idea of purposely disobeying him. Would he smack her bottom as he had previously? *Only one way to find out.*

"I think I'd rather stand, thanks anyway," she replied, intentionally sounding haughty to wind him up.

He arched a brow at her. "You're forgetting, Gracie."

"Forgetting what?"

"That in the bedroom I'm in control."

His words sent a sensual shiver down her spine. Her clit

throbbed, as if eager to do as Wade commanded. She waited, anxious to see what he would do, more excited than she'd ever been. He smiled and moved away from her, then glanced around the room. His gaze stopped on something, she couldn't tell what. Wade bent and picked the item up, then strode across the room. Her breathing increased with each step he took. As he came to stand mere feet away, she saw a multicolored silk tie. Wade hadn't worn a tie, not in all the time she'd known him. That didn't stop her imagination from going into overdrive, though. "What do you plan to do with that?"

He slid the material between his fingers and smiled. "You can't guess?"

Her pussy dampened. A blindfold perhaps? The idea sent a rush of anticipation through her. Unwilling to give voice to her speculations, Gracie shook her head. What if she were wrong? She already felt so far out of his league.

Wade surprised her when he moved behind her and clasped one wrist in a large, calloused fist. Not a blindfold, she thought. He wrapped the silk around her arm, then grabbed the other and did the same. "Is your wrist sore, baby?"

His voice so close to her ear obliterated her ability to speak clearly. "N-no, not really."

Gracie tested her bonds. It was loose; she could easily get out. She had a feeling Wade did that on purpose. She was securely tied, but still able to escape if she wanted. The thoughtfulness behind Wade's action gave her the bravery to surrender to him once more.

Wade's hands smoothed their way down her sides until they were cupping her hips in a tight, possessive hold. "Mmm, I like you this way. You are mine now, to do with as I please. If you're a very good girl, I'll let you come. If you're naughty, I won't."

Shocked, Gracie turned her head, her gaze searching his for

a hint of teasing. There wasn't any. He appeared deadly serious. "You would withhold pleasure from me?"

"Until you learn, yes." At her frown, he went on. "There's pleasure in the buildup, sweetheart. Your pleasure is mine, always. But at times I think you forget who I am."

She couldn't accept that. "I know exactly who you are. You're the man I've let handcuff me to his bed. You're the man I let spank me. You're the only man I want."

His already intense gaze turned darker. "And I'll be the man to possess you, fully. Binding your hands, it's just the beginning. By the time I'm through, there will be no part of you I haven't touched, tasted . . . fucked. In here you're mine. I will make you scream with pleasure, but I want your total surrender, Gracie."

"I have surrendered. Everything we've done, Wade, it's been beyond description. You've taken me to heaven and back."

"But there's still a part of you that holds back. Admit it."

How had he known? Was he so attuned to her that he could see inside her soul? The idea of letting Wade have total control over her sent a shiver of warning down her spine. Even though she knew that Wade wasn't an autocratic man, that his demanding side only surfaced when they were in the bedroom, it still caused her to hesitate. Letting a man, even one as trustworthy and kind as Wade, see her in such a vulnerable way scared her.

And yet, it turned her on as well. She couldn't lie about that. Not even to herself. Wade would never hurt her. Gracie knew it in her heart. The thought of turning herself over to him, submitting, made her clit throb with the pleasure such an act would bring.

"So serious," Wade murmured as he rubbed his thumb over her bottom lip. "If it's not what you want, tell me, sweet angel. I won't have you feeling forced."

"I like when you take control, Wade. It does scare me a little.

I'm not accustomed to relying on anyone but myself. This is new for me."

His lips curved upward in the most wicked grin she'd ever seen. "A little scared and maybe a little excited?"

She closed her eyes tight and gave him nothing but total honesty. "Yes."

"Mmm, such a surprise you are, Gracie." Suddenly a large palm closed over her pussy through her jeans. She could feel the heat of his skin through the denim, and her eyes shot wide.

"Would you like me to tongue fuck your sweet cunt, Gracie? Would that please you?"

Wade's coarse language spoken in his guttural voice was the single most stimulating thing she had ever heard. There was, of course, only one answer to give.

"Yes."

"Ah, now that's the way I like it. My dick is as hard as a hammer right now. One touch, and I could come."

Gracie didn't speak; she couldn't. Her blood was liquid fire running through her veins.

Wade stepped away; Gracie tracked his every move, excitement a razor sharp edge. "Get down on your knees."

This time Gracie started to lower herself. Wade helped, and it brought to life just how awkward she felt. She couldn't look at him; equal parts embarrassment and arousal flooded her senses.

Wade cupped her chin in his hand and lifted her face upward. Her eyes connected with his. Gracie witnessed the wild frenzy of sexual hunger in the set of his jaw and the heat in his gaze. Knowing she had the ability to affect him so intensely was enough to loosen her up, if just a little.

"Do you know what you look like in this position?"

She shook her head, still staring into eyes the color of dark chocolate.

"You look like my pretty little sex slave."

"No." Her independent streak reared its feminist head at the notion.

"Yes. And you are mine to fuck," Wade growled.

"Wade," she groaned.

He touched the ring in her breast, flicking it in a way that had her clit throbbing. "Will you let me?" he asked, staring at her naked torso.

"I can't think straight when you do that."

"Stop thinking so hard, sweet angel. Let me take you somewhere you've never been. I want to be the first man to pull pleasure from the very depths of your soul. Let me."

Gracie faced the truth then. The moment she'd let Wade tie her hands behind her back, she had been his to touch, to taste, to fuck. "Yes."

Not a single sound came from Wade at her acquiescence. He didn't even appear to be breathing hard. He seemed totally at ease. As he moved his finger away from her breast and began unbuttoning his jeans, Gracie nearly whimpered. Licking her lips, Gracie hungered to suck him into her mouth, to taste him on her tongue.

Slowly, as if he had all the time in the world, Wade unzipped and freed his cock, and finally Gracie could see him in all his magnificence. He was hard and pulsing with life, the bulbous head darkly engorged. Jesus, he looked delicious. It was crazy how eager she was to nuzzle her face against him, to savor his unique scent and flavor.

His cock held firmly in his hand, Wade stepped forward and bent slightly at the knees. "Open those sexy lips, my Fiery Angel."

Gracie tilted her head upward and opened, but when she would have sucked him in, he stopped her with a hand to the back of her head, pulling at a fistful of her hair just hard enough to bring the slightest sting to her scalp.

"Only your tongue. Lick my dick, little Gracie. I want it nice and wet."

Obeying, Gracie opened wide and slipped her tongue out. Letting her eyes close, she tasted the sensitive tip of him. Taking the small bead of moisture that had appeared there into her mouth only teased her appetite. She wanted his come. All of it. Spurting into her mouth, filling her.

"Christ that's good, baby. So fucking good."

Gracie moaned, lost in the pleasure of playing with Wade. Her tongue roamed freely over and under. His cock was silk over steel and so large she wondered how on earth she would ever be able to use her mouth to bring him satisfaction. Slowly moving to the underside, Gracie finally came into contact with the sensitive flesh of his balls. She swiped her tongue back and forth, eager to take them both into her mouth and suck. Wade had given her an order, though, so she held back, moving her wet tongue over the rest of him instead, giving his cock the thorough licking he demanded.

She felt his hand pulling once more at her hair, and Gracie eased away. Leaning back on her heels, she looked up at him. Wade stared at her with the most feral look she'd ever seen on a man's face. He looked ready to explode. To throw her on the bed that sat a mere few feet away and fuck her brains out. Had she pushed him too far?

"You are the sexiest woman I've ever seen. Such a tempting little thing, Gracie," he growled, and then he dipped down, put an arm beneath her, and swung her into his arms. He carried her to his bed and sat her, ever so gently, at the edge. She adjusted her hands slightly, trying for a more comfortable position, but when he began stripping off his clothes, Gracie went still.

The sight of his body would always make her go pliant and mute. He was just too good-looking for her peace of mind. His short, dark hair and just the slightest hint of stubble on his chin emphasized how incredibly rugged and masculine he was. Any woman would drool over him, but only she had the right to touch. The thought sent her heart soaring.

Wade put one knee on the bed and turned to the task of unfastening her jeans and ridding her of the rest of her clothing. Soon, nothing stood between them and sexual heaven.

He pushed her legs wide, and before she could protest, he descended between them and licked her. She pushed forward, attempting to get him closer, to get his tongue inside her as he'd suggested earlier, but he seemed in no hurry.

"Wade, please, I need you so badly!"

He chuckled and lifted slightly. "You are in no position to be giving me orders, *slave*."

She glared down at him and muttered, "Don't make me regret letting you tie me."

"Once I'm done with you, you will crave being tied," Wade whispered. The heat of his breath stroking her clit caused her femininity to throb to life. "Your mouth will water and your pussy will drip with need any time I mention this tie."

"So confident in yourself are you?" She had to struggle to say the words coherently.

"No. So confident in *you*. You're a woman capable of great passion, and I intend to be the man drowning in it very soon."

Now that sounded promising. "Then quit talking and get to work. You've barely scratched the surface," she dared.

He grinned, and her clit swelled. "Ah, just what I love, a challenge." Then his tongue delved deep, and Gracie's thoughts scattered.

21

Wade was exactly where he wanted to be. Between the wide spread thighs of the woman he loved. It'd hit him when he watched her get down on her knees in front of him. Her supplicant position had pulled feelings out of him that he'd never felt before.

He'd always thought himself free of entanglements of the heart. His father had warned him once, when a Harrison man falls in love, it's for life. There'd be no going back. Somehow, he was going to have to convince the willful and independent Gracie that they were meant to be together. That he was good for something other than protection from a stalker. He had a feeling that proving to Gracie that he wasn't her father, that he wouldn't let her down, that she was worthy of love, would indeed be a challenge.

As Wade tasted and teased her, feeling the quiver of Gracie's supple body, he knew that no man could ever touch her in such a way and live. She was his. Her desire was for him to play with and nurture to life, no other. The very thought of any other man using his tongue on her sweet, hot pussy had him feeling crazed with rage.

He lifted up and stared at her nude body. Her eyes were closed, her hands behind her back, securely tied, and best of all she was already in the beginnings of a climax. She looked magnificent and so damn hot he felt singed.

Wade used his thumbs to part her delicate folds, exposing her swollen clit as he did, and then he dipped his head once more and sucked the tiny bit of flesh into his mouth, flicking back and forth with his tongue.

Gracie came undone, screaming his name and arching her back. Wade held her, keeping her from falling backwards, as he swallowed every last drop of her tangy flow.

This time when Wade lifted his head, Gracie was staring at him through half-raised lashes, a sexy hint of a smile on her face. Wade spoke, uncaring how his words affected her. "I hope you understand that I'm a man who doesn't share, Gracie. This curvy body is mine to treasure, mine to love."

Gracie didn't rebuke his claim, only stared. Unmoving. Her eyes seemed to look straight into his soul. No woman had ever been able to do that to him. At that moment in time, Wade didn't care to think too hard on such serious issues, however.

To take his mind off the out-of-control freight train of his thoughts, he slipped his hands beneath her hips, cupped her ass cheeks in his palms, and squeezed. She clenched up on him, drawing forth a grin.

"Remember when I said I wanted to fill this ass with my cock?"

Her eyes went instantly wide with shock, and her mouth dropped open. Ahh, now he had her full attention. "Don't look so scandalized, sweet angel."

That pushed her out of her delirium, and she began to shift and wiggle atop the bed, as if by doing so she could free herself. But he wasn't about to let her go.

"Wade, this is definitely an area that's unfamiliar to me, and I'm not so certain I want to become familiar with it."

"You've never had anal sex with a man?" He held his breath, not quite sure why.

"A couple tried. It simply didn't work."

They'd hurt her. He could see the fear. He hated when Gracie had that guarded look. Wade cupped her cheek, letting his thumb tease her lower lip. "Baby, you trust me with your body, I know you do. I won't hurt you. I would never do anything that made you uncomfortable or brought you pain. Let me show you how well we fit."

A long time passed with Gracie stiff, a frown marring the beauty of her face. Finally, she said, "I will let you . . . try, but I want a safe word."

That had him rearing back in shocked surprise. "And how are you familiar with safe words?" It was a term used by couples who enjoyed bondage, dominance, and submissive-type sex. The idea that she might have done such things with someone other than him, bothered Wade . . . entirely too much. He had no right to inquire of her past relationships. He had a rather checkered past himself and wouldn't relish an inquiry by her. Still, he was just chauvinistic enough to wish that he had been the only man to try such things with her.

Then, her next words had him sighing a little too vigorously in relief.

"I read it in a romance book. The heroine was experimenting and wanted to play the sex slave to the hero. They used a safe word, which meant that if she spoke it aloud, the lovemaking stopped instantly." She explained, as if tutoring him. "So, I want a safe word."

"You read some very interesting books, little Gracie," he murmured, amused and turned on at the same time. "There's something you don't know, though. Safe words are for both the dominant and the submissive. If the submissive wants something the dominant isn't comfortable with, then he can use the safe word to stop the play."

"Oh, I didn't know that. Do you want that option?"

Wade chuckled. "No, I'm certain you won't push me to a point that I'm uncomfortable. But, you only need to say 'stop,' Gracie, and I'll stop. We don't need a safe word. At least not with this particular sex act." His dick swelled painfully as they talked; images bombarded his head, making him want to flip her to her stomach and slide into her tight, puckered opening.

She smiled, and some of the tenseness left her shoulders. "And here I was all prepared to shout 'Bambi.' "

Surely, Wade had not heard her correctly. "Huh?"

Gracie laughed, her body relaxing even more as she grew comfortable with their conversation. "It was the first thing that came to mind. Don't ask me why."

Unaccountably charmed by her in that moment, Wade leaned toward her and pressed his lips to hers. So soft, like butterfly wings. He could sip at her for hours. "Another time we'll use 'Bambi.' I promise," Wade whispered against her mouth, their hot breaths mingling. As he locked his gaze with hers, Wade slowly lowered his head and kissed her gently between the legs. She moaned beautifully for him. Lifting to his feet, Wade noted that Gracie's gaze never wavered. She watched his every move, her anxious expression cutting through the haze of his lust the way nothing else could. Tenderly, he wrapped his hands around her waist and moved her to the center of the bed. Careful of her cast, Wade maneuvered her until she lay sprawled out on her belly; he arranged her legs wider. The sight of her would be stamped on his memory forever. "Are you uncomfortable? Is your wrist okay?"

"I'm fine. I'd all but forgotten about my wrist."

Wade stared down at her lying in the center of the rumpled bed, the low light of the bedside lamp turning her skin a creamier shade. His beautiful Gracie, all spread out for his pleasure, her luscious body and plump bottom mere inches away from his eager fingers and cock. He nearly whimpered like a whipped pup.

"You are a feast, baby."

She turned her head to speak, and Wade helped her by moving her silky, dark hair away from her face. "I'm too plump. I'm sure you've been with women in better shape, with less baggage too, I'm sure."

Her voice, small and *unsure,* turned his heart to mush. "I'm not going to deny that I've been with other women, but none could compare to you." Wade caressed the length of her back with his palms until he cupped both round ass cheeks. "Your body is the softest bit of paradise I've ever touched. I want to spend days playing with you." When he touched her little pink pucker, Gracie trembled. "I don't want to hear you talk of yourself like that again. I will punish you." He rubbed one palm over her bottom, while he used his other hand to tease the sensitive skin protecting her most forbidden hole. "Remember how I punished you earlier, Gracie?"

Her cheeks heated at the reminder of the erotic spanking he'd given her. "I remember," she whispered.

Impossibly, Wade's dick hardened further. "That little spanking is just the start. Now tell me you believe me when I say that I find you perfect just as you are." A nod was his answer. The sleek skin of her ass was softer than any silk he'd ever touched. So round and firm. So spankable and kissable.

So far away from his mouth.

On his knees between her legs, Wade leaned down and licked one smooth cheek, moving from the crook of her leg to the small of her back. The startled sound that came from Gracie was not so much from fear, but from sexual hunger. He recognized her sounds already. Her needy little whimpers and anxious groans. He wanted to make her scream with a satisfaction that only he could give her.

Wade moved off the bed. "Stay put, baby. I'll be right back."

"Hurry, Wade. I'm about to lose my nerve here."

He touched the cleft of her ass and stroked her intimately. "You'll be a good girl and wait for me."

She didn't speak, but her body told him all that he needed. She was giving him her total acceptance. Wade would treasure it for what it was, a gift.

Not willing to be away from Gracie for even a second, Wade quickly retrieved the body oil he kept in the bathroom cabinet. It wasn't anything special, an off brand he'd bought at the drug store. Soon he would buy her something special. A deliciously scented oil that would mingle with the heat of her arousal.

Resuming his position between the silky thighs of the woman he loved, Wade popped the top of the bottle, watching Gracie closely for any signs of fear or worry. As he poured a small amount of oil into his palm, smoothing his hands together to warm the slippery liquid, he could see a slight blush to her skin. She stiffened a little, her past experiences coloring what they were about to do, no doubt. What had her past lovers done to cause such a reaction? His protective instincts boiled to the surface.

"I would cut off my own arm rather than cause you pain, baby." Her nearly imperceptible nod touched him. His sweet, brave little Gracie.

Wade touched her shoulders first, and he could tell she was surprised. Apparently Gracie had expected him to dive right in. She should know him better than that by now. Wade savored and enjoyed.

Slowly, Wade smoothed his hands over her collarbone next, then the delicate line of her neck received extra special attention. She had an elegant neck, soft and vulnerable. "The bruises are barely visible now, Gracie."

"Mmm, that feels so good, Wade. You have the magic touch."

The husky tone of her voice had the effect of a lick over his engorged cock. Damn, she was potent. As he skated his palms down her arms to her bound wrists, he could feel her hum of pleasure. He massaged the oil into the skin of her good wrist, easing the restraint a little until her arms were now barely tied at all. He didn't need to truss her up to get off. It wasn't about that for him. Pleasure came from her total submission. Her trust in him. That's what turned Wade's blood to molten lava. Knowing Gracie was able to get away, but chose to give all control to him instead, it did things to him. Wild, untamed things.

Once Wade was satisfied that he'd made her as comfortable as possible, he poured more oil into his palms and touched her spine. He took utmost care in massaging each vertebra, feeling her relax even more. He chuckled. "At this rate you're going to be asleep before we even get to the main event."

"Sleep is impossible when you're so near . . . and so naked."

Masculine pride had his chest swelling. "What's your favorite scent, Gracie?"

"Scent?"

"Yeah, I want to buy you some body oil. Something besides bargain brand crap."

Her eyes were closed, a dreamy expression on her face. "Coconut," she answered. "It reminds me of the beach. Sun and warmth. No cares."

Wade leaned down and placed a small kiss on a spot on her back that he'd already massaged. "Coconut it is then," he murmured against her slippery skin. "When this is all over I'll take you to my beach house in Miami. You'll like it there, sweetheart. It's secluded. And there's a great big hot tub."

Her eyes drifted open, and she looked over her shoulder at him. "You have a beach house?"

He shrugged as he massaged her lower back. "A spur of the moment purchase. Costly, but worth it."

Her gaze narrowed. "You've taken other women there?"

Wade chuckled. "I wasn't celibate before you, Gracie. But, no, I've never taken a woman there. I use it whenever I need to unwind. Get away from all the pressures. Jonas and I own it together actually."

"Oh. It sounds lovely."

"You'll see it soon."

Wade smoothed his fingertips over her hips and groaned. "You're so damn pretty. A warm, sweet treat. *My* treat."

"Mmm. It's not easy to talk with you doing that. Oh, my, Wade, you're incredible."

Wade grinned, feeling cocky and turned on at the same time. He let his fingers drift over the small indentations above her bottom. "So, *slave,* would you like your reward now?"

She grinned, peeking at him through eyes half-closed. "You mean this isn't it?"

Her playfulness sent all his blood south. Gracie was sexy as hell when she played. "Ah, but this is only the beginning." Wade's slick fingers slid between her ass cheeks and stroked up and down over her tightest opening. He needed to ensure the delicate skin was completely coated with the oil. When he slipped a single digit into her a bare inch, Wade saw Gracie bite down on her lower lip.

"Shh, pretty baby. Let me love you." Tamping down his own needs proved harder than Wade had imagined. He needed to fill her with his cock. He wanted to own every inch of her.

"Wade, please. I can't think straight."

Her pleas tore straight through his control. "Easy. Gentle and easy, Gracie. For now, I want you nice and slick so that when my cock slides into that tight little ass it will feel so fucking good. I'm going to fill you up. Every inch of me, Gracie. You will crave this type of lovemaking once I'm through. I promise you."

"Oh, God, it just feels so . . . I don't know how to describe it."

"Forbidden," Wade helpfully supplied. "You are *my* forbidden pleasure, Fiery Angel."

She mumbled something that he couldn't quite make out. Wade continued to tease her inner tissues with his finger and said, "The warmth from my finger and the oil, mixing with the sensitive nerve endings just inside of you here"—he wiggled his finger for emphasis, rewarded by a moan from Gracie—"it's making me want my cock there. It's going to be so good. Spreading you open and pumping into this pretty little bottom. Tell me, do you want more? Do you want my cock?"

"Yes, Wade! I want you there, please."

"Not yet, Gracie. I need to make sure you're ready for me. Two fingers now."

Slowly, allowing her body to adjust to the invasion, Wade slid a second finger into Gracie's tight heat. He thrust in and out, then scissored his fingers, stretching her farther. She moaned and spread her legs wider, pushing backwards.

"Mmm, now you're ready," Wade ground out, barely maintaining control over his body's need to bury itself inside the woman he loved. On fire and aching for release, Wade couldn't wait another second.

He reached for the bottle of oil once more and slicked some over his throbbing shaft, already swollen and dripping with precome at the thought of being inside his pretty red-haired vixen. Gently, Wade separated the round globes of Gracie's backside and touched the head of his cock to her entrance. Slowly, aware of every little tremor of Gracie's body, he moved a mere inch inside. It was such sweet torture to hold back from thrusting deep. Fucking her hard and fast, the way his body so desperately craved.

"Wade."

Her breathless voice caressed his senses and made him want to howl in triumph. Her body vibrated beneath his, and as he slipped in another inch, she whimpered and bucked wildly.

"Easy, pretty baby. We're going to build the pleasure. One inch at a time. I want you to feel me there, even when I'm not. I want you craving it."

An inch more and suddenly Gracie thrust herself backwards, taking control of their lovemaking in a way that both surprised and pleased him. Her body bowed, and he had to clutch her hips to keep from going in too far too fast.

"No, Gracie," he growled, his tone brooking no argument. "This virgin ass is so very tender, sweetheart. I don't want to hurt you." Wade refused to cause Gracie even an ounce of pain—despite the primal instincts battering at him to fill her completely.

Holding her hips firmly, keeping her still for his slow invasion, Wade heard Gracie let loose a needy little whimper. The yearning, delicate sound turned his heart to mush, and he gave her another heated inch of hard flesh, unable to deny her. In the same instant, he took his right hand from her hip and toyed with the lovely little bud of her clitoris. Fascinated, he watched the play of emotions on her face, as she became a slave to her body's delicious sensations. She moaned and pushed against him as her orgasm took her. It was sheer ecstasy to bring her to all new heights of pleasure. She was ten thousand more times the woman than any other.

"Mmm, such a hot little ass," he snarled. "Do you want it? Will you let me fuck it good?"

"Yes, damn it!"

A rumbling growl escaped him at her feral response. "As you wish, baby." He pushed himself the rest of the way inside her tightest opening; her muscles sucked him in, and her flesh immediately tensed.

Wade swore a blue streak, the pleasure-pain of her body's clutch both glorious and tormented.

"Ease up, damn it."

"I-I can't," she cried.

Wade reached up, tore the tie from her wrists, and flung it away. At once, Gracie threw her arms out to her sides and grabbed hold of the blanket. He stroked the sweat-soaked hair away from her face, then covered her body with his own much larger frame, folding himself around her protectively. He kissed her upturned cheek and felt her muscles relax the slightest bit. "That's a good girl," Wade praised her. He littered her with kisses, making a slow path to her neck where he bit the smooth column. He got an eager response for more from Gracie. Wade was only too happy to oblige.

He licked and suckled, relishing the wild sounds she made, before beginning a gentle rhythm with his hips. Unhurried, Wade built the pace until his hot flesh slapped against hers.

"Mine," he groaned.

She didn't speak, didn't bother to deny or confirm his claim, only licked her lips and pushed against him, joining in the rhythm of their beautiful dance. Soon, he felt himself swell, and his balls drew up tight. One more thrust and he was there, his cock erupting inside of her, hot jets of his come filling her. Suddenly Gracie shouted his name, as she joined him with her own climactic finish.

Wade just barely kept from collapsing on top of her. Bracing himself on either side of her body, Wade gingerly pulled out of her, then moved to lie down beside her. Her breaths came in short pants; her entire body flushed a pretty shade of pink. Wade smoothed his palm over her ass, then dipped his finger between the cheeks. Feeling the sticky warmth of his come did things to him. Crazy, possessive things. "My pretty little angel."

"You've destroyed me."

He chuckled. "Baby, that goes both ways." He watched her turn over, her eyes drowsy. He stroked one pierced nipple with the backs of his knuckles. "I can't get enough of you. I'll never get enough."

She grinned and leaned toward him until her lips were within kissing distance. "That goes both ways too."

Then, shyly, sweetly, she pressed her mouth to his. Damn, the woman was an addiction. White-hot and every bit as lethal as TNT.

And Wade was more than ready to go up in flames.

22

Wade woke, instantly alert to the knowledge that he was alone. Gracie. His heartbeat sped up as the icy-cold fingers of fear traveled down his spine. Just as quickly he pushed the fear away, and his army training kicked in. He glanced at the clock next to the bed. Two in the morning. He listened for some indication that she might be in the bathroom or maybe had decided to raid his fridge. But there wasn't any sound at all.

That worried him more.

Leaving the bed, he found his jeans in a crumpled heap on the floor and pulled them on. As quietly as possible, he opened his nightstand drawer. Grabbing the Ruger he'd tucked in there after returning from the shooting range, he cocked it and took the safety off. On silent feet he moved toward the doorway, letting his senses scan his surroundings. It'd be hard for her stalker to get through Wade's security system, as it was state of the art, but he wasn't taking chances with Gracie's life. He took a step, then another; that's when he heard it. A shuffling, like paper. Wade leaned his head through the doorway and looked to the left. There, tucked in a chair in front of the bookcase,

Gracie sat all curled up like a cat, reading. Wade let out the breath he hadn't been aware he was holding. She glanced up, smiled—and frowned when she spied the gun.

"Wade?"

"Damn, baby. You nearly gave me a heart attack."

"Uh, I couldn't sleep."

Wade ejected the bullet and flipped the safety back in place before placing the bullet and gun on a table. He came toward her; angling his head he read the title on the spine of the old, worn book she held close to her chest. "So, you decided to read a little Poe?"

"I love Poe."

Wade crouched in front of her. "You can read it in bed."

Wrapping his arms beneath her, he lifted Gracie out of the chair and carried her back to where she belonged, all tucked up close to his side. Warm and safe.

"I didn't want to wake you. You look so peaceful when you sleep, Wade."

"I'm peaceful knowing you're close," he growled, as he sat her on the bed and waited until she scooted over before getting in beside her. He flicked the sleeve of the T-shirt she wore—his T-shirt, he noted with satisfaction—and said, "In my bed, you sleep naked. Off with it."

She batted his hand away and frowned. "No, I'm cold."

"I'll keep you warm." Her frown turned fierce. He softened his tone and tried for persuasion instead of force. "I'll read Poe to you if you take off the shirt."

Her eyes widened. "You will?"

Ah, now he had her. "If you take off the shirt, yes."

Like the cat that had spotted the mouse, Gracie grinned. She handed him the book. He took it and waited. She pulled the shirt over her head. Like a heat-seeking missile his gaze zeroed in on her pretty piercings. Christ, he was fucking obsessed with those shiny bits of gold. "I should make it a rule. No clothes in the bed. Ever."

She laughed and lay back against the pillow. "I'm waiting for my bedtime story."

Wade pulled her close and yanked the blankets over them both. Contentment settled over him. He opened the book, then paused, spearing her with a look of disapproval. "You know, Gracie, only good girls get a bedtime story."

She nuzzled his chest and murmured, "I took the shirt off. I was a very good girl."

"But you left my bed," he reminded her, "leaving me to sleep cold and alone."

"You're anything but cold, Wade. In fact, I'm pretty sure you're the hottest thing I've ever seen."

Her husky voice heated his blood, which had been her intention all along. "Little minx. Be good." He kissed her, keeping it light and quick; otherwise he'd end up dragging her beneath him. Wade didn't think she was up to more sex tonight. He'd taken her hard earlier. Her body needed time to recover.

Or did it?

Opening the book, Wade asked, "Where'd you leave off?"

"I was to the part where Madeline dies."

"Ah, it's just getting good then."

She glanced up at him. "You said earlier you liked Poe."

Wade nodded. "Yeah, he's my favorite. The man had a way with words, even if he was a little warped."

She laughed and settled against him. Wade started to read. It felt right, natural, having Gracie next to him. It was as if they'd done this same thing hundreds of times. Several pages later, Gracie stopped him with a hand on his chest. "You're a wonderful reader, Wade."

He felt his face heat at her praise. "Thanks."

She reached up and took the book from his hands, then

placed it on the table next to the bed. "Tell me about your army days."

He rubbed her arm and tried to take his mind off the tempting swell of her breasts pressed against his side. "What do you want to know?"

"Why'd you enlist?"

He thought back to those days. Damn, it seemed so long ago now. Another lifetime. "My dad was in the service. I always admired him. Wanted to be like him. I joined up right out of high school. Christ, I was so damn young."

"When did you meet Jonas?"

"In basic training. He called me a pussy. I punched him. We've been friends since."

"You both joined Special Forces together?"

He nodded. "We were adrenaline junkies. The danger was addicting, exciting. Special Forces seemed a natural progression. It didn't take us long to realize how young and foolish we'd been."

"Why? What happened?"

Her fingers kept sifting through his chest hair, distracting him beyond reason. If he could just get her to move those curious fingers a little lower. Damn.

"Taking down terrorist organizations has its rewards. But when you come across a kid with an M16 ready to kill you—hell, eager to kill you—it puts things into perspective real quick." He thought of Jonas. Wade couldn't help but cringe when he thought of the hard-edged man cuddling up to his baby sister. Deanna was too damn innocent for a man like Jonas.

"I can't imagine what sort of life would lead a child to do something like that."

"They're raised to hate. To fight. It's all they know. It's an ugly world for them." He paused as the faces of those kids swam before his eyes. "Jonas and I grew up fast. I've always known that life wasn't all roses and sunshine, but until you're forced to make a decision that could save hundreds by taking out the one—"

Gracie's hand on his cheek stopped his outpouring. She forced his face toward hers. Pretty green eyes filled with compassion snared him in an enticing web, effectively yanking him back to the present. "You did what had to be done, Wade."

"Yeah." He swallowed around the lump in his throat and gave her the bloody truth, one he'd had to learn the hard way. "There are a lot of nasty people out there, Gracie. Most live by one rule: kill or be killed."

"I'm sorry. I didn't mean to dredge up bad memories."

He pressed his lips to her hair, inhaling her fresh, feminine scent. Springtime. That was his Gracie. "It's okay. I don't regret it. Freedom comes at a price. It's important to remember that always."

Gracie shifted against him, and he groaned. Without thought, Wade tugged her face up to his and kissed her, hard, forcing out thoughts of blood and death and replacing them with thoughts of the sweet flavor of her lips, the beautiful sounds she made when she was aroused. His name was a plea on her lips. When her fingers delved into his hair, holding him firmly against her, Wade was a goner.

Wade raised his head and looked at her. Gracie's eyes were half-closed, face flushed. He knew she was ready for him. "Christ, you taste sweet, so deliciously sweet."

"You taste even better. Like warm apple pie."

He chuckled at her description. "Apple pie, huh?"

Gracie blushed. "It's true. You taste sweet and spicy and warm. I love your kisses, Wade."

I love you, he ached to admit. Wade held back the words that were sure to send her running and moved on top of her, his arms on either side of her head, caging her in. "You can have as many as you like. No calories. No guilt."

She grinned and wrapped her arms around his neck. "My favorite sort of treat."

Reaching between them, Wade grabbed Gracie's hand and brought it to his cock. "Feel what you do to me, little Gracie. Feel the way I ache for you, the way I need you." Her small, slender fingers, nervous at first, relaxed finally and wrapped around his engorged flesh. She squeezed, as if familiarizing herself with his weight and size. Her talented hand stroked in a slow, torturous rhythm. Wade's voice was thick and unsteady when he gritted out, "Enough baby. I'll never last."

She ignored him and stroked once more. Wade took over, pulling her hand away gently. "Naughty little tease." Lowering his head, he pressed his lips to the swell of one breast, worshiping her with his mouth. "Satin and cream. And mine." His tongue darted out and brushed the tip of one, before circling the areola. "Yeah, definitely cream." Another lick. "Topped with little drops of cherries." Then he gave in and sucked, long and hard, biting down just enough to make her squirm and moan.

"God, Wade, it feels so good when you do that."

"You mean this?" And he continued to lick and nibble on the other breast.

"Oh yes, that." She arched her back as if attempting to get even closer to his voracious mouth. She squirmed under him, agitated, needing something just beyond her reach. When she began caressing the length of his back, her cool fingers sparking off flames everywhere they touched, it was Wade's turn to moan. The woman turned him inside out. His lips journeyed down her ribs and stomach. His hands clutched her full, womanly hips, massaging little circles with his thumbs. When he slid down farther, tonguing her belly button, Gracie spread her legs, inviting him in. Wade released one hip and touched the springy curls between her thighs. Holding her gaze, Wade began an erotic discovery with his fingers. He rubbed his thumb across her swollen clitoris, enjoying the way her eyes slowly drifted closed, and her breaths began to come in tiny gasps. Holding himself back this time was easier. The release earlier had taken the edge off; now he was free to explore the beauty beneath him.

"Open your eyes for me, Gracie."

She complied, and he thrust one finger into her tight cunt. The green of her eyes glazed over. Her mouth opened, but no sound came out. Wade began moving in and out; feeling her muscles clench around his finger was a sweet kind of torture. She was warm and wet and welcoming. He glided a second finger in and felt her body stretching to accommodate. She began to move against him, her inhibitions a thing of the past now. Wade let his thumb tease the tiny bud of her clit, rubbing back and forth, as he pumped her tight passage with his fingers. Caught up in the fires of ecstasy, Gracie undulated against his hand, throwing her head from side to side, pleading with him, begging him as her body began that rapturous climb toward completion.

"I need to taste you, baby." Wade slipped his fingers out of her, then moved down her body, never breaking eye contact. His tongue darted out, and he licked her from clit to ass. Ambrosia.

"So damn tasty."

Wade pulled Gracie's legs over his shoulders and began lapping at her succulent pussy. He ran his tongue over her hard bud and flicked it back and forth. She shamelessly mashed her lower body against his face. Her fingers dug into his scalp. Wade groaned and slipped his tongue into her tight passage, the rhythm akin to what he wanted his dick to do. His hands closed over her breasts and squeezed. Gracie arched off the bed. Wade pinched her nipples and tugged at the little gold adornments. Gracie screamed his name, bursting all around him in a magnificent climax.

Seconds passed before Gracie opened her eyes. At the knowledge that he'd thoroughly pleasured Gracie, a sense of predatory satisfaction took him. He gently placed her legs back down onto the bed. Captivated and more aroused than he'd ever been, Wade positioned his cock at her slick opening and thrust forward, penetrating her in one smooth movement.

"Wade! Oh, God, yes!"

He swallowed her cries with kisses meant to soothe and held himself still while her body molded around him. His muscles strained, sweat dripped down his back. Angling his head, Wade began trailing little kisses everywhere at once. Touching his lips to her temples. Her eyelids. The delicate slope of her chin. He moved his hand between their bodies and began stroking her passions to new heights. Surprise registered on her face as she felt herself becoming aroused all over again. His caressing mouth moved lower, to her clavicle, then over the small indent at her throat. Lingering there, Wade sucked the velvety soft skin into his mouth, bathing her with his tongue. Gracie moaned and twisted beneath him. Her quickened breathing amplified his need a thousand times.

He pulled his mouth away. "So fucking sweet. You take me to heaven every single time I sink into you, Gracie."

Wade began a gentle glide, building the fires deep within her body, allowing her to feel his fullness a measure at a time. Gracie wrapped her arms around his torso, her legs around his waist. He felt her shyly stroke his back, her shaking fingers an indication of her excitement. With her entire body enfolding him in her intoxicating web of sensuality, Wade felt something inside him give way. As if a barricade had been torn down, he emitted a low growl of possession and pushed harder, faster, into her inviting wetness, continually toying with her swollen clit. She arched upward, pressing her breasts against him as she soared over the precipice once more. Her whimpers fueled his hunger. Damn, he was starved, and she was a fucking buffet.

Wade pumped harder, driving her supple body into the mattress, oblivious to anything but satiating both their needs. Gracie's nails scored his back; the sharp pain tore at his control.

Anchoring one arm beside her head, Wade smoothed her hair away from her face with the other, then kissed her, letting her feel every ounce of his passion. Gracie tasted of a juicy forbidden fruit, and he wanted to eat her up. In that moment, Wade had an inkling of what Adam had faced in the Garden of Eden.

Gracie reached up and cupped his face between her hands, a soft, dreamy smile on her face. Her gentleness sucked the air right out of his lungs. She was so sexy and willing, and Wade wanted to hold the image of her like this in his head forever.

He began pushing inside her heat. Tears sprang to Gracie's eyes. He paused.

"What is it? Are you sore, little baby?"

She shook her head, eyes closed tight. "I've never experienced such pleasure," Gracie whispered.

Her words made Wade want to howl at the moon. Honesty forced him to admit, "Me neither. Only with you, sweetheart. Only my Fiery Angel could make me feel this damn good."

Wade moved then, slowly at first, then faster. Gracie's arms came around his back, fingernails bit into his flesh as she matched his rhythm stroke for stroke. It was the final touch. Wade threw his head back and let out a low, rumbling growl. His body flared to life. The untamed sounds Gracie made had his dick swelling even more. His balls drew up tight. His larger hips pounded against Gracie's softness as he fucked her with feral abandon.

"Come for me again, sweetheart," Wade demanded.

The tight hot fist of Gracie's cunt held his cock captive. She pushed her hips upward. Once. Twice. Then shouted his name as her climax washed over her, bathing his cock in liquid fire.

"Christ, yes!" Wade shouted. Flexing his hips, he thrust deep, and then he was joining her.

She moaned and clutched his forearms until her body settled back to earth. Only after she lay limp on the soft sheets did Wade allow himself to slip out of her. He levered himself up and stared down at her. "It must be the red hair," Wade blurted out. Gracie opened her eyes and stared at him as if he'd lost his mind. Hell, maybe he had.

"I figure it must be all this sexy red hair," he explained, "that makes you such a wild thing in bed."

Gracie rolled her eyes. "You're the one with all the wicked ideas."

He chuckled and grabbed a fistful of the object in question. "Blondes and brunettes are invisible to me now. The only thing that'll do it for me is a pretty, little, red-haired angel."

Gracie was quiet, and Wade wasn't sure it was the good sort of quiet or the *he's moving too fast* quiet. And he didn't want to know either. Instead of pushing, like he usually did, Wade moved to lie next to her. It wasn't until he had her back snuggled up against his front that she finally spoke.

"You've ruined other men for me too, Wade. And that scares me."

Her quiet voice did him in. Wade didn't want to hear that she was too afraid to give him a chance. Too afraid to try for more than a good time between the sheets. Instead, he stroked her hair and murmured, "Shh, baby. Just sleep. It'll all work out, you'll see."

Even as the words left his mouth, he wondered if he spoke the truth or if he was merely fooling them both.

23

The next morning Gracie sat at Wade's kitchen table, her laptop open in front of her. She peeked out of the corner of her eye at the quiet man seated in the chair beside her. He was completely engrossed in her blog. He'd gone through every post for the past four months, and she was about to jump out of her damn skin. Gracie knew what was in so many of those posts. Her, going on and on about the hottie she was infatuated with. The friend of her boss at the massage therapy office where she worked. Gracie's nerves were shot. There was no way Wade could misread that to mean any other man than him. Finally, he finished the last post and sat back, his gaze seeking hers. He grinned.

Yep, the cat was definitely out of the bag.

Crossing his arms over his chest and looking as if he'd just discovered gold, Wade said, "So, you've got the hots for 'Mr. Hard & Dangerous.' Anyone I know?"

Angry that he'd found her out, Gracie snapped, "You're supposed to be looking for clues about my stalker."

He quirked a brow and pointed at the computer screen. "He hasn't commented. The blog is a dead end."

The news was as disappointing as it was surprising. "How can you be so sure?"

"You go on and on about another guy, Gracie. There's no way he would have sat back and kept quiet. At the very least you would've gotten an angry e-mail from him about it."

Gracie slumped in the chair. "Damn. I really had hoped we could find something, anything."

"We still have the e-mails. I want to go over those next." He leaned forward in his chair and placed both hands on her thighs and squeezed. His warmth seeped right through the jeans she'd pulled on earlier. "So, is Hard & Dangerous anyone I know, baby?"

His cocky attitude had her speaking without thinking. "No. You wouldn't know him. But it doesn't matter because I've decided he's too arrogant for me. And annoying. He's very annoying."

He had the nerve to chuckle. "Oh, yeah?"

Gracie batted his hands away from her thighs. "Definitely. In fact, if I saw him right now, I'd probably hit him or something."

He leaned back, his ornery grin speaking volumes. "Brings out the worst in you, does he?"

To give herself something to do, Gracie started fiddling with the keys on her laptop. "I don't know about the worst, but he does bring me to violence quite often."

"That's not the tune you were singing in that last post. In fact, I believe you said something about wanting to eat him up because he's *so* delicious."

Her temples started to pound. "I've amended my earlier assessment of the man." Hoping to change the subject, Gracie stood and went to the fridge. "I'm hungry. We never had breakfast." She pulled the door open, then bent to see what sort of groceries Wade stocked. She saw a package of lunchmeat and a container of sliced cheese. Sandwiches would do the trick. "Want me to make lunch while you go through the e-mails?" When no response was forthcoming, Gracie turned her head to see if Wade had heard. He was watching her, his eyes dark with passion. He looked her over from head to toe, pausing for a heart-pounding few seconds on her upraised backside. Her too large backside, she thought, which was facing him in the broad light of day. Oh, God. Gracie quickly straightened and closed the refrigerator door. Wade shut the computer, then stood and came toward her. Every one of her survival instincts screamed for her to move away. Retreat. Instead, she seemed frozen in place. The closer he came, the faster Gracie's pulse beat. She backed against the counter, clutching onto the edge to keep from melting into the floor.

Once Wade was a few inches in front of her, his strong, masculine scent filling her senses, he growled, "Tell me the truth. Have you changed your mind about Hard & Dangerous?"

Gracie hadn't expected him to take her so seriously. All of a sudden she seemed incapable of lying to him. Still, she wasn't willing to give him that much leverage over her either, so she merely shrugged and let him decipher for himself what it meant.

Wade backed up a step, jaw clenched tight, the muscles in his forearms flexing as if he were trying very hard to keep from pouncing. The image of him unleashing all that untamed passion brought her back to the night before. He'd strummed her body like an expert. No man had ever taken such care, spent more time pleasing her.

"Turn around." Wade's deep voice allowed no room for argument.

And still, Gracie pushed. "Why?"

Wade planted both hands on the counter beside her, caging her in. "Do as I said, Gracie."

In that moment in time, Gracie knew the truth. Wade owned her. Irrevocably and completely. She would do anything for him. The notion sent a jolt of fear clear to her soul. No man should ever have such power over a woman.

On shaking legs, Gracie turned and faced the kitchen cabinets. Waiting, for what she didn't know, proved to be a lesson in patience. It seemed like an hour passed before Wade spoke again. This time, his words had her pussy creaming.

"You lied to me, baby," he whispered, his lips caressing the shell of her ear. "As far as I can see there's only one thing to do about that."

Gracie braced herself, anticipating the spanking she knew Wade would deliver. Only nothing happened. "Wade?"

"Hush, Gracie. I won't be rushed." When large hands cupped her buttocks and squeezed, Gracie groaned. "You wanted me for months, but you turned me down. Time and again. And then you have the nerve to lie about it to my face. That's very naughty." He caressed her through the denim, and Gracie knew a kind of torment she'd never experienced before. She ached to have his hard, calloused hands against her flesh. Warming her with the erotic spanking she knew was coming.

Still, he took his time.

"So many times I went home after one of your rejections and was forced to take myself in hand. Do you know what that means, Gracie?"

She couldn't speak, couldn't think. His hands kept petting and kneading. She shook her head from side to side, already losing the thread of the conversation.

"It means, my Fiery Angel, that I unzipped my jeans and pulled out my cock," he whispered. "I had to wrap my own fist around it. Your image stayed in my head while I stroked. Your denials too. I came, vowing that someday soon it'd be your pussy I pumped full of my seed, instead of a damn tissue."

"Oh, Wade," she whimpered, as the image he'd created with his words flitted through her head.

"And finally here we are." Wade's big, warm hands cupped and massaged; he was driving her insane with his words and touches both. "I've fucked this tight little ass. I've filled your hot cunt. And you've taken me to heaven with that pretty mouth of yours. Unfortunately, you had to go and tell that little fib about not wanting me."

"I-I can't help it. I'm not used to feeling so . . ." She simply couldn't put into words the way he made her feel.

"Vulnerable?" he helpfully supplied. Gracie nodded, knowing that's exactly what had her so scared. "You think it's any easier for me? You can't breathe without my taking notice of it, Gracie. Everything about you fascinates me."

Facing away made it easier to speak her mind, Gracie realized. For the first time, she let down the walls protecting her heart. "You're too intense, Wade. I don't know what to do with you half the time. I feel like a five-year-old going to kindergarten for the first time."

"These are feelings we can work out. There's no rush. I don't need you to be a relationship expert. I only need you to be you. Open. Honest. Willing to embrace what we could have together."

She had no words. Wade already knew how she felt about relationships, so reiterating it seemed pointless. Instead, she stayed silent and waited.

Several seconds went by before Wade murmured, "So stubborn. Soon you'll see that I'm a good bet, sweetheart." One strong arm wrapped around her waist. "Until then, there's the little matter of your discipline."

Gracie's legs trembled as Wade unbuttoned her jeans. The zipper went down next. He pushed, and the material slid down over her hips to pool at her ankles. She felt him grip her panties and yank. The fragile silk tore in two. She moaned, more than ready to step out of her jeans and give him complete access to her body, but he stopped her with a hand on her hip.

"No. Stay still. I like you like this. Shackled at the ankles and at my mercy." Wade rubbed his palm over one cheek, and Gracie tensed. "God, I fucking love this ass. So round and creamy. I want to see it all pink, Gracie. I want you to have a stinging reminder of what happens if you ever choose to lie to me again."

Gracie took a single breath, then yelped as Wade delivered the first hard swat to her bottom. She grabbed the counter harder and waited for the next, her clit throbbing and swollen, juices spilling down her thighs. She didn't have to wait long before Wade's palm came down a second and a third time.

"Reach down and play with your soft little pussy, Gracie. Do it now."

Helpless against the sensual assault, Gracie did as Wade commanded. She slipped her hand between the counter and her body and cupped her mound.

"Fuck it with your finger, pretty baby. Get yourself off while I spank this ass."

"Wade," she moaned, even as she glided her middle finger into her hot, wet opening. So close. She could come so easily.

Wade slapped the left cheek of her rear two more times, then switched to the other and paid the same attention to it. Over and over, Wade alternated between hard and gentle swats. Soon, Gracie was begging and writhing, her finger deeply imbedded in her pussy.

"Damn, you're hot," Wade growled as he massaged the sting away with his palm. "So pretty. So naughty. You love this don't you? Admit it to me."

As an answer, Gracie pushed her hips backwards, giving him better access to her ass. Her name passed his lips in a rough demand seconds before his hand landed on her stinging cheek once more. "Come for me. Let me see it."

Given permission, Gracie moved her finger farther inside the heat of her pussy. Her body gripped the digit, sucking at her finger. Wade brought his hand down on her once more. Over and over. Gracie pumped herself faster, teasing her clit at the same time, while Wade delivered the stinging swats she craved. Unable to help herself, Gracie glanced over her shoulder. Wade stood behind her, his gaze on her ass, every inch the dominant male lover she'd imagined him to be. Knew him to be. She inched another finger in, watching as Wade's gaze sought out hers. What she saw in his eyes curled her toes. Her sweet, demanding lover, aching to bring her pleasure. Her gaze darted to his crotch, and she saw the erection his jeans couldn't even begin to hide. God, how she wanted to suck him. To swallow his seed. Her mouth watered at the erotic thought.

Wade growled low and wrapped an arm around her middle, holding her tight. "I want my cock feeling that hot squeeze of yours, Gracie."

"I want that, Wade. Very much."

He shook his head. "No," he bit out. "You lied. No cock for you. Come. Do it now."

As far as punishments went, Gracie had had worse. The forceful command seemed to do the trick, as Gracie felt her body climbing higher and higher. She pumped her own pussy with her fingers. Just when she thought she couldn't take another second of the pleasurable torture, Wade spanked her backside once more. Hard. Gracie's body bowed as she exploded, screaming his name over and over.

"That's the sweetest damn sound, baby," Wade said, his voice deep and rough, as if ready to come himself.

"Hey, I wanted to—"

Gracie froze at the familiar male voice. It did not belong to Wade.

"Oh, fuck!"

"Out, goddamnit!" Wade shouted, even as he moved to stand behind her, protecting her with his larger body.

She heard the sound of shuffling feet. "Fuck, I'm sorry. Fuck!"

Wade slammed his palm down on the counter beside her. "Out, Jonas! Now!"

"Uh, right. Shit."

Gracie heard a door slam shut. She slumped against the counter. "Oh. My. God." Her face was sure to be as red as her ass right now.

"I'll kill him. He's dead."

Gracie heard the rage in Wade's voice, and all she could think about was stopping the runaway train of his anger. "Uh, I'm sure it wasn't intentional."

He kissed the top of her head and grumbled, "I'm still gouging his eyes out."

Gracie pushed her hips backwards. Wade got the hint and moved away. She reached down and pulled her jeans back up. The denim scraped over her sensitive reddened flesh. She winced. Crap, that wasn't at all pleasant. She attempted to ignore the sting as she buttoned and zipped.

Turning around, she saw Wade staring at the closed door leading to his PI business next door, a frown marring his brow. She reached up and cupped his check in her palm. He turned and stared down at her. "I can't believe I'm saying this, but I'm sure he's as embarrassed as we are."

Wade's eyes widened. "You're defending him? He just saw your ass, which is red as hell from the spanking I just delivered, and you want to make excuses for him?"

Put that way, Gracie had half a mind to kill Jonas herself. "I . . . He must have had a good reason for walking in here after you told him to knock from now on. Maybe it's about my stalker."

Immediately, Gracie knew it was the right thing to say. Wade's gaze shot to the door connecting his office to his home. He ran a hand through his hair and bit out, "Go upstairs and pull on something more comfortable. I'm going to talk to Jonas."

Gracie bit her lip, unsure if that was guy code for "I'm going to beat him into the ground," or not. "Is this your way of getting me out of the way so you can punch him?"

Wade looked back at her. To Gracie's relief some of the rage was gone. He was definitely still pissed, but it was no longer at the boiling point. "Baby, Jonas and I have known each other for a long time. Trust me; he'll expect what's coming."

She rolled her eyes. "I don't understand men at all."

He closed the little bit of distance separating them and cupped her bottom in his palm. She sucked in a breath. "Sore?"

"Yes."

"Pull on a pair of my sweats, pretty baby." When she hesitated, he said, "I promise to ask questions before I start beating on him."

For a possessive, hard-edged man like Wade, Gracie figured the promise was as good as it was going to get. Rising up on her toes, Gracie pressed her lips to his and murmured, "No blood, please. I can't stand the sight of it."

He smiled, but she noticed it was strained. "Go, before I forget he's even here and drag your sexy red ass up those stairs."

Gracie didn't need to be told twice. She went. By the time she was on the upstairs landing, she turned and realized Wade was already gone. She really hoped he didn't kill Jonas. Besides the blood, she didn't want to be the cause of the men's long friendship coming to a sudden halt.

24

When Wade walked into the office, he saw Jonas pacing back and forth, oblivious to the fact that he was no longer alone. Wade stayed across the room. Hell, if he moved closer he'd end up breaking his promise to Gracie.

His hands fisted at his sides in an effort to keep himself under control. "You'd better have a damn good reason for not knocking, asshole."

Jonas stopped and turned. The only thing that kept Wade's anger in check was the red color staining Jonas's cheeks. Gracie had pegged it. Jonas was embarrassed as hell.

"Shit, Wade. I wasn't thinking."

"I picked up on that part already. The question is why weren't you thinking?"

Jonas pulled a flash drive out of his jeans pocket and held it up in the air. "We had a visitor at Gracie's apartment last night. The camera picked him up."

Wade tensed. Could this be the break they'd been waiting for? "Her stalker?"

Jonas nodded and went to the desktop computer, pulled out

the chair, and sat. "Yeah, but don't get too excited. The crafty little bastard hid himself well. A hood over his face, gloves, not a spec of skin showing."

He popped the flash drive into the slot. Wade strode across the room and knelt down, his gaze riveted to the computer screen. The front door to Gracie's apartment came on the monitor. Within a few seconds a figure appeared on her front stoop. Jonas was right. There was no way to tell who the midnight caller might be. Hell, he couldn't even swear it was a man. "Looks about five feet seven, give or take. Maybe one hundred and seventy pounds."

Jonas nodded. "And no way to tell his race. If it even is a he."

Wade leaned forward and watched as the shadowed figure lifted his hand to the door. "What the hell?"

Jonas sighed. "You aren't going to like it."

Wade swung his head toward Jonas. "What aren't I going to like?"

"He left Gracie a note." Jonas pointed to the desk. A Ziploc baggie sat next to the keyboard. Damn, Wade hadn't even noticed it there. He'd been too intent on trying to identify the stalker.

Wade picked it up and read the neatly typed note through the clear plastic. "Motherfucker. I'll kill him."

"I want to see it."

Wade and Jonas came to their feet and swung around at the strained feminine voice. Gracie stood in the doorway, wearing one of his army Ts and a pair of dark blue sweatpants. The clothes swallowed her up. They were ugly as sin, but she looked adorable. Young, sweet, and too damn far away from him. Her gaze darted toward Jonas, then away just as quickly. He heard Jonas curse under his breath. Wade held out his hand. Gracie came to him, as if she'd been doing it her entire life, and entwined her fingers with his.

"Uh, Gracie," Jonas began, waiting for her to look at him before continuing. "I'm sorry for earlier. I wasn't thinking."

She blushed and looked down at the floor. "It's okay."

Jonas's lips thinned. When he stepped closer and cupped her chin in his palm, coaxing her to look at him, Wade wanted to protest. Seeing another man's hands on Gracie set him on edge. Knowing they both needed to get past the embarrassment was the only thing keeping him from leaping between the two.

"Gracie, I'm not going to lie and tell you I didn't see anything, but I would never do anything to embarrass you intentionally."

Gracie's head came up, her gaze connecting with Jonas's. "Of course you wouldn't. I know that."

Jonas relaxed and held his hands in the air. "Believe me when I say it won't happen again."

"No, it won't," Wade gritted out as he pulled Gracie in tight against his side. Gracie elbowed him in the ribs and glared up at him. Wade wouldn't be swayed. One slipup was all Jonas would be allowed. Next time he'd find himself on the floor nursing a broken nose.

She rolled her eyes and shook her head. "Whatever. You have something to show me, remember?"

Wade handed her the plastic baggie. "We need to get this to Detective Henderson. I doubt they'll get anything off it, but it's still evidence."

Gracie began reading the note aloud. " '*Did you like the gift I left? Soon, Gracie Lynn. We'll be together soon, my love. Yours Forever.*' " She frowned and handed it back to him. "He's talking about the black rose he left on my kitchen table."

Rage threatened to consume Wade. He knew better than anyone that getting emotional could cloud his judgment, but knowing Gracie was trying to be strong, trying not to let it eat her up inside, tore at his gut. He wanted this over already.

Wade shoved a hand through his hair. "Yeah. That's not why he left the note, though."

"Then what is it about, Wade?" Gracie asked, her voice rising in anger. "I'm so sick of the mind games with this jerk."

Gracie stepped away. Distance, emotional as well as physical. He knew what she was doing, and it made Wade want to put a fist into the wall. Better yet, into her stalker's damn face. Christ, did she think that a few inches of carpet between them would keep him from knowing that she needed him? Hell, no. When would she learn that she wasn't in this alone anymore? He wasn't about to let her erect her little walls. Hell, he'd just barely penetrated a few of her barriers; backtracking now wasn't an option.

Wade tamped down the instinct to drag her close, to know she was safe and prove to her that she could lean on him, that he wouldn't bend under the pressure, and focused instead on the threat. Pointing to the computer monitor, Wade said, "He came straight to the front door, even after trashing your place. He's playing with us. He knows we're watching, but it didn't scare him off. He's trying to prove how smart he is. Preening for you."

Jonas shoved his hands in his front pockets, as if he too had a hard time watching Gracie stand there, separate, alone. "The cops are driving by regularly, and we've got your apartment wired. Yet he still couldn't resist leaving the note."

Fuck this. Wade wrapped a hand around her nape and pulled her close. "This will end soon. I promise you."

Gracie shook her head, equal amounts of anger and fear chasing across her expressive face. "You can't make a promise like that, Wade. This could go on for weeks. Months even. We're completely at his mercy."

"No, we aren't," he ground out. "We still have those e-mails." He kissed her, hard. The flavor of her lips was a subtle seduction that he ached to explore further. Remembering they weren't alone—and that they had a job to do—Wade pulled back and held out his hand. "Come on, let's get to work."

She took his hand, but didn't budge. "The police have been through the e-mails, Wade. I've read them until I'm blue in the face. You've even gone through them. I just don't see what else we could learn from them."

"Jonas and I skimmed them, but we didn't go through them thoroughly. We were more concerned with learning their origin then. And the police may have gone through them, but I'm not sure they were looking too closely."

"Could it really hurt at this point?" Jonas added.

Gracie sighed. "I suppose you're right."

Wade tugged. She relented finally and allowed him to pull her into his adjoining home. He placed a kiss to the silk of her hair and released her. "Want to boot up while I make us some lunch?"

At the reminder of what they'd been about to do before he'd gotten distracted by seeing her ass up in the air, a temptation he hadn't bothered to deny, Gracie blushed. "Uh, yeah."

Jonas cleared his throat and pulled out a chair. "If you're making lunch, I want chicken parmesan." Jonas looked over at Gracie. She'd already sat down at the table and was tapping the keys of her laptop. "You haven't tasted heaven until you've had Wade's chicken parmesan."

"He made cannelloni yesterday. It was delicious." Gracie grinned up at him, and it was all Wade could do to keep from slinging her over his shoulder and dragging her sexy ass right up the stairs.

"He rocks the kitchen, that's for sure."

"I was going to make sandwiches. Something fast so we could get to those e-mails." Gracie and Jonas both pouted. Wade rolled his eyes. "Fine, but you two are on cleanup duty."

25

After lunch—rather, after she'd completely stuffed herself with more of Wade's divine cooking—Gracie and Jonas had cleaned up as promised. She had to admit, working side by side with the flirtatious man had helped dispel some of the nervousness she'd been feeling toward him ever since he'd walked in on Wade spanking her. Oh, God, her rear still stung when she sat. It was an erotic reminder, one that sent little pulses of heat to her pussy.

It was impossible to stay upset with Jonas, she realized, and she had a feeling Deanna was going to have quite a job on her hands if she meant to keep him at arm's length.

As Gracie sipped her second cup of coffee, she watched as Wade and Jonas carefully read each e-mail—for what seemed like the fourth time. "I don't see how we're going to find anything new, Wade. This is getting ridiculous. No name. No indication of where he met me." She threw her hands in the air. "There's nothing! He gives no real details about himself or his life. It's all about me."

Wade pointed at the computer screen. "Here," he said, his voice low and even, "the first one."

Gracie leaned toward Wade, attempting to read the e-mail in question. It was the first e-mail her stalker had ever sent her. "What about it?"

"He says: I saw you for the first time today."

"Yeah, so?"

"And the next one is dated a whole week later, Gracie. On another Monday, when he writes: I've missed you, Gracie Lynn. It's been too many days since we last spoke."

Jonas rubbed his hand over his jaw, frowning at the computer. "It's not another employee at that office she works at. He wouldn't just see her on Mondays if that were the case."

Wade shook his head, pinning her with a look. "Go over your schedule for me again. What do you usually do on Mondays?"

"I get to work at about eight in the morning. Lunch at my desk usually. I get off at five in the evening and go to the store."

His eyes narrowed. "And that's it? You go to the store and then head home?" Wade prodded.

Gracie didn't even have to think. Her schedule was so routine that she could probably go through the motions with her eyes closed. "No, I go to Charlie's. That little market I told you about."

"To get lunch meat and cheese. Only on Mondays."

"Yeah, I—" Oh, God. Horror struck as Gracie followed Wade's train of thought. "He works at Charlie's Market."

Wade covered her thigh with his hand and squeezed. "I don't want to get too ahead of ourselves, sweetheart, but that's what it looks like to me." He tapped the screen. "For the first several correspondences he e-mails either on Monday night or Tuesday morning. After he's seen you. It's only after that when he begins the everyday thing."

Jonas sat back in his chair and drank the last of his coffee, before standing and bringing it to the sink. "Who do you talk to at that market, Gracie?" he asked, as he rinsed out the cup and placed it in the drainer. "And not just the people who stand out. This guy, I don't think he's going to be obvious."

Wade nodded. The hand he had on her thigh began to caress and stroke, sending her thoughts scattering. "Jonas is right. I'm betting this asshole is someone you've barely even smiled at."

Gracie stood, needing the distance to think straight, and tried to bring up the image of each employee at the little meat market. Stopping there after work on Mondays had always been the bright spot in her day. She hated to think of her stalker tainting that too. "It's a small store. A mom-and-pop type place. The owner, Charlie, who always cuts my meat for me, is a seventy-eight-year-old man who flirts way too much for his own good." Gracie smiled when she thought of the ornery old man she'd come to think of as a friend. "His wife, June, usually works in the office, but she'll pop her head out to say hi whenever I come in—and to chastise Charlie for his flirting. A few stock boys, high school kids, I think. I think their granddaughter is the cashier." Gracie shook her head. "No, there's no one there capable of doing this, Wade."

Wade stood—his hard, powerful body drew her attention like a moth to a flame—and came toward her. "Don't bet on it, Gracie. The world is full of seemingly normal people who lead wicked lives when the sun goes down. Some of the shit Jonas and I have seen since hanging our shingle would have you losing faith in mankind real quick."

Gracie stood still as Wade's gaze took her in from head to toe, stopping for a heart-pounding few seconds on her breasts. She'd slipped his T-shirt on and gone without a bra. Could he see her nipple rings? A part of her hoped he could. It would serve him right to feel as turned on as she was. A part of her, the more reasonable part, hoped he couldn't. After all, if he could see them, so could Jonas.

"We need to go to that market," Jonas said from behind them. He was in the same room, but he might as well have been in another county for all the attention they paid him.

Wade raked his fingers through his hair, a muscle in his jaw jumping in agitation. "Feel like visiting Charlie and June today?"

Gracie wrapped her arms around her chest, hoping to chase out the chill those words evoked. Would she finally come face-to-face with the man who'd tormented her for two months? It seemed so impossible. That it could be so easy seemed almost anticlimactic.

Gracie turned and headed toward the stairs. "Just let me change. I'll only be a few minutes."

"Gracie?" She turned at the worry she could hear in Wade's voice. "It's going to be okay. I won't let anything happen to you."

Smiling, though Gracie was sure it fell a little flat, she said, "I know. After all, you'd be a lousy bodyguard if you did."

"This is it? This is the market?"

Gracie sat wedged between Wade and Jonas, staring at the old brick building through the windshield of Wade's pickup truck. She'd been in there so many times. "God, it looks so normal, so harmless." She closed her eyes tight, as if by doing so she could make it all just go away. When she opened them again, nothing had changed, of course. "How could a man capable of running me off the road, breaking into my apartment, and tearing apart my things possibly work with people as kind as Charlie and June? It's inconceivable."

Wade wrapped an arm around her shoulders and pulled her in close to his side. His lips pressed against the top of her head as he growled, "Don't try to make sense of it, baby. That'll just drive you crazy."

"Besides," Jonas added, "this could be a dead end. Right now, we're just checking out a lead."

Gracie looked up at Wade and saw that his face was tight with concern. She glanced over at Jonas and witnessed the same worry in the lines of his forehead and the set of his jaw. The knowledge that both men cared about her, wanted to make this easy on her, warmed Gracie's heart. She wasn't alone. She wouldn't be going in there meeting her nightmare by herself. And for that she felt like the luckiest woman alive.

Gracie unbuckled her seat belt and cupped Wade's cheeks in her palms, then brought his head down for a light kiss. "Thank you for being here with me," she whispered. Looking over at Jonas, Gracie smiled. "Both of you."

"Hey, how come he got a kiss and I didn't?"

"Find your own woman, Phoenix." Wade's low rumble had the ability to curl her toes.

"I tried," Jonas grumbled, "but you had to go and play the big brother card on me, remember?"

Wade slammed his palm down on the dash at the reminder that Jonas wanted Deanna. "Someone other than my sister, damn it!"

Jonas cursed under his breath.

Gracie snorted. Neither man was seeing the obvious. If Deanna chose to date Jonas, no one would stand in her way. As far as Gracie could see, bullheadedness ran in the Harrison family.

She patted Wade's thigh and tried to steer them back to the nasty task ahead of them. "Let's get this over with. You two can argue later."

"There's no argument," Wade groused, as he unbuckled his seat belt. "It's settled. Jonas can save his depravities for someone who's *not* my sister."

Jonas chuckled and opened the truck door. "You just don't like the idea that she might actually like my depravities." He stepped out and closed the door. When his words registered, Wade exploded.

"I swear if he goes anywhere near Deanna, I'll castrate him!"

"Wade?"

"What?" he answered, his gaze never leaving Jonas.

"Deanna is a big girl, and Jonas isn't that bad from what I can see. Would it be so horrible if they hooked up?"

"Yes." His gaze glittered with icy menace as he watched Jonas through the windshield.

And that, Gracie supposed, was that.

Wade slung his door open and left the truck, then turned and grabbed her around the waist and helped her down. "Come on. It's time to see if our friendly neighborhood market is into hiring crazies to stock their canned goods."

26

The bells above the door tinkled merrily as Gracie entered the little market. Wade held the door, his body close behind her with Jonas in front. They were both in military mode. She could see it in the way they had her boxed in. Both men were quiet and watchful. Gracie rolled her eyes. What did they think would happen? That suddenly her stalker would jump out of an aisle with an Uzi?

As Gracie started toward the counter at the back of the store, where she noticed Charlie wrapping up a steak for a customer, Wade put his hand on her shoulder, pulling her to a stop.

"Keep your eyes peeled," he whispered. "I want you to check out every employee."

Gracie nodded and tried not to look too obvious when she let her gaze scour the small store. There were only five aisles of goods, one cash register, and the deli situated along the back wall. One young female cashier stood at the front, talking on a cell phone, while a stock boy stacked cans of baby formula on a bottom shelf. She couldn't tell much about him from her angle. She willed him to stand and turn around so she could see his face, but it wasn't happening. Gracie scanned to see if there was anyone else working today, but all she saw was Charlie and the elderly woman he was chatting up. She shook her head and smiled. Charlie was such a huge flirt.

As if hearing her thoughts, Charlie's head shot up. He grinned when he spotted her. He handed the wrapped steak to the elderly woman, then waved her off. Gracie waited for the woman to head toward the cash register before stepping up to the counter.

"Well, if it isn't our sweet Gracie. What brings you in on a Tuesday?" Before she could answer, Charlie's sharp gaze landed on the cast covering her wrist. His head swung toward Wade, then Jonas. He frowned. "What happened?"

Gracie shrugged. "I was in a car accident. A fractured wrist, but I'm fine otherwise."

Looking her over for more injuries, Charlie frowned and his eyes narrowed when he asked, "Is that where the bruise on your cheek came from?"

Crap. Gracie hadn't realized it was still so noticeable. She'd been so preoccupied with the thought of maybe finally finding out who her stalker was that she hadn't bothered with makeup. "Yeah. I lost control and went off the road. Unfortunately, my car is totaled."

"Damn, Gracie. I'm real sorry to hear that."

"It could've been worse. The seat belt and air bags helped."

"Hey, June!" Charlie shouted, in his usual subtle fashion. "Get out here, woman, we have a visitor!"

June popped her head out of a doorway along the right wall and grinned. "Hi, dear, what brings you in on a Tuesday?"

Gracie laughed. "I'm that predictable?"

"Every Monday like clockwork," Charlie and June said in unison.

Slumping at the confirmation, Gracie muttered, "Wow. I am so boring."

Wade snorted. "Hardly," he growled, staring down at her with unmistakable arousal.

"Who are these two handsome devils?" June said, eyes glazing over as she took in Gracie's two tall, powerful companions.

"Charlie, June, this is Wade Harrison and Jonas Phoenix. Friends of mine."

Jonas and Wade both offered their hands. Gracie wanted to laugh when she noticed June sigh as she shook Jonas's hand. "You have very good taste in friends, Gracie."

Charlie groaned. "You're old enough to be their mother, June."

June planted a fist on one round hip. "Doesn't stop you from flirting with young Gracie here, though, does it?"

Gracie saw where this conversation was headed and decided it was time to intervene. "Charlie, if it wouldn't be too much trouble, I'd love to get a pound of that Swiss cheese of yours. I've had a serious craving for it lately."

"No problem, dear. And how about some smoked turkey while I'm at it?" He winked and added, "My treat."

She heard Jonas chuckle. "No way am I passing that up," Gracie said. "Thanks, Charlie."

Charlie beamed and went about cutting up the cheese and turkey. June took in Gracie's appearance and clucked her tongue. "So, are the bruises really from a car accident?"

"You heard that, huh?"

"I've found it's wise to eavesdrop on all of Charlie's conversations."

"Ditto," Charlie said from the meat slicer several feet away.

Gracie laughed at the older couple. They were so much in love, but they razzed each other constantly. How wonderful would it be to have that sort of relationship? And oh how easy it was for Gracie to picture Wade as the other half.

Mentally squashing that thought, Gracie answered, "Yeah, they're really from a car accident."

June clucked her tongue. "You look awfully tired, young lady. Everything okay?"

It warmed her to know the woman cared enough to ask. "I'm fine, really. Just have a lot going on lately." Boy, wasn't that an understatement!

June pointed a finger at her, her tone turning motherly. "Are you still working two jobs? I thought we talked about that. You need to stop letting your dad lean on you so much."

Gracie grimaced. June always did have a way of getting straight to the heart of the matter. "I know, June. I will, I promise. It's just . . . hard."

June glared at Wade and Jonas. "You're her friends. Can't you see she's working herself to the bone?"

Jonas shifted, as if uncomfortable under the woman's scrutiny. Wade merely grinned and took Gracie's hand in his own. "Gracie tends to do what she wants, ma'am."

June's head shot up, pride filling her gaze. "That she does, that she does."

Turning her attention back to the reason they were there, Gracie asked, "So, June, I'm curious how many employees you have. I have a friend whose daughter was looking for a job." Well, it was just a little lie.

"We're a small operation, Gracie. The two stock boys and Traci are really all we need. But tell her to come fill out an application, and we'll be sure to keep her in mind."

"Thanks, I will. Two stock boys?" Gracie pointed to the guy in the far aisle, who was still stocking canned goods. "I only see the one."

"That's Matt. Good kid. He's going to school. Some sort of art program. George is the other. He's a whiz with computers."

Gracie's heart sped up, and Wade's hand tightened a fraction. She wiggled her fingers, and he relaxed his hold. "George?"

June nodded. "Yeah, George Lusk. He doesn't work on Tuesdays. This is just a part-time thing for him. He comes in on

Mondays to help with the new shipments, then every Wednesday and Friday."

"I see." Charlie handed her the wrapped meat and cheese she'd requested. Gracie smiled. "Thanks for the freebie, Charlie."

"Anything for you, dear." He looked over at Wade, noticing the way his hand was wrapped around hers. "Take care of our girl. I'd hate to see any harm come to her."

"Yes, sir, I will."

After paying for the cheese, Gracie followed Wade back out to the truck, Jonas trailing close behind. Wade lifted her in the air and placed her on the bucket seat, then waited quietly while she scooted to the middle, making room for him to slip in behind the wheel. Wedged between the two men once more, Gracie mulled over June's words. Wade put the truck in gear and drove out of the parking lot. She couldn't help but notice the way his sexy thighs flexed beneath the tight jeans he'd pulled on that morning as he worked the clutch and gas, his powerful hands wrapped tightly around the steering wheel. She peeked out of the corner of her eye and realized Jonas was every bit as pensive, every bit as on edge. Both men's demeanors had changed as soon as they'd left the store. In that moment, Gracie could so easily see why they'd decided to become soldiers.

"So, what did you think?" Gracie asked, desperate to break the tension-filled silence.

Wade gripped the wheel harder. Gracie was very much afraid he'd rip the thing right off the dash if he weren't careful. "I think I'm going to see what I can find out about Lusk," he snarled. "I want to look into Matt, too, but I don't think he's our guy."

Jonas slung an arm over the back of the seat and looked over at Wade. "And we should fill Detective Henderson in, too. Maybe he can do some digging."

Wade didn't reply. Instead he asked, "Are you busy tomorrow, Jonas?"

Jonas grinned, but it wasn't a pleasant look in the least. "Free as a bird. What do you need?"

"After I get Gracie to work, you and I are going to see what else we can find out about George."

Jonas winked at her. "You got it, man."

Gracie didn't like the sound of that. What exactly did Wade have planned? "Find out more? What are you planning, Wade?"

Wade sent her a hard look before turning back to watch the road. Gracie shivered. There hadn't been any warmth in his eyes. He was cold, lethal, and appeared ready for battle. The transformation startled her.

"There's nothing to worry about, baby. Jonas is going to work his magic on the computer. We're going to see what we can dig up about both guys. I'm going to do a little surveillance. If George is our guy, we're going to need to find some proof. Something to connect him to you."

Gracie let his words sink in before replying. "I don't see what you could possibly learn that might prove he's the guy behind the hit-and-run and the break-in. He's been pretty clever."

"He's obsessed with you, Gracie," Wade gritted out. "At the very least he'll have pictures of you. And that hit-and-run was bound to fuck up his car." He shrugged. "I need something so Henderson can pull the bastard in and ask him some questions."

She could see the logic in all that, but it still bothered her. Wade could be putting himself in danger, and she wouldn't allow that. "Why you? Shouldn't we tell the detective about all this and let him do the investigating?"

Wade reached over and caressed her thigh. Warmth seeped through her jeans, and she relaxed a measure. "Yes, and we will. First, I want to see what I can learn about this guy. I want something solid." As he pulled onto his street, he said, "We don't want this prick falling through the cracks. I want to gather as much evidence as I can."

"And if that doesn't work, we'll just dig a big hole and bury the motherfucker," Jonas said, his voice a little too serious for her peace of mind.

Gracie wrapped her arms around her chest. "You're both so bloodthirsty. It's freaking me out."

"This isn't about blood," Wade said, his voice low and all the more powerful for it. "This is about protecting what's mine."

Hearing Wade proclaim that she belonged to him sent a thrill through her. Knowing he could get hurt terrified her. If anything happened to him, it'd be like losing the ability to breathe. "I don't want anyone hurt because of me, Wade. Please, just call Detective Henderson. Tell him what we learned. Let him do his thing."

Wade pulled up to his home and shut off the engine. He turned in the seat, and their gazes clashed. "You need to have a little faith, Gracie," he whispered. "This is what I do. I'm not going out there half-cocked. Surveillance. That's all it is."

"Yeah, he's the levelheaded one," Jonas said. "I'm the loose cannon in this outfit. Why do you think he wants me steering a wide path around his baby sister?"

Wade cursed and glared over her head at Jonas. Gracie laughed, letting go of some of the fear that had her stomach in knots. "You're going to get your comeuppance some day, Jonas."

Jonas chuckled. "Hey, if she's a tall, sexy brunette who goes by the name of Deanna, then I'm all for getting my comeuppance."

Wade reached around her and smacked Jonas on the back of the head. "Quit thinking about her, dickhead."

"Not a chance, buddy." Jonas quickly exited the truck and started up the walk, leaving Gracie alone with Wade.

She turned toward him, scared all over again. "I don't want you going after George. Please, Wade. We have no idea what he's capable of."

Wade took her face between his palms. "This is what I do, Gracie. Don't ask me to stop being a private investigator. I can't do it. Not even for you."

She shook her head. "Of course not, Wade. I would never ask that of you. But I'm scared."

"I know, sweetheart, but there's no need. I'll be okay. It's time to finish this. I want you safe. I want it done."

"I want it done, too. And I want you safe. Just remember that when you're out there tomorrow."

"I will." He caressed her lower lip with the pad of his thumb. "Besides, knowing you're waiting for me is enough incentive for any man to use caution."

She pushed at his chest, but he didn't budge. "If you get hurt, I'm making you sleep alone."

"Mmm, that's my Fiery Angel," he murmured as he brushed his lips over hers. As always, Gracie melted.

27

"I don't like leaving you here unprotected. You have the mace I gave you?" Wade stared at the tall structure with resignation. Two of them. He had things to take care of, and Gracie had a job to get back to. Still, a sense of foreboding rode him, and he didn't like it one damn bit.

"Yes, I have the mace. And your number is on my speed dial. I'll be in an office building full of people, Wade. Nothing is going to happen to me."

He took in the sight of her. Her hair was up in a ponytail, and she wore a tight, black skirt and white silk blouse. They'd gone shopping after dinner the night before, and she'd purchased several new things. Like the pretty bra and underwear set. The color matched her eyes. However, she'd refused to wear it with the white blouse, claiming it would show through. Wade had managed to wiggle a promise out of her that she'd wear the pretty satin bits for him tonight.

Christ, she looked good enough to eat. As his gaze lingered on her breasts, he smiled. "The chain I ordered for your piercings is supposed to be delivered today."

She blushed and smoothed a hand over her skirt. "I know."

He cupped her chin and lifted her gaze back to his. "You'll wear it for me, won't you, baby?"

"Yes."

Her breathless voice turned his dick to granite. Damn, how he wished they were back in bed. He'd woken her early this morning, needing to feel the heat of her surrounding his cock, holding him tight. He'd needed the connection, he realized now. He loved Gracie, and he was scared as hell that she might never feel the same for him.

It was Wednesday, and this was their first time apart since the shit had hit the fan. Wade was loath to let her out of his sight. Being honest with himself, Wade admitted that it only partly had to do with protection and had more to do with Gracie's having time alone. Time alone to think about things. To think about him. Would she still want him around after eight hours apart?

"I'll be here to pick you up at five and take you to Cherry's. Don't wait outside; I'll come in and get you."

Gracie rolled her eyes. "We went over all this already, Wade. I'm not stupid, and I don't plan to take unnecessary risks."

He raked a hand down his face and sighed. "I know you're not. I'm going to worry until we get this bastard, though. I can't help that, Gracie."

"And I'm going to worry about you, so you'd better check in often."

He smiled at the demand. Knowing she cared went a long way toward allaying his fears. "I'm just on a fact-finding mission today. Nothing more."

As he watched, Gracie took his hand in hers and brought it to her mouth. She placed a gentle kiss to his knuckles before whispering, "Do you have plans for lunch?"

"No," he said, his voice hoarse with need.

"Pick me up at noon, and we'll grab a burger together. Sound good?"

"Sounds perfect." Wade let his gaze travel to her chest. "Maybe we can slip in a quick make-out session afterward."

The color in her cheeks darkened. "Maybe."

Wade's control snapped. Leaning down he took her lips, hard, demanding. Claiming her. He knew his attitude was primitive, but he couldn't seem to stop himself. Gracie pressed her soft curves against him, fanning the flames. Her lips parted on a sigh. Wade took it as an invitation and sank his tongue into the warmth of her mouth. Their tongues mated. He gripped her lower lip between his teeth and nibbled on her, letting his hunger for her show. Gracie moaned his name. So accepting. So sweet and tempting. The arousal behind the single word yanked Wade back from the edge.

He cupped the back of her head, both of them gasping for breath. "I need to get you out of this truck," he growled, "before I forget where we're at and take you against this seat."

Gracie's emerald gaze snared him. "Tonight you can finish what you started."

"With pleasure, angel."

Wade opened the door and stepped out, then lifted Gracie to the ground. He waited for her to push her purse up her shoulder, before kissing the tip of her nose. The fact that she was already looking forward to the night to come tamped down some of Wade's fear. "See you at noon."

She nodded and headed toward the entrance. He waited until she was safely inside the building before he got back behind the wheel and slammed the door shut. He took out his cell phone and dialed Jonas.

"This better be good, Wade."

Jonas's voice was gruff. As if still asleep? Wade checked his watch. It was ten after eight, but Jonas had always hated mornings. "Where are you?"

"In bed," he snarled. "Like most normal people."

"Get to the office."

"Time to do some digging?" he asked, his voice more alert now.

"Yeah," Wade said, as he slid the key into the ignition. The truck roared to life. "I want this shit over with, damn it."

"Me too. It about killed me seeing Gracie so worried yesterday at the market. This asshole needs to be behind bars."

"You'll get no arguments from me. Just remember one thing."

"What's that?"

"George Lusk might be a dead end."

Jonas snorted. "My gut says he's our man." There was a pause, then Jonas added, "By the way, I did a little checking into that other employee. Matt Goodger is twenty-three years old and lives about half an hour from the market. I think we can officially rule him out."

Wade wasn't surprised by the news. "What'd you learn?"

"Well, for one—and this is a biggie—the dude's not into women. In fact, he's been with his partner, a guy by the name of Rob Elliot, for the last five years. They're both art students. And from what I could dig up, they pretty much live and breathe the stuff."

Wade frowned. "When did you have time to find all this out?"

"I couldn't sleep last night. Figured I might as well do something productive."

"Thanks, man," Wade said. He was damn lucky to have a friend like Jonas.

"No problem."

"See you in a few." Wade flipped the phone shut and put the truck into gear. He hadn't said it aloud, but Wade had been feeling the same way about Lusk. Since the moment they'd realized the significance of the dates on the e-mails, Wade had felt like they were closing in on Gracie's stalker. Unfortunately, stalkers were sneaky little bastards, and they tended to be difficult to keep behind bars. They were careful. Finding enough evidence wasn't always easy. Wade was determined that one way or another, Gracie would be safe. Soon.

Jonas had spoken the truth the day before. If George Lusk turned out to be their man, but there wasn't enough evidence to bring charges against him, then they'd just bury the fucker. One of the first things they'd learned from their black ops days: there are plenty of ways to make a man disappear without a trace.

"Damn, I love my job."

Wade rolled his eyes. "You get way too much joy out of hacking into state computers."

"We all have to find our jollies somewhere."

Standing behind Jonas's chair at the computer, Wade said, "This is why I don't want you around Deanna. You're a hairsbreadth away from turning into a sicko."

"I take pleasure in my work. What's wrong with that?"

Wade smacked him on the back of the head. "Quit messing around and get me the address and license plate number."

Jonas jotted something down on a sticky note and held it in the air. "You're no fun at all."

Wade snatched it out of his hand and read the address. "This is close to that market."

"Just a few streets away." Jonas hit a few keys, and the computer screen went black. Standing, he reached for the digital camera on a shelf over the desk. "So, are we going spying?"

Wade looked at his friend. They'd been together for years, and they'd always had each other's back. Knowing it was personal for Wade this time around had him admitting, "I'm emotional about this one, Phoenix."

"So, I should make sure you don't shoot the asshole before the police have a crack at him?"

Wade chuckled. "Yeah, something like that."

Jonas let out a long-suffering sigh. "It's always about the details with you." He slipped the knife out of the sheath on his belt loop and flipped it into the air, catching it easily. "If it were up to me, we'd do our own interrogation."

Wade checked the gun he had strapped into his chest harness. "Gracie had it right when she said you were bloodthirsty."

"Hey, she included you on that one."

Wade took in Jonas's appearance. He wore a black T-shirt, old worn jeans, and army boots. Wade had pulled on a long-sleeved black shirt, jeans, and black work boots. "Christ, check us out, would ya?"

Jonas gave him the once-over and frowned. "What?"

"We look like we're going out on mission rather than doing a little surveillance work."

Jonas tucked the knife back into its sheath and checked the camera's memory. "Just because we like to be prepared, doesn't make us bloodthirsty."

"No, but it does make us a little different from most folks."

Jonas cocked his head to the side and stared at him. "You thinking of taking on safe, easy cases now that you're with Gracie?"

The very thought made Wade cringe. "Hell, no. I'm just saying that Gracie has a point. I mean, what woman wouldn't be a little reluctant to hook up with me? I'm damned possessive. Protective to the point that it's annoying. And I'm this close to solving Gracie's stalker problem with a bullet. That's not normal, not in anyone's book."

Jonas grinned. "And yet she hasn't told you to go to hell yet."

Wade turned and headed toward the door. " 'Yet' being the operative word there," he muttered.

He hadn't intended for Jonas to hear, but apparently he had because he was pulling him to a stop with a hand on his shoulder. Wade glared back at him until he dropped his hand. "Listen, Wade. Gracie seems pretty taken with you. And she doesn't strike me as the wilting flower type either. She's put up with a lot over the past few days, and she still holds her head up high. She's a tough cookie."

Wade thought about Gracie's dad, the shitty way she'd grown up. Never knowing a mother's love. Having to take care of a father who didn't deserve to breathe the same air as her. She was tough, but she was also easily bruised. "She's beautiful, passionate, and so damn smart it makes my head spin. She's my Fiery Angel."

Jonas narrowed his eyes and crossed his arms over his chest. "You're in love with her."

Shit, had he said all that aloud? Then again, now that it was out in the open, it felt good. "Yeah," Wade confessed, "I'm in love with her."

"Does she know?"

Wade shook his head. "I didn't want to spook her. Hell, we haven't even gotten a chance to go on a real date, Jonas. Everything has been happening so damn fast."

Jonas slapped him on the back. "Then I say we get this fucker, so you can take that pretty little thing on a date. The sooner you tell her how you feel, the sooner I can start thinking of my own love life."

Wade opened the door and stepped outside. "If you start on your Deanna campaign again, I'll hit you."

Jonas threw his hands up in the air and slid past him. "I'm not. It's just . . . She's different. I like Deanna. She pretty much hates my guts, though, so there's really nothing to talk about."

Jonas seemed so sincere, and that surprised Wade more than anything. He'd never seen his friend get serious over a woman before. "She doesn't hate you," Wade said, knowing he shouldn't encourage Jonas, but unable to let the man believe something that simply wasn't true. Wade set the security alarm, then locked the door, and headed for his truck.

Once on their way, Jonas turned and asked, "How do you know she doesn't hate me? Has she said something?"

Wade was waiting for the question to pop up. "No, not in so many words." He pressed on the gas, anxious to get to Lusk. "Deanna likes to get under your skin. She only does that if she's attracted to a guy."

Jonas grunted. "She's definitely under my skin."

Hearing the desire in Jonas's voice had Wade counting to ten. It was either that or punch him. "Jonas?"

"Yeah?"

"This is the part where you shut the hell up."

"Right. Sorry."

Wade sighed. "It's not that I don't want you with Deanna. It's just that I don't want to see her get hurt. Don't play with her feelings."

"You have my word."

And Jonas's word was as good as gold. Still, Wade made sure they understood each other. "I'll have more than that if you break her heart."

"Noted."

With that settled between them, Wade turned his attention back to George Lusk. With any luck, they'd find proof that he was Gracie's stalker. They'd be able to turn him over to the police without any problems. And Wade would be able to spend his evening loving Gracie. But that little prickly feeling he'd felt earlier hadn't gone away. And that, Wade knew, was a very bad sign.

28

The first few hours back to work had seen Gracie playing catch-up. If she'd known what awaited her, Gracie never would've taken Monday and Tuesday off. When she finally had a few minutes to think straight, Gracie picked up her cell phone and sent a text message to Wade, letting him know she was looking forward to their lunch date. Oh, God, she missed him something terrible. Gracie wondered if he were feeling the same way or if having her out of his hair was a relief. The text he sent back had her heart racing.

I'M HUNGRY, ANGEL. FOR U. MISS YOU BUNCHES.

She sent one back asking how they were doing with Lusk.

AT HIS HOUSE NOW . . . HE'S DEFINITELY THE GUY. TELL YOU MORE AT LUNCH.

Gracie had to read the message three times before she would believe it. It was really happening. After two months of dealing with the jerk, they were finally starting to close in on him. Soon it would be over, and she'd be able to concentrate on her relationship with Wade. And why did that thought send her into a panic? *Simple,* Gracie thought, *because this is the first time you've been in love.*

On a whim, Gracie flipped her cell open again and dialed Cherry.

She answered on the second ring. "Hello?"

Gracie took a deep breath and let it out slowly. "Cherry, it's Gracie."

She laughed. "I know, sweetie; I saw the caller ID. What's up? Everything okay?"

Gracie picked up a pen and started doodling. "Everything's great. In fact, we may finally have a lead on my stalker."

"That's wonderful news!"

"Yeah, but that's not why I'm calling. I need to talk. Do you have a minute?"

"I'm in between clients right now. What's wrong?"

"It's Wade. I-I think I'm in love with him." Why did it seem so ludicrous out loud?

"Ah, I see. Have you told him?"

"God, no!" Gracie's face heated, and suddenly she couldn't catch her breath. Crap, just thinking about telling Wade she was in love with him was giving her an anxiety attack! "He'll think I've lost my mind, Cherry. I mean, we've only spent a few days together."

"First of all, Wade won't think you've lost your mind, so get that thought out of your head. Second, stop trying to look at this logically. Logic and love don't always go hand in hand. I know they didn't for Dante and me. He walked into my life and swept me right off my feet."

"When you know, you just know. Is that it?"

"Yeah."

"But what if he doesn't feel that way about me?" She paused, then added, "I mean, I'm sure he doesn't. Men don't fall in love that quickly, right?"

"I don't know about that. It sure didn't take Dante long to figure out I was the one for him. Actually, I was the hesitant one."

She hadn't known that about Cherry and Dante's relationship. It was hard to imagine any woman wavering with a man like Dante. He was so kind, so giving. And then there was the sexy, hard, dark-haired Italian part. "You were?"

"It's tough when you've been hurt before, Gracie," Cherry said, her voice softer now. "It's hard to let someone else in. There's always that fear of getting burned all over again."

Cherry had been married, and it hadn't ended well, but that didn't explain Gracie's reluctance to lay her feelings on the line with Wade. "I've never been in love. That's not what this is about."

"No, but you've been burned, sweetie. Your mother leaving you. Your dad's drinking. It's hard because you're afraid to let yourself trust. It'd be difficult for anyone with your circumstances. But Wade's a good man. Give him a chance."

Knowing Cherry was right had Gracie slumping against the desk in defeat. She'd kept people at arm's length her entire life, too afraid to care. After all, she hadn't been enough for her own mother, and her father cared more about alcohol than his own daughter. That Wade could want her, that he could possibly love her . . . It seemed too good to be true. "Why is this so hard? I wish I could let the past go and just grab Wade and tell him everything."

"It's hard because the past has a lot to do with who you are now. Just don't let it rob you of something as wonderful as love. Don't let them take that from you, Gracie."

She started to tell Cherry she was right, but her phone made a pinging sound, indicating there was a call waiting on the other line. "Cherry, I need to go, but thanks for letting me unload on you."

"That's what friends are for."

Friends. Gracie smiled at the word. "I'll see you tonight."

"If you need the evening off, it's fine. We're not super busy today."

"No, it's okay, but thanks." Gracie glanced down at the doodles she'd made on her day calendar. One word scrawled over and over: Wade. Good Lord, she was in so deep.

"Okay, then, see you tonight."

When she heard the pinging sound again, Gracie quickly switched over to the other line. "Hello?"

"Ms. Baron?"

"Yes, this is Ms. Baron. Can I help you?"

"This is Frank Gaetz. I'm a friend of your father's. He asked me to call you."

She wasn't aware her father even had friends. Concerned now, Gracie asked, "My father?"

"Yes, ma'am. He's been in an accident. It's pretty bad."

Gracie paled. "Oh, God. Where is he?"

"He's at Saint Mary's Hospital."

Saint Mary's was just a few blocks away. "I'll be there as soon as I can." Gracie slammed her phone shut and shot out of her chair. After grabbing her purse from beneath the desk, Gracie headed toward the elevator. She stopped short when she realized she had no ride. Damn! Wade was her ride, and he wasn't due for another hour. Gracie looked around the office and spotted her boss, Marie, explaining something to a coworker. She headed toward her. "Marie?" The gray-haired woman looked up and smiled. "Can I talk to you for a second?"

"Sure, Gracie." Marie closed the distance between them. "What do you need?"

"I just received a call. My dad's been in an accident." Gracie's hands shook as she thought of her father lying helpless in a hospital bed. He might have been a drunk, but he was still her father.

"Oh, no!"

"I need to go to him, but I don't have a car. I hate to trouble you—" Gracie stopped midsentence. She hated to ask the woman for a favor after she'd been generous enough to give her the time off after the accident. But what choice did she have?

Marie held her hand in the air. "Think nothing of it. Just let me grab my keys."

Gracie stopped her before she could rush off to her office. "You have that conference call at noon with those suppliers. You can't miss that; it's much too important."

Marie frowned. "Shoot, I forgot about that."

"If I could just borrow your car? Normally I wouldn't ask, but I'm really worried about my dad."

"Of course, Gracie. Don't know why I didn't think of it myself. Let me get my keys. Be right back."

Gracie watched her hurry off, grateful all over again for having such an understanding boss. When Marie came rushing back to her, handing the keys over, she said, "Will can swing by and get me. Go ahead and keep it until morning."

"Thanks, Marie. I'll take very good care of it, I promise."

Marie tsked. "You're the most reliable person I know, Gracie. I'm not worried."

Gracie smiled and thanked her again, then headed for the elevator. She hit the Down button and waited. The elevator doors opened, and another man was inside, but she barely noticed him. Her mind was on her father. The last she'd heard her father didn't have a license. So, how could he have been in an accident? As an afterthought, Gracie sent Wade a quick text, explaining where she was headed.

GONE TO ST. MARY'S. DAD'S BEEN IN AN ACCIDENT.

As the doors opened, Gracie tucked her phone into her purse and sprinted across the parking lot, easily locating Marie's black BMW. Just as she hit the Unlock button, a hand closed over her mouth. A sweet-smelling odor filled her mouth and nostrils. She tried to scream, but no sound came out. Gracie reached into her purse, hoping to grab the mace Wade had insisted she carry that morning, but the words filling her ears sent a chill down her spine, freezing her in place.

"I'm very disappointed in you, Gracie Lynn. I thought after that last lesson I was forced to teach you that you'd be more circumspect in the company you keep."

No, it couldn't be. Gracie struggled harder, kicking out with her legs, using her fingernails to claw at the hand clasped tightly over her mouth and nose. She heard him curse, but he didn't release her. She fought harder, tried to kick him in the shin, but her legs felt like rubber. What was wrong with her? Suddenly, her vision blurred. Oh, God, he'd drugged her. Gracie felt herself being lifted into the air, and then there was nothing but darkness.

29

"Jesus, this guy is seriously twisted, Wade."

Wade stared around the small, dark room, anger twisting his gut at the sight before him. The walls were papered with pictures of Gracie. All four walls were covered with them. Gracie heading to work. Gracie talking on the cell phone at the market. Gracie coming in and out of her apartment. Wade stepped closer to the bed, staring at the wall above the oak headboard. "Fuck, these are from outside her bedroom window!"

Jonas came closer and cursed. "He's been watching her. A lot."

Wade fisted his hands at his sides. "I'm going to kill him, Jonas. There won't be anything left for Henderson, because I'm going to gut the bastard."

Jonas grunted in agreement, then frowned as he looked around the room once more. "Look at the bed, Wade. The nightstand. The dresser. Unless I'm misreading the message here—and I highly doubt that I am—he's readied the place for her."

Wade walked over to the nightstand. A pink brush with the

tag still on it sat next to the phone. A bottle of light pink finger-nail polish and matching lipstick were placed on a little silver tray. On the bed lay a long white dress. Demure white heels were placed on the floor directly in front of the dress. Wade turned to Jonas. "What the hell? Lusk think he's going to marry her?"

Jonas pointed to a bottle of champagne on the dresser across from the bed; a box of condoms sat next to it. "I think that's the plan. As crazy as it sounds, I think he's set the stage for their wedding night."

"Son of a bitch."

Wade's cell phone started to vibrate, interrupting his build-ing rage. He yanked it out of the holder on his front jeans pocket and flipped it open. It was a message from Gracie, let-ting him know she was looking forward to their lunch date. Damn, how was he going to tell her about this? The pictures of her in various stages of undress alone would make her feel vio-lated, much less the crazy scene he was staring at now. Wade sent her a quick text, telling her he missed her. He'd have to think of a way to explain all this. Knowing how upsetting it would be for her had Wade cursing. Again.

"She's been through enough," Wade bit out. "These pictures are going to . . ." He couldn't bring himself to finish the sen-tence.

Jonas slapped him on the back. "Let's get some pictures of our own, then we'll head to the station and fill Henderson in on what we've found."

Wade waited as Jonas walked around the room taking sev-eral shots of the bed, the dresser, the walls. After he'd finished, they headed out the back door. They'd parked a street over, careful not to be seen. When they'd realized Lusk wasn't home, Jonas had gone to work on the lock. It'd only taken a few sec-onds to get inside.

After they reached the truck and were on their way, Wade

said, "We can't just walk into Henderson's office and show him pictures that we took of Lusk's bedroom, which were taken *after* we broke into his house, by the way."

Jonas shrugged. "He doesn't have to know how we managed to get the pictures. For all he knows, we befriended Lusk, and the man invited us into his home."

"Fuck it. I don't care what we have to do or say. I just want this guy taken care of."

"One way or the other he will be," Jonas promised, his voice ice-cold.

"One way or the other," Wade repeated the vow as he gripped the steering wheel and took the corner faster than he should have. The prickly feeling, the one that told him something bad was about to happen, hadn't gone away.

Within minutes they were standing in Detective Henderson's office, watching as the seasoned detective flipped through the pictures on the digital camera. They'd already filled him in on everything they'd learned about the market George worked at, which Gracie visited every Monday, like clockwork. Once the detective reached the end of the pictures, he quietly placed the camera on the desk and looked up. "How did you say you came to be in Lusk's bedroom?"

"We didn't," Wade ground out, not bothering to explain further. He didn't care what happened to him, as long as Lusk was arrested. Keeping the freak away from Gracie was his number one objective. Nothing else mattered.

A muscle in the detective's jaw jumped angrily as he pushed away from his desk and stood. "You say he works at the market that Gracie goes to every Monday. Does she remember him?"

Wade raked his fingers through his hair, his instincts firing at him that something wasn't quite right. "No. Gracie has no idea what he even looks like."

The detective let out a breath. "Is there anything else I should know before we investigate this guy?"

Wade couldn't have heard him right. "Investigate?" Wade yelled, as he stepped forward and planted his hands on the desk. "He needs to be behind bars, detective. Drag his ass in for questioning!"

"We can't pull random people off the street just because you say so, Harrison!" he yelled back. "It doesn't work that way. We need probable cause."

Jonas pointed to the camera. "Did you see those pictures? He's set the stage. He's going to take her. My guess is soon."

Henderson held up his hand. "He's obviously off his damn rocker. And we're going to do everything in our power to keep him from harming Gracie. But you need to leave the rest to me. This has to be legal or the scum walks. Is that what you two want?"

Wade's temper boiled over. "Son of a bitch! I fucking knew this would happen." Wade's cell phone vibrated, interrupting his murderous thoughts. He yanked it off the clip and read the words on the little screen.

Jonas stepped closer. "What is it?"

"It's a text from Gracie. She says her dad was in an accident. He's at Saint Mary's Hospital. She's taking her boss's car and heading there now."

"I've got a bad feeling here, Wade."

Wade did too, and it was getting worse by the second. He started tapping the small keyboard. "I'm telling her to wait for me." He hit Send.

"Good plan."

Within seconds he received a reply. Only it wasn't from Gracie. "He's got her. That son of a bitch has Gracie."

"What? How?" the detective asked, as he moved around the desk.

Wade handed Jonas the phone. Jonas read the text aloud. " 'Too late. Gracie Lynn is mine now.' "

Wade and Jonas took off running, the detective hot on their

heels. "He'll take her to the house," Wade shouted over his shoulder. "He thinks he's safe there. He doesn't know we're on to him."

The detective caught him by the arm and pulled him to a halt. "I'll call for backup," he gritted out, "but you two need to stand the hell down. This is a police matter."

Wade shot him a glare. "No way in hell is that happening."

"Ditto," Jonas growled.

Henderson seemed at war with himself for a moment, and then he let Wade go. "Christ! Fine." Before Wade could turn to go, Henderson jammed a finger against his chest. "But if you go in there in the state you're in now, you're liable to get Gracie killed. Think, goddamnit!"

Wade smiled. Henderson paled. "Trust me, detective, my thinking has never been more clear."

30

Gracie's head hurt, but she couldn't understand why. She tried to open her eyes, but that only seemed to make the ache worse. Tugging on her hands and feet, Gracie realized she was very effectively bound. She remembered everything then. The call about her father. It'd been a ruse, but she'd been blinded by worry. She'd rushed out to Marie's car without thinking about her own safety. A hand had slammed down over her mouth. Gracie's eyes shot wide, and she looked across the room and came face-to-face with her stalker.

"Oh, good! You're awake," he said, a maniacal smile lighting his face as he stood across the room, watching her. "I wasn't sure how long that nasty stuff would knock you out."

Gracie licked her lips; they were chapped, her mouth dry. "You drugged me," she muttered. Her throat felt as if it had been scraped raw.

"Yes. I'm sorry, but it was necessary."

Gracie looked at George, taking note of his filthy appearance. He had dirty, sandy blond hair parted down the side, and if Gracie had to guess she'd say he was in his mid-thirties. He looked as if he hadn't showered in weeks. He wore a black hooded sweatshirt and jeans. He couldn't have been taller than five foot seven. He was thin, almost painfully so. This was the man who'd been sending her e-mails? The person who had run her off the road and had torn up her home? Somehow she had expected someone more sinister. Someone bigger, meaner. This guy looked like an accountant. He was so normal in appearance, so completely average. And yet he was clearly insane. He was also a complete stranger. How was it possible to attract such obsessive attention, and yet she couldn't even remember seeing him at Charlie's Market?

"Why? Why me?" Gracie had to know what she'd ever done to warrant such fanatical interest.

He moved away from the doorway then. With each step he took closer, Gracie's heart beat faster. Once he was standing beside the bed, fear like she'd never before felt filled her. She could see it then, the vacant look in his eyes. He was completely insane.

"You know. You already know the answer to that question, Gracie Lynn."

She shook her head as frustration started to edge out the fear. "I don't understand any of this! Please, just let me go." Even as the words spilled out, she knew it was futile. He would not be letting her go. Wade would come, she thought, hope blooming. When she didn't show for their lunch date, he would come looking for her.

"Why would you want to leave?" George asked, as if genuinely confused. "We love each other. We're going to be married." He picked up a white dress that had been on the bed next to her. She hadn't even noticed it lying there. Gracie looked it over, then let her gaze travel around the room. She saw it all then. The champagne, the condoms, the pictures of her. Oh, God, there were so many. Thousands of them.

"Do you like it? I did it all for you."

He wanted to know if she liked it? Gracie started to tell him where he could shove the damn dress and the rest of his crazy little plan, but she stopped herself. Pissing off a madman while bound was not a good plan. Instead, she lied.

"It must have taken you a very long time to do all this. I'm flattered." Bile rose as she spouted lies. "Of course, it's going to be difficult to put the dress on if I'm tied to this bed." She smiled and wiggled her fingers for emphasis. "Maybe you could let me up? So I can try it on, I mean. It's so lovely."

"Not yet. We have a few things to discuss first."

"Oh?"

"I'm not pleased with you, Gracie Lynn. You let another man spend the night with you. You betrayed me."

Gracie watched as George took a gun out of the pocket in his hoodie and placed it on the nightstand. "I-I didn't mean to upset you, George."

"It's his fault." George shook his head, his voice shifting to a higher pitch. Almost feminine. "You were so perfect before. He's tainted you. He's tainted my Gracie Lynn. I can't let that go unpunished." He pulled a knife out of his pocket and flipped it open. "You understand, don't you? This is for your own good, my love."

As he sat down on the bed beside her, Gracie started to shake uncontrollably. "No, please."

The point slid over her blouse, beneath the top button. He sliced, and the button fell away. "It's for your own good. Soon, you'll be perfect again. Soon, Gracie Lynn."

Gracie started to struggle, but the ropes had no give. Another button popped free. When she felt cold metal against her chest, she screamed.

"Jonas, go around the back. We'll go in the front," Wade instructed.

"You're a civilian, damn it. You'll hang back until backup arrives."

Wade and Jonas exchanged a silent look. Jonas nodded and took off around the side of the house. Henderson glared at Wade. It was ignored. "His bedroom is down the hall, the first room on the left."

The detective tested the doorknob, but it didn't give. "We need to do this right. We can't just storm in there."

Wade's patience snapped. "She's in there, and he could be—" A bloodcurdling scream rent the air, cutting him off midsentence. Gracie. Fear mobilized Wade into action. He body slammed the old, beat-up door. It gave way easily under the brutal assault. Wade took off through the living room and down the hall, barely aware that the detective was right behind him. Wade stopped at the sight inside the barely lit bedroom. Gracie, sprawled out on the bed, blood covering her chest. It dripped down her side to the pristine bedspread. Her gaze landed on him, and tears filled her eyes.

Wade crossed the room in two strides. "Oh, God, baby."

"Wade, watch out!"

Wade turned his head in time to see George Lusk standing in the adjoining bathroom, gun raised, tears spilling down his cheeks. Reacting purely on instinct, Wade lunged across the bed, protecting Gracie with his larger body. He felt a sharp sting in his left bicep seconds before the room erupted into chaos. Wade looked up to see Jonas holding George by the throat, knife poised directly over his heart.

"You got him secured?" Wade snarled.

"He moves, he dies," Jonas promised, his voice low, menacing.

Henderson cursed and came over to the side of the bed. "You've been shot, Wade."

"No!" Gracie cried, struggling under his weight.

Wade lifted off her and went to work on the ropes securing her wrists to the headboard. Once free, she flung herself against him. "You can't die, Wade. Please, don't die."

Wade wrapped his arms around her. Damn, he was shaking like a friggin' baby. "Shh, sweetheart. I'm fine. It's just a graze. I've had worse during my army days." He pulled back and looked down at her. Blood coated the front of her blouse. "Oh, baby. What did he do to you?"

Gracie shook her head and wrapped her arms around his neck, squeezing him tight. Wade could feel the wetness of her tears soaking the front of his shirt. They mingled with the blood, tearing another layer off his self-control. "Baby, I need to see it. I need to know how bad it is. We need to stop the bleeding."

She tightened her hold on him and shook her head harder. "He only managed to cut me once," she said, her words muffled by the front of his shirt. "It's not deep, Wade."

Not deep hell. He would see that blood on her chest in his nightmares for years to come. Wade glanced over to see Henderson untying Gracie's ankles. She was completely free now. Wade slipped his arms beneath her knees and behind her back, then stood, lifting her. Wade spared Jonas a grateful look, knowing that if not for him, Gracie could be dead. Hell, rushing into the room the way he had could've gotten them all a bullet. Jonas only grinned and tightened his hold on Lusk, who continued to wail like a toddler whose toy has been snatched away. Wade had a powerful urge to cross the room and hit the son of a bitch who had made Gracie's life a living hell for the last two months, but the man was just too damn pathetic.

Wade quickly dismissed him and turned his attention back to Gracie. "I'm taking Gracie to the hospital."

Henderson stepped in front of him. "We've got Lusk dead to rights, Wade. Kidnapping, assault, and whatever else we can stick him with. He's going away for a long time."

Wade glared at the detective and moved around him. "Just so you know, Lusk walks, I'll be going hunting. Remember that."

"Guess I'll just have to see to it that that doesn't become an issue."

"You do that," Wade muttered, as he walked out of the room. Gracie cupped his cheek. "I really can walk. The cut on my chest, it's not that bad. You've been shot, Wade. You shouldn't be carrying me."

"Hush, damn it. I'm not letting you go, Gracie. I'm never letting you go."

Gracie relaxed against him. "I knew you'd come for me."

"Always, angel." He kissed the top of her head. "But be warned, after we're both patched up, you and I are going to have a little chat."

Gracie stiffened against him, but stayed silent.

31

"I want to see her. I want to see Gracie."

"Just one more stitch." The doctor stuck him again, and Wade winced. "There, that's the last one." He unwrapped some gauze and started to cover the dent the bullet had left in Wade's arm. "You're lucky that bullet only grazed you. This could have been a lot worse."

"I'm aware of that," Wade bit out. "It doesn't change the fact that I want to see Gracie. Now." He wouldn't believe she was okay until he saw her with his own eyes.

"She's fine, you know," the doctor said, as if reading his mind. "That cut on her chest was pretty shallow. Didn't even need a stitch. Just a few butterfly bandages."

Wade was fast losing his patience. "So you've said, but if I don't see her soon, I'm going to get violent."

The doctor had the nerve to chuckle and pat his arm. "You're done." Wade got off the bed and started for the door. As soon as he stepped into the hall, he saw the whole crew coming at him. Dean, Deanna, his mother, Cherry, and Dante—they were all converging on him. "What the hell?"

Wade's mother wrapped her arms around him, squeezing him tight. When she pulled back, he could see the worry on her face, and he felt like a complete shit.

"Jonas called. Are you okay?"

"I'm fine, Mom." He patted her on the back and felt her trembling. "Just a little graze on my arm, I promise. You made a trip for nothing."

"Jonas told us you'd be fine, but I wanted to see with my own eyes that my son wasn't lying half-dead."

Suddenly Wade was a little kid again. He leaned down and kissed her cheek. "Sorry to worry you, Mom."

Deanna hugged him next, then smacked his chest. "I thought you learned how not to get shot when you were in the army. What happened, big bro? Going soft?"

Wade snorted. "Love you too, sis."

Dean chuckled. "Don't let her fool you. She's been worried sick about you ever since Jonas called her."

Wade quirked a brow and grinned. "Is that right?"

Deanna glared at her twin. "Big mouth."

Dean ignored her and slapped him on the back. The jarring sent lightning streaking down his arm. "Glad you're okay, bro."

"Thanks," Wade muttered, willing them gone so he could get to Gracie. Regardless of what the doctor said, he wouldn't sit easy until he saw her. Cherry and Dante took their turns next. Wade's patience finally gave way to worry for Gracie. "Look, I really appreciate your all coming down, but I'm sort of in a hurry."

Dean nodded. "Yeah, we heard about Gracie."

His mother stepped to his side. "I'd very much like to meet the woman my son is willing to take a bullet for."

Oh, hell. "Mom, I'm not sure—"

"I want to meet her."

Wade had heard that tone before. There'd be no changing

his mother's mind. He sighed and caved. "Come on then." Wade went to the other end of the emergency room where Gracie lay in a bed, eyes closed. She looked so pale, too pale. Wade moved up beside the bed and pushed a lock of hair off her forehead. Her eyes shot open. She smiled, then glanced around him, and the smile was quickly replaced by confusion.

Wade leaned down and placed a gentle kiss to her cheek. "How are you, baby?"

"I'm fine. My chest stings a little, and my head hurts from the chloroform, but knowing it's finally over . . . it's such a relief, Wade."

Wade bit back a curse. "I didn't realize he'd used chloroform. The son of a bitch could've killed you if he'd used too much."

She nodded. "The doctor wasn't real pleased either." Her gaze darted back and forth among the mass of people positioned around her bed. "Um, did you want to introduce me, Wade?"

No, he didn't. He'd much rather have Gracie all to himself. He had things to say, and they wouldn't wait. Wade moved a foot to the left, letting his mother come up to Gracie's side. "Gracie, this is my mom. Mom, Gracie Baron."

Gracie smiled and sat up straighter. "Hello, Mrs. Harrison. It's nice to meet you. Well, the circumstances are unfortunate, of course."

Wade's mother frowned in concern. "You've had a rather rough go of it lately, I hear."

Gracie winced. "Yeah, it's been a little crazy. If not for Wade and Jonas, I don't know what I would've done." Gracie's eyes, still swollen from crying, looked up at him with love. At least that's what it seemed like to Wade. Maybe he was deluding himself. Damn, he needed to get her alone and find out.

His mother smiled up at him, pride clearly visible. "My son sure knows how to keep things from getting too dull."

"I'm sorry he was shot. It's my fault. It never should have come to that."

"From what Jonas told me, you were an innocent in all this."

"I just wish it hadn't ended the way it did."

His mother patted Gracie on the hand. "Seems to me, it ended just right. You're both safe, and the bad guy is behind bars."

Gracie sighed and relaxed against the mattress. "Yes, it's over. Thank goodness for that."

"Hey, mind if I intrude?"

Wade looked up to see Detective Henderson at the foot of Gracie's bed. He looked tired and in bad need of a vacation. "What's up, detective?"

"I thought you two might want to know Lusk confessed to everything. The man spilled his guts."

"Good," Wade growled. *Saves me the trouble of killing him.*

"And there's also this." He came toward Gracie and handed her a plastic evidence bag, a piece of paper inside. Gracie took it, her brows scrunched together. "Do you recognize it?" the detective asked.

She shook her head. "It looks like a raffle ticket, but I don't remember filling it out."

The detective shoved his hands in the pockets of his navy slacks. "Lusk had it in his pocket. We found it when we searched him. He went ballistic when the officer took it from him. According to Lusk, you filled that out at Charlie's Market. He said you intended it for him." The detective shrugged. "Of course, he's off his rocker, but at least now we know how he obtained your e-mail addy and mailing address."

"And my middle name. There was a space for it, and I'd simply filled it in." Gracie said, staring at the slip of paper. "Oh, God, I remember now. The raffle was to win an e-book reading device. I can't believe he's had it this whole time."

Wade took the bag and looked its contents over. The paper was so badly wrinkled, it was hard to make out the words. Hell, it looked ten years old, rather than a couple months. "The first contact," Wade mused aloud, as he handed the baggy back to the detective. "He must have seen this as a sort of love note."

Henderson nodded. "He said as much when we talked to him. He's certifiable."

Gracie wrapped her arms around her chest, tears filling her eyes. "Then it's really over."

Wade took her uninjured hand in his and squeezed gently. "It's over, angel."

"It seems so . . . surreal."

Wade's mother spoke up. "When you get to feeling better, Gracie, I'd love it if you could come out to the house for a visit."

"That would be lovely, Mrs. Harrison."

She clucked her tongue and fingered the strap of her purse. "Oh, please, it's just Audrey. Mrs. Harrison makes me feel ancient."

Wade leaned down and kissed his mother on the cheek. "Thanks for coming, Mom."

She crossed her arms over her chest. "You'd better take better care of yourself from now on, mister."

Wade grinned, his first real smile since seeing Gracie covered in her own blood. "I'm made of steel, or didn't you know that?"

"Ha! Your head maybe."

Dean stepped up and took their mother by the elbow. "You can lecture him later, Mom. We should let Gracie rest."

"Bring her for a visit, son."

"I will, but no home movies. You'll only scare her off."

His mother winked. "No promises."

Wade shook his head and watched his family leave. He

could hear Deanna and his mother plotting, but Wade was simply too grateful that Gracie was safe to care what the two women had in store.

He turned to see Cherry hugging Gracie; both women had tears in their eyes. Dante stood close by, quietly watching the display.

"I'm so relieved you're both okay," Cherry said in a wobbly voice. "When Jonas called I was so scared."

Wade took Cherry by the shoulders and pulled her in for a hug. "Everything's going to be fine now. Lusk is going away for a while."

"From the sounds of it, he'll be heading for a maximum-security psychiatric hospital," Dante muttered.

"That'd be my guess."

"It's so bizarre. I mean, I thought I'd recognize him. I thought at the very least he would look familiar."

"You don't remember seeing him at the market?"

Gracie pushed a hand through her tangled hair. "No. He's a complete stranger. And yet I somehow managed to attract his attention." She looked at Wade. "How is that possible?"

"He fixated on you," Wade stated. "Maybe you smiled at him one day or said hi. Whatever it was, however mundane, he took it as a sign that you were attracted to him. Again, he's crazy. Don't try to figure it out."

"Wade's right," Cherry said, as she stepped backwards and into Dante's waiting arms. "There's no way to know for sure why he ended up so obsessed with you. Let's just be happy it's done."

"Come on, little one. We should let Wade and Gracie have some time alone."

"Of course, you're right," Cherry said. "And don't worry about coming to work tomorrow. In fact take as many days as you need."

"Believe it or not, I *want* to come back to work. I'm ready to take my life back. I feel as if it's been in limbo ever since this all started."

"I can understand that, but don't push yourself too hard. A day of rest will do you good."

"I agree with Cherry," Wade said, adding his two cents. "Situations like these can sometimes hit you all at once and leave you feeling drained. Right now the adrenaline is still pumping."

"Yeah, you're probably right. We'll see how I feel tomorrow, I guess."

Cherry leaned down and whispered, "Call me and let me know how it goes."

Wade was curious, but stayed silent. After Dante and Cherry were out of the room, he looked at Gracie. "When can you leave?"

Gracie started to pick at the blanket, as if nervous all of a sudden. "The doctor said to just rest a little bit, to let the effects of the chloroform wear off."

Wade pulled up a chair and sat down. "It's time we talk, Gracie." He looked around the emergency room and shrugged. "This is as good a place as any, I suppose."

"Before you say anything, I have something to tell you."

Wade's chest tightened. Was she done with him? Now that it was all over, would she give him the brush-off? "You do?"

Gracie bit her lip, her fingers tangling in the bedspread. "I know we've only been together for a short time, and with everything that's happened you'll probably just think I'm crazy. I wouldn't blame you if you did, I mean, I've never done this before and I'm not sure—"

"Are you blowing me off?"

Gracie's eyes widened. "What? No! I-I'm trying to tell you, well, what I mean is—"

"Blurt it out, baby. Like a bandage, fast and painless."

She frowned. "I would if you'd stop interrupting me."

Wade chuckled at her disgruntled tone. Hell, he wasn't sure if she was about to kick him to the curb or not, and still she managed to make him laugh. "Sorry, sweetheart. The floor's all yours."

"I love you." Gracie said between clenched teeth as she continued to glare at him.

Wade's entire body went still. "Come again?"

"I said, I love you. Even though you drive me crazy and I'd like to clobber you right now, I love you."

Wade shot out of the chair and hovered over her. Bracing himself on his hands beside her head, he whispered, "I love you too, my Fiery Angel."

Gracie blinked several times. "You do?"

Wade pressed his lips to hers. Soft and warm and so damn intoxicating, that was Gracie. He lifted slightly, letting their breaths mingle. He could see the green fire in Gracie's half-closed eyes; the sight had his blood pumping faster. "Yes, I do. I've never told another woman those three words."

"It's happened so fast," she said, her gaze filling with alarm. "And I don't know how to be in a relationship, Wade. I'm scared I'm going to mess this up."

"I told you, I don't need a relationship expert. I only need you, open and willing. We'll figure out the rest together."

She smiled and kissed him. It was quick, too quick. "I was so afraid you didn't feel the same way. I talked to Cherry about you, you know. She told me I should go for it. I'm glad I listened to her."

Wade cupped Gracie's cheek and smoothed his thumb over her bottom lip. Damn, how he wished they were back at his place. "I'm sending that woman a dozen roses. I owe her big time."

"There's still a lot unsettled. My apartment, my car. My dad. I come with a lot of baggage, Wade."

"It's nothing we can't handle together, Gracie." He kissed

her forehead, her cheeks, then let his lips sip at hers. Soon they were both panting. "Right now the only thing I want to do is get you home. The rest can wait."

"Yes, home. That sounds heavenly right now." Wade stood and held out his hand; she took it and started to lift up, then stopped and frowned.

"What is it? Are you in pain?"

"No, but there is one little problem."

Baffled, Wade asked, "What's that?"

Gracie smiled wickedly. "The little matter of your punishment."

"Er, Gracie . . ."

She quirked a brow, and Wade fell silent. He had a sudden vision of Gracie dressed from head to toe in leather and wielding a flogger. It was a damn good vision.

"You said I could spank you if you cursed. I've been keeping count. You've cursed a lot, Wade."

Wade took her head in his hands and held her still for his kiss, this time harder, more demanding. He pulled away and growled, "Let's go home, my Fiery Angel."

"Yes." Gracie smiled. "Let's go home."

Epilogue

Five weeks later . . .

Gracie slammed a cupboard door, frustrated and hungry at the same time. "I've searched this entire kitchen, and I still can't find your cannelloni recipe."

Wade tapped his temple. "It's all up here, and it's my little secret."

He was sprawled out on the couch reading Poe's "The Murders in the Rue Morgue." After they'd showered together, he'd pulled on a pair of loose-fitting gray sweats and nothing else. As Gracie stared at his powerful chest, so beautifully displayed, her body temperature spiked. And an idea began to form.

Crossing the room, Gracie said, "I could get you to talk. I have ways, Wade." She straddled his thighs, sighing when she felt the length of his cock nestled against her pussy. Wade would always have that effect on her, she knew.

Wade tossed the book aside and wrapped his hands around her waist. "No doubt you do, pretty baby."

She smoothed her palms over his chest, then moved them over his rib cage to his tight abs. "How's the arm?"

270 / *Anne Rainey*

Wade rolled his eyes. "Like I told you this morning and yesterday, and every day before that, it's healed."

"Sorry. It's just . . . I'll never forget hearing that gun go off. Knowing you were shot." Gracie shuddered as she thought of that day. So much had happened since then. She'd made living with Wade a permanent situation. Her renter's insurance had come through, so she'd managed to replace a lot of the things Lusk had destroyed. Wade had pitched in by surprising her with her very own e-book reading device—filled with the rest of the books she'd lost in the break-in.

"I'll never get that image out of my head of you covered in blood." He looked at her from head to toe, as if searching for injuries. When he took her hands in his and kissed first one palm and then the other, her clit swelled. "Is this wrist giving you any problems, sweetheart?"

She shook her head. "It's fine. Not even a twinge. I am so glad to have that cast off. The itching was driving me nuts."

He bobbed his eyebrows. "Sooo, wanna fool around?"

She laughed and slid her hand beneath the elastic waistband of his pants, encountering his already hard cock. "Thought you'd never ask."

"Keep doing that and the fun won't last."

She leaned forward and licked the shell of his ear, then whispered, "Have a little control."

He cupped the back of her head, holding her in place. "I have plenty of control. But when there's a naughty little vixen on my lap, playing with my cock and whispering in my ear, my control takes a siesta."

She started to tell him she loved it when he lost control, but her cell phone rang. Gracie frowned. "I don't want to answer that."

The hand Wade had at the back of her head tightened. "Then don't."

Her cell phone rang again. "I have to, Wade. It could be

Cherry."

Wade cursed. "It's probably your dad. Leave it."

Gracie moved off his lap. "No, I can't keep avoiding him. It's time to settle things."

She went to the kitchen table and grabbed her cell phone. She didn't recognize the number, but that didn't mean anything. Her father was always borrowing someone else's phone. When it rang a third time, Gracie flipped it open.

"Hello?"

"You've been screening your damn calls, haven't you?"

Gracie sighed at the belligerent tone. "What do you want, Dad?"

"They're threatening to kick me out, Gracie. I need the rent paid."

"No," Gracie said. Oh, God, her heart hurt. It shouldn't be this painful, she thought.

"What the hell do you mean, no?"

"I'm done, Dad," she answered, holding her ground for the first time that she could remember. "No more calling and asking for money. I'm finished."

"You ungrateful bitch!" he screamed, his words slurring just enough to tell Gracie he was already halfway to being drunk off his ass, and it wasn't even noon.

"Call me whatever you want, but I'm serious. You either get help for the drinking or lose my number. Either way, I'm done."

"You can't do this to me. I raised you! I kept a roof over your head when no one else wanted you!"

Gracie felt each word like a slap to the face. Her gaze shot to Wade's across the room. Immediately he was in front of her, his arms around her in a protective embrace. "You have a choice to make, Dad. If you can sober up, then we'll talk." When he started cursing her, her mother, her grandmother, God, Gracie hung up.

"I'm so sorry, baby," Wade said.

Gracie tossed the phone onto the table and buried her face in Wade's chest. The tears came, and it wasn't pretty. Once she'd cried herself dry, she pulled back and stared at Wade's damp pecs. "You're all wet."

He cupped her chin and raised her head until their gazes met. "I'm so damn proud of you right now."

"It hurts, Wade," Gracie admitted, her voice hoarse with emotion. "I don't feel very good about what I just did."

"I know. He's your father, and that doesn't change—no matter what. But you took a very necessary step today. Like you told him on the phone, he has a choice to make. The ball's in his court now."

Gracie smoothed her palms over his hard chest. "Wade?"

He kissed the top of her head and murmured, "Yeah, baby?"

"Make love to me."

"Always, my Fiery Angel," he vowed. "Always."

Then he picked her up and carried her up the stairs to their bed, where they made love for the rest of the afternoon. It was, Gracie thought, the best way to spend a Saturday afternoon.

Turn the page
for a sizzling preview
of Lorie O'Clare's
TEMPTATION ISLAND

An Aphrodisia trade paperback
coming August 2011.

Ric Karaka stepped onto the front porch of the large, old house and breathed in the morning air. He loved the smell of the island. It brought back memories, the first good ones he'd had, from after high school when he'd originally come to Lanai, one of the smaller Hawaiian islands. The fresh air, often mixed with the aroma of some nearby flowering plant or tree, had an erotic edge to it.

He didn't regret living on the banana plantation, although he was still getting accustomed to all the silence and space. It was a far cry from the inner city in L.A.

"Life goes on," he reminded himself, voicing the mantra he'd used for years as he stretched, then tested several of the floorboards on the old porch as he headed down the stairs. The first half of his life made hell dim in comparison, but Ric had always found the energy to push himself forward. "You never would have thought you'd be here, though, did you, old man?"

Ric was only thirty, but he didn't see any reason to try clinging to his youth. He hadn't started enjoying life, or learning how to move ahead in it, until he'd let go of his childhood. Not that years in foster homes, being used so a family who didn't want him could receive a government check every month, had been much of a childhood. Once he managed his emancipation at seventeen, Ric had finally taken charge of his own destiny.

Thirteen years later, he hadn't made any mistakes yet. The old banana plantation didn't look like much right now, but with funding, he'd turn the place around. Sweat and sore muscles didn't bother him when they came from hard work. He wasn't running from anyone anymore, and he knew who he was.

Ric's full name was Ricardo Karaka. It wasn't until he reached college, managing grants so he could attend UCLA, that he had learned anything about who he was and where he'd come from. He was the son of Julio Karaka and Maria Winston, two people who'd loved the hell out of each other but were ripped from life before they were really able to live it. Ric was all that was left of both of them. He didn't resent their dying, especially since he never knew either of them. And he didn't resent the state for taking him in and placing him in foster care.

Julio Karaka came from a family of farmers. The Karaka family dated back generations here on the island. The moment Ric had discovered that, he'd hopped on a plane and flown to Lanai. The chances of him not being related to all of them, with such an odd last name, were slim to none. And he'd been right. There were still quite a few Karakas around on the island, although none of them farmed anymore. Meeting his father's side of the family helped explain his coal-black hair and dark skin that got even darker when he worked outside in the summer.

His mother, though, had been a blonde goddess. Ric remembered the first time he saw her picture. No wonder his father had fallen head over heels for the rebellious daughter of a billionaire.

It wasn't until he came to the island that he learned that

much about either of his parents. His grandparents, Pedro and Alicia Karaka, took him in for a while. But when they lost the banana plantation, there was barely enough food, or room, for the two of them in the small house they had moved into on the other side of the island. During the time he stayed with them, he had learned a lot about the hot, sultry romance between Julio and Maria.

Ric had politely listened to Alicia as she fanned herself and looked at him dreamily as she told him how Maria Winston had become smitten with her oldest son. Julio didn't care about her money, and Maria didn't blink an eye when her family cut her off for marrying a poor farmer's son. The Winstons never knew Julio and Maria had a son, since Julio's death had cut them off from Maria.

Ric had managed the research and learned the details about his birth. Maria had been pregnant and alone. Her family had disowned her, although Ric would never know why she didn't turn to the Karakas. Maybe she believed they wanted nothing more to do with her. Possibly she'd been extremely depressed after her husband's untimely death. She could have been destitute, penniless. Whatever the reason, she gave birth to Ric in a hotel room all by herself. The motel maids found him crying in his dead mother's arms the next morning. His mother had lived in a home with several other women for a while while she was pregnant. According to the records that followed him through life, Maria's roommates said she knew she was having a boy and named him Ricardo. She had called him Little Ricky while he was in her womb. Ric never went by Ricky, but he got more than many orphans received. He knew his name.

All of that was ancient history. Ric survived, grew up, went to school, and managed a loan from the bank to buy back the Karakas' banana plantation. It got him a warm welcome from his father's side of the family, since the farm had been lost in a foreclosure. His grandparents and uncles weren't convinced he would make a good farmer and were even a bit more cautious when he told them he would turn it into a bed-and-breakfast. The Karakas were well known in the local community. Today they might be poor, but they were proud. When he shared with his grandparents and two of his uncles, Juan and Jose, his plan to renovate the old plantation house, their silence spoke volumes. They feared their newfound grandson and nephew would bring shame to their good name.

Ric turned as the screen door behind him opened, then shut with a bang. Colby, his bloodhound mix, sauntered to the edge of the porch and stared at the land in front of the house.

"They'll learn soon enough I don't discuss plans if they aren't solid," he said, reaching to scratch her head as she stared up at him with soft, brown eyes. Colby might not say much, but she was the best addition he'd made to the large, rambling old house so far. He watched her prance down the steps, then follow her nose as she started a spiraling pattern through the yard. "It's Karaka land. Can you smell that?"

Colby wagged her tail and continued her urgent sniffing until she found the right spot to take care of her morning business. He wasn't sure what had compelled him to take in the bloodhound mix when she'd shown up at his door shortly after he'd moved in. No one knew who she was or where she'd come from. Ric understood her plight.

Colby was an orphan, just as he'd been. She had no family, no home, no roots. Ric had lived on the streets long enough to know there was no such thing as coincidence. Colby's gift for tracking had brought her to the one house on the island that needed a family. Ric once believed he would find the perfect girl, have kids, and be the perfect father he never had. That dream was long gone. Ric and Colby were family, and together they would show his newfound family, and enemy one on the island, just how successful he could be.

Timing was everything. Ric knew how to keep his credit

score high enough to do business. And right now, times were hard. He'd qualified for the loan and convinced the family who bought it off the bank for next to nothing to sell it to him.

As one of his foster mothers used to brag when she'd come home from her Realtor job—ignoring him and the other foster kids and drinking with her husband—"Location, location, location."

His negligent foster parents had nurtured him more than they'd ever know. Ric stared off the front porch, down the long, one-lane driveway leading to the highway that circled the island, and at the endless ocean beyond. He had location nailed down. Some might see this old house and the untended land as an eyesore and a wasted investment.

There were still pineapple bushes growing on the property. Ric had no intention of turning it back into a farm, though. He might plant a few banana trees just for atmosphere. It was going to take a lot of hard work to turn the place around. Sweat labor would be his saving grace. That, and a solid investor.

He had the first, and by the end of the day, he'd have the latter.

Colby finished doing her business at the same time that someone pulled off the highway into his driveway. She bounded across the yard, baying loudly as her ears flopped, and she ran toward the old faded blue Buick Skylark. Ric made sure the door was locked and the screen door secure before following his dog to greet his grandparents. They knew he was going to meet Samantha Winston today, his maternal grandmother, with whom he'd been exchanging letters for the past few months. The last thing they would do was tie him up so he couldn't get business under way.

Ric was a realist. He prided himself on the fact. No one knew his private excitement to meet another family member—his mom's mother. He's barely slept a wink last night. When he had, it had been filled with heaving stories about his mom, stories that would bring him closer to the woman who died giving him life. He would soon know more about the woman he'd been clinging to during the first few hours of his life.

Anyone would think him weak with thoughts like that. Ric had been clear and to the point with the Karakas and Samantha Winston, his grandparents, concerning this meeting today. He wanted this meeting to discuss a business venture—the bed-and-breakfast. Samantha would hear the details in person. The Karakas already knew, and they thought he was crazy. Samantha wouldn't think he was crazy. She was a very successful businesswoman.

Ric had done the right thing, keeping the letters between him and Samantha business related. His mom's mother spoke the language of big business. Ric couldn't wait to meet her. He knew he got his ability to turn a dollar from her.

Pedro Karaka climbed out from the driver's side of his Buick and patted Colby's head as he walked around the front of the car, then opened the door for his wife, Alicia.

"Ricardo!" Alicia Karaka extended her arms, greeting Ric as if it were the first time they'd seen each other and not less than twenty-four hours since he'd been at their place on the other side of the island. "So today you take on the Winstons," she said, not waiting a minute before jumping into her reason for being there. "You remember what we told you last night, your grandfather and I. These are not good people. Keep your head high and remember you are a Karaka, good blood and good people." She reached him and clasped his face, squeezing it with her damp, arthritic hands as she grinned up at him.

"I'm half Winston, too," he reminded her, smiling down at her leathery face and twinkling dark eyes. There weren't many people on this planet capable of giving unconditional love so easily. Alicia Karaka was one of them.

"And half Karaka, which is why I'm not worried one bit,"

she said, laughing and giving his head a little shake before releasing him. "Now, what are you going to say?"

"Mother," Pedro Karaka complained under his breath, giving her a hard side glance before shifting his attention to Ric and looking apologetic.

"Shhh, shhh." Alicia didn't look at her husband but waved her hand at him dismissively.

Pedro ignored the gesture and the command to be quiet. "We came to wish him the best of luck," he said, sounding as if it weren't the first time he'd reminded his wife why they were stopping by Ric's place unannounced.

Another day Ric might have been amused. Alicia and Pedro were good people. Some might even claim he was blessed to have them as grandparents. But Ric saw them as a repeated reminder as to why he would never get married; why he'd quit the dream of his childhood to be a good father and husband someday. They spoke over each other, interrupted each other, and went off on tangents, losing focus as to what they were originally talking about.

Ric wouldn't ever get stuck in a mess like that. His grandparents had spent a lifetime together and had nothing to show for it. They were broke and lived in a shack.

"Of course we wish you good luck." Alicia ignored Colby when the dog walked between her and Ric. "And we want you to know how proud your papa would be if he were alive today."

Ric had heard a lot of that since he'd moved to the island almost a year ago. It wasn't the easiest thing for him to wrap his brain around. If Ric got his practicality from his father, then his dad wouldn't be proud until Ric accomplished his goals. He was simply moving forward, securing his success and his roots into place.

"Thank you, Grandmother." There wasn't anything else to

say. When she simply beamed up at him, Ric leaned forward and gave her a gentle hug.

Alicia wasn't going to have anything to do with that. She wrapped her arms around Ric and held on as if her life depended on it. His grandfather, Pedro, nodded as he watched his wife.

"Give us a call when you get home," he said, apparently deciding his wife had clung to Ric long enough and slowly began peeling her away from him. "Your grandmother will worry until you do."

Alicia made a clucking sound as she swiped her hand at Pedro, as if she would hit him several times for suggesting such a thing. A simple sidestep on his part and he avoided her efforts. She continued waving Pedro off as she turned to the car.

"Are you sure this is what you want to do?" Pedro asked, turning from his wife and pulling on his multicolored shirt. Once, the old man probably had hair as black and thick as Ric's, but strong streaks of silver dominated it now.

Pedro asked as if there were other options. Ric wanted to tell him this was standard practice in business. A venture this size didn't get off the ground without financing. He could go to the bank and take out another loan, hopefully. But he'd only paid a year on his mortgage so far, and as it was, the money he'd saved was quickly dwindling. If Samantha Winston financed this project, once the bed-and-breakfast was up and running, he'd be able to pay off the mortgage and pay her back with money left to live on. He'd crunched the numbers enough times to have them memorized.

"Everything will be fine." It was a line he'd learned from the foster mother he'd had through part of grade school. "Don't worry," he added. Then, again not sure what to do, he extended his hand. "I'll call you two once I'm done."

Pedro was old-school, and stubborn as hell. No one could get the old man to see any viewpoint other than his own. More

than once, Ric had explained why he was approaching Samantha Winston. He had no clue how Pedro ran his farm for all the
years he did when he appeared to be so staunchly against borrowing money. And God forbid the old man understand a line
of credit.

"You would think after a year you'd understand the concept
of family, boy," Pedro said, ignoring the extended hand and instead taking Ric by the arm and walking with him toward the
driver's side of the car. "Sometimes I think you got every lick of
stubbornness your grandmother could pass down through her
blood. We're going to worry. We're going to support you. And
we're going to ask questions and butt our heads into your business on a very regular basis. I've been over this with you. Your
grandmother is living proof of this."

Ric watched Colby as she circled around Pedro, sniffing his
pockets with each turn. Pedro absently stroked the dog's head
but kept his stern, watery gaze on Ric. He wouldn't admit
Pedro had a point, especially when it wasn't the issue at the moment. He wanted Pedro to understand business, and Pedro
wanted him to understand the concept of family, something Ric
had never had prior to a year ago and what many people didn't
seem to give the same value to, at least as far as he'd seen. Ric
stood a better chance of explaining business to his grandfather
than the other way around.

"I understand," he lied, and the look Pedro gave him proved
he saw through the lie. Ric patted his grandfather on the shoulder and held the car door while Pedro got in. The old man slid
a large piece of jerky out of his pants pocket and tossed it to
Colby. "I'll be sure and let both of you know how things went
as soon as I'm done visiting with her."

"Don't make it all about business, boy," his grandfather said,
wagging his finger at Ric. "Take time to know your blood."

Pedro and Alicia Karaka backed out of Ric's driveway, the
old man taking it at a snail's pace. Ric waved after them for a

moment, then turned to his dog, who was on the trail of some rodent and already heading across the field where neglected banana trees and rows of pineapple bushes grew.

"You ready, Colby?" he yelled.

Colby bayed loudly, one of her ears inside out, as she gave up on her hunt and came bounding toward Ric's truck. She pranced around in circles until Ric opened the passenger door for her. She leaped into the seat and immediately sat facing forward without giving him a second glance.

"All right, girl," Ric informed Colby as he climbed in, then revved the engine. "You're going to chill in the truck while I tend to some business. You know the drill."

Her response was to lean forward and sniff the glove box where her bone was kept, a reward for not chewing on his upholstery when Ric left her in the truck. He waited until his grandparents had pulled out onto the road, then made a U-turn in the driveway and headed for town.

Joe Seal, whom Ric had met right after moving to the island, moonlighted as a bellhop at the Four Seasons at Manela Bay, one of the two hotels on the island. He had his eyes open for Samantha Winston's arrival. Joe had called Ric the night before and confirmed that the Samantha Winston party had arrived as scheduled and, it appeared, with more servants than usual. Ric guessed she might have quite an entourage with her. This was the half of his family that was loaded.

Not that he had any desire to drain her dry. And he expected her to be wary, to not trust him, and to anticipate that he wanted her money. His story was too stereotypical. Long-lost relative shows up on the doorstep looking for handouts. It would be what he would think if the tables were turned. No one had ever given him a handout his entire life. Not so much as a meal. And that wasn't what he was asking for now. Corporations like Winston Enterprises invested their money in smaller companies all the time. No, Ric wasn't after a free ride.

Ric had given the old woman time to relax after her flight. Now it was time for her to know her grandson. He still would want to meet her even if he didn't need her to invest in his new business. And, truth be told, he admitted to himself as he gripped and released the steering wheel and realized he was already in town and hadn't even turned on the stereo, he would have been a hell of a lot more nervous meeting her if it weren't for his business plans. The banana plantation kept him focused, helped his mind stay where it belonged—on sensible, level-headed matters. Otherwise, he'd be stepping into unfamiliar territory, which was not something he liked doing.

Although somewhere around eighty years old, Samantha Winston still had an active hand in the huge line of restaurants and hotels her family owned around the world. She was owner and CEO of Winston Corporation. Shortly after arriving on the island and meeting his grandparents and uncles, Ric had learned enough about his mother's side of the family to start researching. It hadn't been hard tracking down Samantha Winston. She owned several homes, and he learned from reading tabloids and *People* magazine, which did an extensive piece on her almost five years ago, that she lived in Minneapolis during the summer, Houston during the winter, New York during the spring, and Los Angeles in the fall. None of that appealed to him as much as studying her business portfolio. In her earlier years, Samantha Winston had taken her father's business and quadrupled its value.

A woman after his own heart.

Ric knew the moment he explained his plans to her, she would be more than willing to invest in him. He didn't need to play the long-lost relative. There was no point. He would speak as a shrewd businessman spoke to another shrewd business-person.

Ric wasn't an idiot. The bed-and-breakfast would make it.

Samantha understood business, and she'd see what Ric saw—
the perfect business in the ideal location.

The Four Seasons, which was one of two hotels on the island, was designed for the very wealthy. He'd grown used to
the flashiness of the rich and famous, as well as the recluses,
who were probably even wealthier and who came to Lanai to
escape the paparazzi and other invasions of their privacy. He
pulled into the hotel parking lot as a Rolls-Royce pulled out.

Ric waved at Joe Seal, who stood in his black hotel uniform
in the parking lot, talking to a kid Ric didn't know. Ric parked
his truck off to the side of the parking lot, opened the glove
box, and took out the massive rawhide bone he'd purchased the
day before after Colby had finished off her last one.

"Try and make this one last at least until I get back," he said,
handing the bone over to Colby.

She accepted her bribe not to eat the truck's interior and
looked at him with her jowls sticking out over the bone. Colby
winked at him. Good enough answer, he hoped.

"Be good," he ordered, lowering both windows a few inches
to give Colby fresh air, then hopped out of his truck, locked it,
and headed across the parking lot toward Joe.

"Slow morning?" he asked, extending his hand and shaking
Joe's.

"It's been off and on. The morning tourists are already out
and about the island. It won't pick up again until this afternoon." Joe gave Ric an appraising look and rocked back on his
heels. "So you're here to meet the old lady?" Joe asked, falling
in alongside Ric as they started toward the entrance. "Your
grandmother, huh?"

"It's time for her to get to know her charming grandson."
Ric wasn't ready to announce his intentions of trying to get her
to finance converting the old banana plantation into a bed-and-
breakfast.

"Well, she hasn't left the hotel today. I haven't seen her, but hope to. She's a good tipper." Joe grinned and scratched his short dark brown hair. He was a big guy, stocky but not heavy, and shorter than Ric. He was tan from working with his father-in-law and was, according to his wife, Susie, quite the stud. Ric didn't see it but wouldn't argue with Susie. "Fill me in on all the details later. If I don't go home with some kind of tidbit for my wife, she'll drown me with questions until she makes me call and ask for a total recap."

Ric snorted, knowing Joe wasn't exaggerating. The couple times Ric had been over to Joe's house, Susie had spent the entire time on the phone talking to someone about how she was not a gossip. "I'm sure I'll see you when I leave. You'll have to bring the kids out to the place when you get some time off."

"Whenever that might be," Joe grumbled, although he didn't look put out and rocked back on his heels again. Work was hard to find. Joe wouldn't complain about too many hours. "Let me know when you're ready to reroof that old house. I can't believe you're living out there the way it is now."

"I manage, and will do. Hopefully soon." He'd heard enough comments about his choice to live in the dilapidated plantation house. He was saving money by not paying a second mortgage or rent. Not to mention by living there he had discovered other things that needed fixing that he might not have noticed until after he'd opened his doors for business.

Ric waved at Joe over his shoulder as he strolled into the lobby. He had only been in the hotel a couple times, the last time to help lay carpet with a job he got with Joe several months ago. Just as the last time, Ric entered a different world as he walked across the lobby. He didn't want to be impressed, but breathtaking was the best way to describe the hotel. Although most of Lanai was breathtaking. After living in the inner city of Los Angeles all his life, he'd seen enough ugliness. Beauty, whether it be skin deep or to the bone, surrounding him every day sure made life seem a lot easier. It was a good thing Ric understood that anything that appeared easy was usually a hell of a lot harder than something that appeared complicated.

Melinda Sadey worked the front desk and had her eyes on Ric the moment he had arrived on the island. Although he'd flirted with her on a few occasions when he'd been to the bars, she wasn't his type. Melinda was somewhere between forty-five and fifty-five years old and preferred her men a bit on the younger side. Ric had no intention of ever touching the woman but didn't mind casually flirting until she gave him the room numbers of the three rooms booked under Samantha Winston.

Room 201 was a large suite and reserved with very specific instructions. The other two rooms, 211 and 213, were smaller suites alongside each other down the hall from Samantha's room. Ric didn't care to speak with her entourage. He got out of the elevator on the second floor and walked to the end of the hallway to the large suite, then rapped firmly on the door.

After knocking a second time, Ric reluctantly approached the two other doors. He didn't want to speak to hired help, but possibly Samantha was in one of the rooms. He stepped to the nearest of the two and again knocked.

A thin, short-haired man, who was probably in his forties, answered the door at room 213. He didn't say anything but simply stared at Ric, as if it wasn't his job to speak and therefore he had no intention of doing so.

"Are you Marc Waters?" Ric asked, and knew by the wary look the man gave him that he was. "I'm here to see Samantha Winston," he added before Marc could say anything.

"That's not possible." Marc cocked his head and made it look like he was trying to look down at Ric. His tone was rather nasally, stuck-up sounding. "Who are you and what do you want?"

"I just told you what I want," Ric said, keeping his own tone civil in spite of the urge to push past the man and see if Samantha was in the room. "And I'm Ricardo Karaka, her grandson."

Marc made a snorting noise and began shutting the door. "Nice try, but Ms. Winston doesn't have a grandson. If she did, I would know."

"I am her grandson." Ric didn't like doors being shut in his face. He held his hand out, stopping the door. "Her daughter was my mother."

"Ms. Winston's daughter is dead."

"I know. I killed her."

Marc Waters stared at Ric, apparently not having a snooty comeback for that comment. Ric cringed inwardly, aware of the possibility that Ms. Winston might very well be in the room, listening to the conversation. It wouldn't surprise Ric, from what he'd learned of the lady's personality through her letters, that she would screen callers, taking advantage of her presence not being known and gathering what she could about them before agreeing to meet them. She had mentioned once in her letters to him that a woman in business had to be ten times more shrewd than a man, and as she'd put it, especially in her time, when women weren't involved in business.

Ric pushed the door open so he could see into the hotel room. Marc Waters instinctively took a step backward. It sounded as if he yelped under his breath. His eyes grew large as he sucked in a breath. If the man thought Ric would get rough with him, that wasn't Ric's fault.

"I've exchanged quite a few letters with Ms. Winston this past year." He kept his voice low, almost whispering. "She didn't know I existed before that, and I wasn't aware I had family. She told me the dates she would be on the island, and I agreed to come meet her." He had no intention of getting rough with anyone. It wasn't his fault he stood six foot two and the man before him was possibly a bit over five and a half feet and one hundred fifty pounds dripping wet.

"Sir, I've already told you," Marc said, stepping back farther, then turning and almost running to a phone on a round table in the middle of the room. "Don't make me call security."

Ric stared at the imbecile facing him, waving the phone at him like a weapon. "Would you like the number?" Ric wasn't sure if the man was going to start crying or piss his pants.

Marc Waters humphed, straightened, and looked to his side, through open glass doors that led to the bedroom half of the suite. "All I need for you to do is leave, Mr. Karaka." The man pulled his attention from whoever was in the bedroom and boldly stepped toward Ric. "Ms. Winston isn't here. I can't change that for you."

"When will she return?"

"She isn't going to return because she never came here in the first place."

"Marc? What's wrong?" a woman asked, peering around the opened doors. Her question was unnecessary, since if she'd been in that room the entire time, there was no way she'd missed Ric and Marc's conversation.

The woman had incredibly captivating hair. Golden high-lights wrapped around darker auburn strands. It flowed past her shoulders in thick, heavy curls. She had it pulled back at her nape, but the hair tie constricting those locks wasn't strong enough to confine all of it. Loose strands contoured her face. Ric had never seen such beautiful hair on a woman.

She looked at him and her blue eyes brightened. Her lips were naturally red and moist. She pursed them, looking as if she would blow a kiss. His insides tightened. She was beyond rav-ishing. Her high cheekbones and cute, slender nose helped show off her intoxicating beauty. There was something about her, beyond the obvious sexual appeal, that made Ric's dick stir to life. If he stared a moment longer, desires way too dark for someone who was probably related to him would surface and fog his focused thinking. He needed to remember why he was here.

"Is something wrong, Marc?" she asked, rephrasing the question as she gave Ric an appraising once-over.

"Nothing!" Marc waved an impatient hand at her. "Go into the room and close the doors."

The woman tilted her head, looking amused when she shifted her attention to Marc.

Ric immediately wanted her attention back on him.

"I said now." Marc apparently needed reassurance he was the man to listen to in someone's eyes. His chest puffed out when the young lady disappeared behind the connecting doors and closed them behind her.

"We were supposed to get together today." It wasn't completely a lie. He'd told Samantha in his last letter to her, which he'd mailed just a couple weeks ago, that he would contact her once she arrived on the island. "There wasn't an exact time set for our meeting, though," he added. "Now what do you mean she never came in the first place?"

"Samantha Winston isn't on the island." Marc had retrieved his balls and stalked around Ric to the door, then opened it, making a gesture with his hand. "Leave a card with me and when we discuss matters with her next, I'll let her know you were here."

Ric turned slowly, the small man's words not sinking in. "She isn't coming to the island?"

"Samantha Winston decided not to travel at this time. Apparently meeting you didn't seem that important to her."

Marc's words cut deeper than if he'd stabbed Ric with a knife. It took more than a moment to master the rage that took over the rush of desire from a moment ago. Samantha Winston wasn't coming. She'd changed her mind and decided not to visit the island. The truth hit him in the face but was damn hard to accept. Samantha had said they would meet and hadn't struck him as a woman to go back on her word.

"It's time for you to leave, Mr. Karaka," Marc said sternly. "We'll make sure to tell Ms. Winston you stopped by."

It had been the letters. They were such an odd way of communicating. It had tricked Ric and he'd fallen into the trap. No one wrote letters. They e-mailed, texted, talked on the phone. The only letters that existed were junk mail. No one read them, just threw them away without a second look.

Samantha Winston's letters had given him the power to dream. She'd been inquisitive about his past, present, and future. Her perfect penmanship and the quality writing paper she'd used had added to the personality of her he'd created in his mind. Although he hadn't mentioned converting the old banana plantation into a bed-and-breakfast—he'd wanted to discuss that with her in person—the many other ventures he'd told her he'd undertaken over the years had impressed her. Samantha Winston had expressed her opinion of Ric. She'd thought him intelligent, levelheaded, and driven.

Without Samantha Winston's backing, the hotel would take a lot longer to do. If the place didn't start making money within the next year—if not sooner—Ric would be forced to find a full-time job to make the mortgage. He wouldn't have time, or energy, to restore the house. He'd be stuck in a dead-end job.

He'd been one hell of a goddamn idiot.

His movements were stiff when he turned from Marc, left the hotel suite, and took the stairs instead of the elevator to the lobby. It wasn't enough to ease the rage growing inside him.

Ric wanted to hit something, pound it until it didn't exist anymore. He was a fool. The humiliation rose like bile in the back of his throat. Nothing had ever pissed him off more. Ric had banked on sealing the deal based on letters with Samantha. His grandfather was right: Ric didn't get family.

He ignored Melinda's singsong voice when she called out his

name. The bright midmorning sunshine annoyed the hell out of him for the first time since he'd moved here. The only thing worse than dealing with an idiot was behaving like one.

"Ricardo! Wait!"

Ric spun around before reaching his truck, the anger on his face apparent enough that the young lady he'd damn near drooled over in the hotel suite slid to a stop. She looked at him, her face flushed, while her unique hair color captured the rays of the sun and added to her radiance.

The smallest amount of sanity crawled back into his brain. "It's Ric, and what?" he demanded.

"Samantha told me you would be one of the appointments."

"I'm flattered I'm not the only appointment she blew off."

She wasn't very tall. He could see her crooked part and how strands that were different shades were pulled back, crossing over each other and confined in her hair clasp. Her skin was creamy white, not tanned like most women he knew. Her sleeveless blouse was silk, her skirt probably also pricey. It was a bit odd that she was chasing him down instead of sending the skinny, obnoxious man to do it for her. He wondered how she was related to Samantha Winston.

Or maybe they weren't related. Possibly this pretty young thing was Samantha's employee. She just indicated she knew the old lady's schedule. Her bright, beautiful eyes looked up at him with interest and curiosity. But how much curiosity? She had the edge on him. She would know if they were related since she'd overheard him tell Marc Waters he was Samantha Winston's grandson. Ric stared into her blue eyes, accentuated with a golden brown shade of eye makeup. Eyeliner drew attention to her eyes, making them look larger. She wore a lot of makeup for an employee, but didn't behave like a rich girl raised with servants at her beck and call.

"My name is Jenny, Jenny Rogers." She stuck her hand out, her arm straight, and waited for him to take it. "You're Ricardo

Karaka, or Ric. I overheard you when you first came into the room and spoke with Marc."

"And how are you related to Samantha?" he asked, wrapping his long fingers around her small, warm hand.

"I'm not." Her mouth was open to say more, but she didn't.

Ric held her hand in his and brushed his thumb over her wrist. Her heartbeat trembled under his touch, beating rapidly when he held her hand a moment longer than he normally would when shaking a stranger's hand. She wasn't nervous, at least not to the point where her palm would be damp. He made her cautious, though.

"Why did you come after me?" he asked, keeping his voice low. He didn't see Joe at the moment, but if Ric was spotted carrying on a conversation with a hot lady no one knew, it would take moments to hit the island grapevine.

When he released her hand, Jenny clasped her fingers together. Maybe she was nervous. He was usually dead-on when deciphering the mood of another person. Something about this sexy lady, with her many different shades of auburn hair, was harder to reach. It was as if she were one person on the surface and an entirely different person deep down inside.

"Can we speak inside? Possibly in the lobby?" Jenny gestured with her hand.

He cocked his head, imagining what she might want to discuss with him. "What's wrong with right here?"

Jenny glanced at the ground, then shot furtive looks at the surrounding parked cars. His truck was just a couple cars away. Colby must have been content with her bone because she hadn't spotted him and started howling. Ric kept his gaze focused on Jenny's when she finished her scan of their surroundings and returned her attention to him.

"I'm supposed to attend all of the meetings and functions Samantha was going to attend while she was here," she said, then paused, staring at him.

"Okay . . ." he said slowly. How the hell was she supposed to stand in for a man meeting his grandmother for the first time?

She wrinkled her nose when she tilted her head, as if she didn't understand his response. Since he simply accepted what she'd just told him, he didn't see any reason to elaborate. And he didn't mind just staring at her. Jenny Rogers was easily one of the sexiest women he'd ever laid eyes on. He wondered if her rather vanilla outfit was her natural attire or if she dressed differently when not under the charge of the Winston entourage.

"What I mean is I'm seeing appointments, then reporting back to her."

"What do you report to her?"

"My impressions mainly. That seems to be all she wants."

"I'm to be interviewed before I am allowed to meet my grandmother?"

"You're on her appointment list. If she was supposed to meet you, I guess you get me instead." Jenny glanced up at him and gave him a small smile. She looked down at her hands before he could hold on to her gaze. Was she blushing over the double meaning that could be read into her words? Was she really that innocent? She was still hot as hell with an interesting accent. He'd guess Minnesota, but it wasn't strong the way some in that region spoke. He liked the way it sounded, though.

Hell, he was even attracted to her modest attire. The straight-cut gray skirt she wore ended just above her knees, and her sleeveless blouse was tucked into her skirt and showed off her slender waist. Her hips weren't too round, but she didn't appear too skinny either. Her creamy white skin wasn't pale, just natural looking.

Ric knew women. For years he'd made them his most focused project. And at a young age, possibly younger than many men, he'd figured out the type of woman who most satisfied him. Upper-class, hesitant, brainwashed, demure ladies weren't it. Unless he saw something inside them, like something he saw in Jenny, hinting that a darker side existed.

There was a particular quality a woman possessed indicating she wasn't as vanilla as others. Ric had managed more than once to pull desires out of a lady she never knew existed within her. He didn't think that was the case with Jenny.

Jenny Rogers was an illusion, right down to her simple Midwestern name. She was doing her best to appear modest, well bred, polite, and sophisticated. She shot him quick, furtive glances, suggesting she was shy, uncomfortable in his presence. Yet he would swear on his mother's grave Jenny was putting on an act.

If that were the case, what else might she be playing?

"No thanks," he said, and turned from her. Ric reached his truck, reminding himself no matter what might lie under the polite, modest layers of this auburn beauty, the point still remained Samantha Winston wasn't here. He needed to think, redirect his course, and talking to a sultry goddess with mysteries lying beneath her surface wouldn't help his case.

When Ric reached for the door handle, Colby sat up, her ears high on her wrinkled forehead, and assessed the situation. The moment Jenny approached his side, touching the side of his truck, Colby let out a baying howl. It was her protective bark, although Ric couldn't tell if she was protecting his truck or her bone.

Jenny didn't jump back or appear startled by the dog. "Oh, wow, a bloodhound," she breathed as if they were her favorite breed.

"Yup." He had half a mind to open the door and "accidentally" let Colby slip past him, just to see if he could break Jenny's soft-spoken, sophisticated act.

"Ric, Mr. Karaka," she said, dismissing Colby and focusing on him, this time not pulling her gaze from the side of his head.

"I know you're disappointed. Samantha Winston had quite a few appointments set up for her time here." She hesitated, chewing her lower lip and obviously choosing her words carefully. "I understand your meeting was quite a bit more personal than her other appointments." Again she paused. "But if you're willing to talk to me, possibly share with me how you discovered Samantha Winston or maybe something about your past . . ."

He looked at her, knowing his expression was hard and his temper seethed beneath his barely contained composure. He wanted to pound his truck. He wanted to take off and tear around the island, releasing the steam and fury building inside him. And he didn't care if Jenny saw how quick tempered he could be. It didn't bother him if she witnessed some of his aggression, and it definitely wouldn't be all he could release. What he didn't expect was for her eyes to widen, her round, moist mouth to pucker when she sucked in a breath. There was no way she couldn't see how mad he was right now, but instead of cowering or politely dismissing him and returning to her perfect world of order and old money, she stood there and faced his fury.

Ric lowered his gaze slowly, curious if showing her more than his anger might make her back off. He let his attention travel hungrily down her body, taking in her full, round breasts pressing against her sleeveless blouse. He couldn't see her bra, although it was obvious she wore one. Her nipples were hard, even though it was warm outside. A loose strand of hair fell free from her clip and drooped around her face, curling against her long, slender neck. He was being a prick and he knew it, but damn her anyway for trying to appease him when she didn't have a clue how Samantha Winston not showing up destroyed plans he'd been foolish enough to believe he could pull off in the first place.

"You want to spend time with me and know me better?" he growled.

"You had an appointment with Samantha, and I'm supposed to see to all her meetings," she said, basically repeating herself as if the words were a mantra she was holding on to in order to maintain her civility.

"Meeting with you wouldn't be the same as meeting with an old lady who is a grandmother I've never met," he informed her, purposely lowering his voice and taking a step toward her.

Jenny stood her ground, tilting her head to hold his gaze. He saw the slender vein at the top of her collarbone pounding with her heartbeat. It was barely visible at the edge of her shirt but was tantalizing nonetheless. Ric imagined yanking the sleeveless shirt out of the way, possibly popping a few buttons off, and tasting her smooth, creamy flesh.

"I understand."

He seriously doubted she did. "I'll return at eight tonight. Be outside the hotel when I pull in by the front door," he ordered, forcing his attention from her and opening his car door. Ric pushed Colby back and climbed into his truck. "Oh, and wear something nice," he added, then closed his door before she could finally tell him to go to hell.